I0775002

# Devil
# IN THE BOOKSTORE

## S. COURTNEY

*TW: Death, blood, gore, violence, language, explicit sex scenes, exhibition. If it's one of the seven deadly sins, it's probably here.*

This is a work of fiction.

Names, characters, places, and incidents either are the product of the author's imagination or are used fictitiously. Any resemblance to actual persons, living or dead, events, or locales are entirely coincidental.

Copyright © 2024

All Rights Reserved.

No part of this book may be reproduced in any form by an electronic or mechanical means, including information storage and retrieval systems, without permission in writing from the publisher, except by a reviewer who may quote brief passages in a review.

Cover Design:

Interior Design: Zakrzewski Services

# CONTENTS

# PROLOGUE

<u>From the Desk of Levi Asant:</u>





**Deep chuckle from the darkness**

What do we have here?

A curious little book bee.

Do you know where you are?

Doesn't matter now.

I heard…

Good girls go to Heaven…

Welcome to Hell.

You will report to my room at the end of the hall to be ravaged.

But for my naughty little book sluts, the playroom is to the right…

**growl**

For you to get on your knees and…

Enjoy the Devil's playground.

-Levi

# CHAPTER 1

## LEVI

"LEVI!"

My father's voice thunders throughout the cavernous halls. It makes my skin crawl and takes my demon out of the pleasure of torture. I revert to my human form, donned in a custom-tailored black three-piece suit. I snap my fingers, and my current victim disappears, but I've only moved him to *Mons Cultri,* which translates to *the mountain of knives.* It's a cruel game of darts; if they land in the middle of the bullseye, they get out of the game, but my minions never aim for the center. They aim to toss them toward the patch of running chainsaws to witness the most damage. They are as sick and sadistic as their master, and that pleases me and my demon.

"LEVI GIDEON!"

It's universal knowledge that parents emphasize their level of irritation by adding your middle name. Undoubtedly, he goes out of his way to torture me. I look down at my watch and sigh. It's too fucking early in the morning for this.

And I got to do this shit sober?!

I groan as I hear his customized Kenneth Cole Oxfords approach my study. He told me how limited edition they were, along with the other 35 pairs. He said he borrowed someone's ultra-exclusive VIP pass to the flagship store, where he spent a fortune. I'm sure he killed the guy. He bragged how each is embossed with 'TDK,' right where the hem of his pants end, for The Demon King. He's adamant that every little detail matters to catch the ladies.

My father is a master at manipulating minds. He finds it more entertaining to make me wait than simply appear in my office.

I'm not in the mood for his pointless bullshit. I pour three fingers of scotch because fuck humans and their judgmental rules. Restrictions that were created by weak, pathetic flesh bags who can't handle their drink. Unlike a superior specimen such as myself. They are quick to sin once the devil's elixir hits their tongue.

I drink for my sanity.

If you had to deal with my father, you'd drink, too.

I stare out the window, so I don't have to face his self-righteous cockiness head-on. I should be hashing out my plan to gain the greatest gift of all, but instead, my dad keeps me busy handling company business while watching millions suffering eternal torture for the sins of their past.

What HE deems a sin is ridiculous. We call it a good time; it sends an endless torrent of entertainment...and work.

Oh, don't seem shocked. There are way more sinners than saints up there. That whole civilization is doomed.

So much so we've implemented various torture activities to keep our demons busy, including a barren wasteland where the unfortunate are strung up and left in the sun to grow their thirst until they're almost hysterical; they happily open their mouths when they see the ladle, not knowing they are being fed molten lava or lead instead of water, burning them from the inside until the contents burst from their throat or abdomen.

There's also the cemetery of perpetual suffering where they perform the ritual of wrapping the bodies in gasoline-soaked linen, setting them on fire, and then entombing and burying them. They unearth them, douse them, set them on fire, and bury them again when the demon sun rises. They repeat the cycle every two days for all eternity or until they beg for another form of punishment, because our sun is half as fast as the one above.

We have plenty.

I save specific sinners for my hellhounds; they have acquired tastes, and I enjoy spoiling my babies.

They are magnificently terrifying creatures, towering at nearly triple the size of an average Doberman. Their ears replaced by majestic ram's horns, and fiery cascades envelop their bodies, even revealing their bare ribs. There's no need to tip off PETA; that's just how they are designed to look. I assure you; they eat very well.

The sight of them is striking, their presence commanding attention. The crackling sound of the engulfing fire fills the air, intensifying the fear that grips onlookers. These beasts emit scorching heat that can be felt from a distance, sending shivers down the spine.

I enjoy dropping the blood-soaked offerings into an endless maze, watching them chase and rip apart their next feeding. So deliciously bloodthirsty. Seeing the remnants of their last digested victims makes them even more malicious.

They are loyal creatures; I've been raising them since they were pups, and we are currently breeding the next generation. They keep me sane after dealing with my father.

"I shouldn't have to call you twice!" My father bellows, bringing me out of my thoughts.

I swear under my breath. He picks his own seed to torture, as if he doesn't have millions to choose from. I take another pull of scotch and bask in the little peace I have left.

The door forcefully opens, disregarding the vintage cherry wood doors, brass knobs, or the rare mosaic wallpaper they slam into. He had no respect for my personal space, but what did I expect from Satan?

"Disrespecting me in my home?" He scoffs. I turn to see him unbutton his jacket and sit in the tufted leather chair by the fireplace, his brow raised, waiting for an answer.

Technically, it is his home, but he annexed this part for me to live and do business, especially after the incident when I lost complete control of my demon. His fault, by the way.

"I'm not in the mood for one of your fake touchy-feely father-son talks. Say your piece and leave me be." I still try to respect him as my elder.

"Such disrespect coming from my own seed!" He tried to feign shock; he was being highly melodramatic. He heads to the bar cart to help himself to my selection of rich, smooth, and highly expensive liquors.

While he pours, I notice his appearance. I'm surprised at his current meat suit selection. Typically, he goes for the dark and brooding, suave type. The type women sell their souls to for one panty-dropping, leg-shaking, multi-orgasmic night. But this look had a completely different vibe. He was shorter than usual. He loved the way worldly women gasped when he walked by, seeing a towering Adonis in their midst, but today, he was barely six foot; I know because I'm six foot. He also chose Northern European features, like Denmark or Norway, fair hair, smooth skin, and deep, green, almond-shaped eyes.

"This is a different look. What gives?" I raised my brow, waiting for the lie.

"Can't I do something different without reason? I bore so easily at being dark and mysterious."

I didn't even try to suppress my laughter. He looked terrible. "You look like Powder!" He wasn't doing this willingly; he definitely was up to something.

I sit at my desk. "Don't bullshit me. *I'm your seed*, remember? So, what's her name? Does she know she's making a deal, selling her soul to ride your dick right into damnation?" I scoff and swallow the last bit of scotch like a shot.

"Well...yeah, she summoned me. She called for the Prince of Darkness."

"Wait, I AM the Prince of Darkness, not you!" I poured myself another glass, knowing he had usurped one of mine. Although I hate being summoned, she was mine to take, not his!

"Uh, you were busy...the devil's in the details. Anyway, she asked me to look like her ex-boyfriend, so I obliged."

Ugh, I hate those. Sad and pathetic, really.

"For a price, no doubt." He was getting predictable in his old age.

"Of course, for a price, I wouldn't look like this for free. Look at me! I look like goddamned Casper, the friendly ghost. Or an unsexy, washed-out vampire. I didn't know what she saw in him until I saw myself naked; it's always the unfortunate-looking ones. She gets a lifetime of her version of happiness and a big dick in exchange for her immortal soul." He tried to gloss over the details quickly, but I heard every deceiving syllable.

"Another one to add to your horde? Awesome... keep them away from my bedroom. Especially Tricia. I keep my hounds at the foot of my bed because she keeps trying to mount me after that one-night stand. She wails like a banshee. Keening and whatnot...wait...she is a banshee, isn't she?"

"Of course she is. I have to keep her busy and out of the house. She's so clingy. What better way than roaming the European countryside? Besides, they must earn their keep to experience endless pleasure from the Demon King." He stated pointedly, like the arrogant ass he is.

"Gross. Well, she was a waste of time. Thank God I'm this close to revealing it all to my mate." He glared at me, but I ignored him. When I was younger, that'd put fear in me, but I've recognized it as an intimidation tactic. Especially when I mention HIM, which is rare, it leaves a weird taste in my mouth. It's not bad, but it's off-putting.

"Yes, this little mate nonsense of yours. You drone on and on about it, yet you do nothing but drag your ass. It's rather pathetic that you feed into this trap. You could have worlds of endless women willing to drain you dry, but you choose to feel that worthless pull. I made that mistake… once…"

He glared at me. I resulted from his mistake. Then he poured himself a heavy drink. We both need a lot of alcohol just to be in the same room.

"Yes, I choose to feel that pull. I know this doesn't make sense to you, but I don't need your input. Haven has to be 25 years old to feel that connection between us. She turns this year, and I will reveal everything to her then."

"And when she says no? Will you finally relish in the multitude of available women at your leisure?"

He's already banking on my failure. "Haven will say yes because I've been coming around this long. Every week for the past two years, building a delicate bond…."

"And hoarding all these useless books. Do you have to buy so many each time?"

"No problem. I'll expand my library space." I snap my fingers, and my west wall expands to another empty floor-to-ceiling bookcase. To temporarily fill them in, I shuffle some books off my other shelves. As I turn around, a smug smile appears on my face. "You didn't say I couldn't expand. Besides, I've always wanted a library." He threw back the rest of his drink, slamming down the glass, about to express his disappointment in me. "Well, this isn't your own Library of Congress for your little book nerd."

He stood and smoothed out his tailored charcoal gray Dior suit and Tiffany cufflinks. "I'm headed topside to claim my victim."

"How long this time?" He knows exactly what I mean.

"Uh, about 42 human years. She'll die at 62 from an aneurysm. At least I'll get half those years of decent sex."

Jeez, she's only 20 years old, too young to be so emotionally invested in one male. He must have been her first. Now she'll belong to my father.

"Half?"

"You know... human women get those female issues. Dryness, lack of sex drive, inability to orgasm, and unwillingness to give a proper BJ. Or if they still want sex, they refuse during their time of the month, as if I've never painted the target before."

"Ok, we're done. Get out!" I walk over to push him quickly out my door.

"Don't knock it until you try it, son. It's indescribable." His eyes roll to the back of his head before this wide Cheshire grin forms.

"Good, keep it that way! Goodbye, Father."

I direct my focus on anything but the end of our conversation. I watch the trainers toss various body parts into the maze, like doggie kibble. My babies deserve treats along the way and have a voracious appetite. They could probably eat until they explode, but I limit them to four or five people or equal in body parts per day.

The handlers know what happens if they don't obey my strict instructions. They become the next victim...and worse, I'd keep them alive while I peel their skin off and dangle their exposed organs while my babies jump up and rip them from their torso like a cruel meat-filled piñata.

I sit at my desk, my body tense, as the intrusive thoughts creep in like shadows, sending shivers down my spine. Why did I even have a mate? Was this punishment from above or a gift? Longing for someone who could see my goodness, only to be rejected because she sees me as a monster.

My father had a mate; he doesn't mention my mother or what happened to her. I know he did something unforgivable to sever the tie, the image of his twisted smile of succeeding haunting my thoughts. Was she his better half, a beacon of purity and good, or just as much of a hellion as he was? I think my sliver of compassion for my mate comes from my mother.

Now, I had to get ready to go topside and see the only human that mattered to me.

# CHAPTER 2

## HAVEN

"Welcome to Book Lair of…"

I stopped abruptly as he walked past, heading towards the back of the store. A wave of sadness washed over me as he walked by without a word, his gaze fixed on the ground, my shoulders slumped in defeat.

"Dragons." I dejectedly finished my greeting.

Even though I'm painfully shy, I love ringing up their books while reading the titles of their selections. I was happy to know they would get lost between the pages of a fantasy world filled with warlocks, dragons, werewolves, and vampires. Or maybe discover a newfound respect for a historical figure or perhaps pick up a new hobby, such as cooking or learning a beautiful language like Italian.

I discover a newfound obsession almost every time. I'm currently in the grumpy next-door neighbor trope. One thing's for sure: all the fiction books I read have a common theme: die-hard romance. I might as well put myself in the heroine's place; no matter how bad her story is in the beginning, because eventually, she gets her happily ever after.

It's the one thing I can't find in real life.

I'm not sure I'll ever find love. I'm barely social and living most of my life in an orphanage didn't help my social awkwardness. When I was five, my parents died in a car accident. A winter storm hit while we were going to our cabin in the mountains. My dad did his best to stay on the road, but he lost control and hit a tree instead of careening over the mountainside. I was fortunate to have survived without grave injuries, but I lost my memory temporarily. While I was healing in the hospital, they were trying to locate my closest kin, but they found none, and I was offered to the Sunshine & Rainbows orphanage upon my release. Honestly, I only remember being with my mom and dad. I never met any other family unless it was when I was a baby. They'd be strangers like any other person. The orphanage was my best choice instead of foster care.

If you're looking for a sad and abusive story that usually accompanies orphanages, I don't have that. I had a pretty decent time, and I believe my tough experiences were because of puberty rather than my circumstances. While the popular girls were getting into hair and makeup and seeking attention from boys, I was curled up reading a book. I developed a crush or two, but I never had a chance. I kept my head down, barely looking out from my average long brunette hair.

Much like now.

I earned a full-ride scholarship to the University of Maine, got my bachelor's in two years, and then got my master's in library science. I even got some experience in the school library and bookstore. I'm the quintessential bookworm; I thrive being surrounded by shelf after shelf of history, fables, and tales. While at work, I quickly retreat into a fantasy world to avoid reality until someone needs my help.

But they don't need me or even know I exist. I'm living life under the radar. I want to gain confidence to be more approachable, but it is easier said than done.

Just then, a guy in a blue plaid shirt and wavy brown hair walks up to the counter with books about massage and physiotherapy. I guess he was using massage therapy to help heal some physical injuries. He had some nice muscles.

I scan *'Basic Massage Techniques'* and take that moment to sneak a longer look at him. He was taller than me, but I was only 5'3"; a teenager with an active growth spurt would look down at me. I scanned the book about human anatomy and noticed the tattoos on his forearm as it rested on the glass counter. Some are black ink, but a very vibrant one stood out from the dark canvas. It's a blue-green dragon that wraps around his arm with its mouth open, mid roar right on his wrist, shooting out fiery red-orange flames, and I see Roman numerals under its chest.

"It's my anniversary date." His deep voice makes me jump. I realize he caught me staring; that's why he spoke up, and now, I'm blushing. I have this annoying rose color that goes across my cheeks and the bridge of my nose. My blush makes me blush. It's the bane of my existence. I said nothing but scanned his books faster.

"Are you always this quiet? I noticed you looking at my tattoo. It's a tribute to my wife; she loves dragons, and that's the date we were married."

I could hear the adoration in his voice when he spoke about her; what a lucky girl. He was going home to someone who couldn't wait to be wrapped up in his arms. I scanned the Pierce Nelson dragon shifter deluxe edition box set. I have that set; it's beautiful inside. Each book features beautifully detailed illustrations. It is worth the expensive price tag.

"That'll be $292.70," I said, ignoring his question from earlier. He shrugged as he reached for his wallet and pulled out a credit card. I wrapped the books in our signature wrapping paper and bookmark, then handed him the receipt. He smiled while grabbing his purchase. "Thank you. Have a nice day."

I hold up my hand and wave in reply. When the bells signal his departure, I'm even more disappointed in myself. "You, too. Jeez, Haven, that's all you had to say! Ugh!"

After scolding myself, I grab the discarded books on the display next to the counter and the ones left on the tables.

I ended up in the erotic romance section, putting away a book titled, '*The Basics of Bondage & BDSM.*' Curiosity got the best of me, and I opened it up to a set of pictures of a beautiful girl on her knees in pretty black lingerie, hands bound by a tie or silk fabric. She seemed highly sensitive to the man's touch, who gripped her jaw with dominance and authority, but I also saw his unspoken worship of her. Her power over him was much greater than his physical display.

The description read how vulnerable the submissive is to her Dom's will and that a true Dom would never abuse or harm their submissive. My entire body flushed with an enormous amount of heat.

I jumped and almost dropped the book when I heard the bells jingle. I couldn't explain how I knew, but my body knew… he was here. My entire body shuddered, and I bit my lip to stop from moaning like a cat in heat.

There stood the ideal man, incredibly handsome, intelligent, and a lover of literature. He really loved this store because he has been here every week for over two years, dressed to the nines in impeccably tailored suits and the most beautifully detailed pocket squares. I usually focused on those because my heart would flutter once our eyes met, which was so intense.

They say the devil is in the details, which made him one hell of a dresser. He was the only man who took time to speak to me, although I couldn't squeak out more than a handful of words. The power of his aura was undeniable, and it stirred impure thoughts in even the most innocent bookworm, like me. If I were to give myself my purity and virginity, it would be to someone like him.

*Lord, I wish it WAS him.*

Someone who can be gentle and teach me but also be assertive. I imagine his firm hands would guide themselves over my body, showing me where I wanted to be touched, feeling the goosebumps all over me by the heat radiating from his body. The essence of his scent surrounds me, comforting me, but also setting my body ablaze.

I felt that embarrassing blush as I saw him waiting for me at the counter. His deep voice echoed in my mind, calling me towards him.

He smiled when I got closer. "There's my favorite girl." I knew he was just being charming, but I wished I was his girl. I step up to the register.

"And how are you today, Haven?"

"Fine." I squeak out. I noticed his red and gray checkered pocket square; it was pretty.

He sighs at my failed attempt to answer him. "You know, I've been coming here for the longest; when will I get more than two words from you? Hmm?" His voice is upbeat as he tries to coax me out of my shell.

"I'm sorry, Mr. Asant."

"I told you," He tips my chin to look at him, "Call me Levi." Even that brief touch has my mind reeling. His eyes are so dark I don't know if they're brown or as black as an abyss. Either way, I'm losing myself in them.

He clears his throat; he's waiting for an answer. "I'm sorry, Levi. I'm no good at small talk."

"But you can try with me. I don't bite…" He elongated his last word and capped it off with his devilish smile. "Here's my list for this week. You've always been my good luck charm for finding what I need."

He handed over his list, which was shorter than usual, and he saw my shock.

"I'm almost done with that section of my library. Just a few more trips. Then, onto thrillers and mysteries. But romance was always my top priority."

It's like he never wanted to finish that section. Who knew such a man existed? He seemed perfect, almost too perfect. For all I know, he's probably harboring the deepest dark secrets, something unfathomable, yet… I'm still captivated by him.

"I'll, uh, be right back."

"Alright, don't take too long." He didn't sound demanding, like hurry; I have somewhere to be. No, it sounded more like hurry back, or I'll miss you.

If only.

I nod as I head back to the romance section in the back of the bookstore.

He needed two limited edition books, *'Favor'* and *'Fire of Roses'* and the box set of *'Renditions of the Heart,'* a trendy and hard-to-come-by set, especially in larger populated areas, but we were a small local bookstore. I wanted a copy, so I ordered a few for the store.

I looked down to double-check the final book title. *'The Basics of Bondage & BDSM.'*

OMG! I didn't realize I had dropped a book until the corner hit my foot. I hissed as I picked it back up, quickly grabbed the last book because I knew exactly where it was, and tried to walk back to the front of the store like I didn't realize the book he wanted wasn't the one I was exploring earlier, fantasizing about myself in such a submissive and vulnerable position with its soon-to-be new owner.

I know Levi would be the ideal Dom. The way he hovers over me at the counter is telling. When I look up, he's smiling. "Did you find everything? That was quick, even for you."

"Yes, sir." I placed the books barcode up and scanned them for the final total. "That'll be $223.47."

***Clack clack clack clack***

UGH! I didn't even hide rolling my eyes as I heard her ridiculously high heels approaching. Who wears high heels in a bookstore? She squeezes into the tiny space with me behind the register, leaning over the counter, pushing me off to the side and in her shadow. Her chest spilled from the low-cut red cardigan. If she exhaled, she'd pop a button.

Cherry takes a pen and slides it between her freshly painted red-stained lips. No doubt she freshened up before she came out of her office after seeing him in the security camera. "Levi, it's so good to see you this week finally! Must have been a significant business trip to keep you away from me." She purred.

I hoped she wouldn't butt her nose in our transaction, but she always does. She flirts shamelessly with him while being condescending to me.

"You could say that. I hoped my favorite clerk wouldn't miss me." He smiled and winked at me.

Cherry rolled her eyes before leering over at me. "Haven's just a silly little worker bee, not worth your attention."

A twisted sense of satisfaction filled me as I played out the image of her face slamming into the glass counter and watching her spit her bloody teeth out onto the floor, a victorious smile curling on my lips. I looked over at Levi, and oddly, his brow raised in surprise as if he had heard my violent inner thoughts.

No, that's crazy. How could that be possible?

"Did you need my help with anything else? We're getting a new shipment of books this Sunday. We're not usually open to the public, but I can make a special exception… for you."

# CHAPTER 3

## LEVI

I'M TAKEN ABACK AND EXTREMELY AROUSED BY THE REVELATION that someone with such a pure soul could have such homicidal thoughts! It has my blood rushing south.

The fact is, I'm being tormented because I can sense everything she feels now. It started about two or three months ago, and I knew it was the official start of the countdown.

It was the night before my usual visit. I was sitting by my fireplace when it felt like my ears popped, and everything became more. My hearing was sharper, my senses keener to her emotions. The moment I walked in and felt my entire body flush, I knew I had synced to her. I also confirmed it when I saw her body mutually shudder.

The range of emotions she goes through daily is intriguing. Right now, she's trying to stay professional, unlike her boss, who takes every chance to throw herself at me. She wouldn't be my type if she had the last pussy in Hell, and my immortality depended on it. My father, on the other hand…

I see Haven look at me and blush across her full cheeks while I listen to Cherry drone on and on. I interrupt her to get a moment's fucking peace.

"No. I'll be in next week as usual." I hand over my platinum card to Haven, and she swipes it before returning it. I immediately felt the mind-blowing sparks she wouldn't feel until she turned 25. It was torture to feel such carnal bliss and torment at once. The pulsing I feel because of it is unbearable.

Haven wraps my purchase up in parchment-like paper and ties them up beautifully with twine and the bookstore's signature bookmark. I love the presentation each time. I kept the bookmarks in a glass canister on my bookshelf. "Here you go… Levi." That pause she took before my name left her sweet lips was deadly innocence. She didn't know the power she held.

"Thank you, Haven. I'll see you next week."

"Have an amazing day, Levi!" Cherry practically screamed, begging for my attention.

I'm currently trying to negotiate with my demon not to make an appearance because he wants to 'scare the annoying whore to death.' His first move would be to turn my eyes obsidian black. We have to stick to the plan to reveal my intentions to Haven, and none of it involves explaining why I can turn into a soul-snatching monster. At least not yet.

I turn my attention back to them both. Haven sighs and looks everywhere but at me, but Cherry hasn't stopped staring. She tries too hard and doesn't get the hint that I'm not interested… not in her, at least. I don't overlook her mistreatment of Haven; it fuels my fire to take her away from this place, but I can't interfere. Not until the big reveal.

Once Haven's mine, no one will mistreat her, and those who have will face dire consequences.

If she came to me, her tear-streaked face reflecting her dim, flickering light, and pleaded for relief from her pain, I would unleash a fiery inferno upon this despicable, wretched world, reducing it to nothingness. The screams of those engulfed in the scorching blaze would echo through the air, mingling with the acrid scent of burning debris as we walked away hand in hand.

I only needed her to live.

I walk behind the building to transport myself to my Earth-placed domicile. It's tucked away, secluded amongst the trees deep within the forest. The building had a strikingly dark, charcoal-colored exterior that made the mahogany wood door look even more malevolent. I'm sure, to children, it looked like an evil witch's lair. Hopefully, that will deter the nasty little pests.

I opened the door to the crimson and black interior; it conveyed stimulating and sexy, more than terrifying. The massive stone fireplace was the centerpiece of the living room. It stretched up the semi-vaulted ceiling and gave an eerie glow against the burgundy velvet couches and black fur rug when lit. The only artificial light was the black wrought iron chandelier with one of the few light accents in the home with the cream candles. I set the books down, recalling her shyly whispering 'Yes, sir' with such fucking innocence.

She didn't know how obedient she sounded. I wanted to whisk her away to the playroom I was now standing in—every toy her curious little heart could desire. I wondered if she even knew what she liked, what made her dripping wet and quiver until she lay exhausted, panting in orgasmic bliss.

I sense my little bookworm has yet to experience the tantalizing sensation of being bound. Oh, but she's curious, so I secretly scribbled that book she was perusing onto the list. She didn't see me observing her from the window when she curiously skimmed the BDSM book lost in the pictures. Her delicate hand ran down her neck to her chest as she read about Dom/sub relationships. Without realizing it, she nibbled on her lips, leaving them slightly swollen and tempting, begging to be taken. Her reaction was precisely what I expected; her blush was blushing. It's nervousness mixed with a bit of shame. The heat washed over her and gave her goosebumps, and I felt her body shiver in delight.

I desperately want to partake in that pleasure with my pet. In my fantasies, she's willing to please me in every way imaginable, but in reality, she's not ready yet.

I hate to admit being flawed like man in this way, but I desperately need relief–a night of empty, meaningless sex with someone equally worthless. I'm the Devil, for fuck's sake! Far superior to these sewer rat humans, but lust is the one sin that plagues all creatures, great and small. Something about that pulsating vibration drives you to the brink of insanity until you scratch that itch.

I accept defeat, walk further into the playroom, shut the door, and hear a purr behind me.

"Mmm, you called?"

I turn to see Aurora sucking on a lollipop in a deep plunge and a high-side split black dress. The plunge stopped at her belly button, barely covering up her massive tits. The sides split up to her hip, which means…

*She's not wearing any underwear.*

Aurora's my steady… burden. To use and defile as I please. She loves to brag that she's banging the heir to the throne. She thinks I gloat about her as well.

This isn't a relationship.

Would you brag about topping off an overflowing cum dumpster? My father thrives on them and the need to drop their panties at his command. I need a bit more decency.

Except right now.

"Bend over, face down." I demand while unbuttoning my sleeves. All my escapades happen here. I keep my bedroom sacred, as pure as my girl. I only want her body wrapped up in my silk sheets, to watch her sleep peacefully under me and her gaze lovingly at me when she wakes up.

Aurora saunters towards the bed while looking at my wall. "Aww, how come you never use your fun toys with me? I love restraints and letting Daddy have all the power…to control me. Mmm…" She perused my inventory with her fingertips.

"Those are for my mate. Stop touching them. Your only purpose to me is facing down. I won't tell you again."

"Hmph…whatever. I don't even know why you're entertaining this mate bullshit, anyway. You could be like your dad and fuck any demon, banshee, or siren you want, but you want to lock away that amazing dick to one pussy? A human one at that! It's absurd. You're losing your touch…sounds like you're getting weak…" She gargled and gasped for air as she tried to pry my fingers from her throat. I should let my claws rip her throat in half, but unfortunately, I need her and that smart-ass mouth, so I let go, and she saunters arrogantly to the bed.

She grabs the fabric panel of her dress and tosses it over, exposing her ass, but she doesn't bend over the bed. Instead, she climbs on top and drops her lower half, leaving her ass dangerously in the air.

That position is my weakness. It gives me the predatory urge to mount and pound her into the bed so hard I wouldn't even care if it caused her pain.

I peel off my shirt while staring at her wide open for me to ravage, but after her insult, I changed my mind. I'm going to punish her by not fucking her.

I unbuckled my pants. "Turn around. On your knees." She spun around and licked her lips hungrily. "Suck it like a filthy whore." She giggled as she knelt and whipped it out, allowing my pants to fall.

She tried to ease into it, but I slammed her face until her nose smashed against my groin, her eyes watered, and her gagging sounded more forced than usual. I zoned out as she did what she does best: swallow me whole.

I was fantasizing about my angel wrapping her sweet lips around me, looking at me with wide eyes for praise, for me to tell her she was such a good girl, my good girl. She would have a worried look upon seeing my dick at first, but I would assure her she was capable of taking all of me.

I glare down to see a grin of satisfaction on Aurora's face, wiping her mouth and licking her fingers. "That's a record for me. Mmm…but you always taste so good."

How long was I out for? Honestly, I didn't feel a thing, but my body clearly responded to her efforts, resulting in my hunger being sated. I didn't even feel embarrassed by how quickly I finished. Aurora is a placemat…no, a place warmer, keeping my needs satisfied until I can claim Haven. And I don't even like to give her that bit of power.

I cringe at the thought that Haven will ask about past conquests and that I'll have to bring up Aurora. Maybe she won't ask; perhaps she won't care as long as she has me.

*Who are you kidding, Captain Delusional?*

Speaking of Aurora, she's still here. She can never suck, fuck, and go.

"Why are you still here?" I reply coldly while pulling up my pants and pouring myself a scotch on the rocks.

"You're kidding, right?! You've never not fucked me, Levi! I worked myself up to feel that perfect demon cock deep inside me…pretty please." She resumes her previous vulnerable position, stroking her pussy and moaning, trying to tempt me.

"Get the fuck out, Aurora! I got what I needed. I'm sure you can find someone to fuck you. We have an entire circle of lustful sinners for your choosing."

Enraged by my lack of concern, she shrieked and stomped her foot. "UGH…go to Hell, Levi!"

I arch my brow and scoff, "Seriously? That's the best you could do?" My attentiveness not to care further ignites her anger. "This is the last time! Don't summon me again, asshole!"

I laugh as she's glaring at me, standing defiantly…

"Aurora, I suggest you make yourself scarce. Know your place. Unless you want to be fed to my hellhounds."

"My place was supposed to be writhing under you!" Her last-minute attempt to convince me.

I saw my demon storming forward; he wanted to strangle her and slowly crush her larynx. I, instead, snap my fingers to make her disappear. She's not stupid enough to come back unless I summon her. As pissed as she is, she'll still be waiting. She'll never stop bragging about banging the future King of Hell, and she won't screw that up.

But soon, I wouldn't have to worry about her satisfying me. Haven will turn 25 and feel that indescribable pull, and when we touch, her body will erupt from the sparks. I didn't have much longer to wait.

And as much as I would love to think this turns out like one of those wretched Hallmark movies with her falling madly in love, I'm not stupid. She is the epitome of purity, mated to her complete opposite.

I am the darkness they warn you about.

She is my light, but there is still a chance of rejection.

I mean, come on, I'm the son of Satan.

But he and I are two different people. As far-fetched as it sounds, I'm not a bad guy.

*Okay…why are you laughing?*

I limit my punishment and torture to those judged by the angels above and those who summon me. My dad entices people to sin. I let them sell their own soul. It's less work because they seal their own fate. They CHOSE this.

My dad thrives on seeing how much corruption he can inflict on the world before they find their home in one of the seven circles.

It may baffle you, but Hell does fill up, and sometimes, we're allowed to perform a reincarnation ritual. However, the last time we did a mass reincarnation, their leader formed the Confederate army, and we know how well that went.

The theory is that a little bad makes the world better; it balances out the good.

I heard about when only good existed on Earth, but that was eventually corrupted with the ease of a mere apple.

The ones granted release usually become repeat offenders and end up back here. It's best that they do. However, the punishment is different because they end up in Tartarus, a realm I've never seen. It houses the absolute worst of the worst. Only my dad knows the path to get there. No one knows what goes on there, and I'm not even sure it exists. My dad isn't the most honest being.

The sound of my phone brings me out of my thoughts.

Speak of the Devil.

"What is it?"

"Rude, didn't I teach you manners?"

"You didn't teach me anything. You hardly raised me. What do you want?"

"Why is Aurora down here screeching about you leaving her high and dry? When have you ever summoned her and not fucked her?"

"And why is this any of your business?"

"Because now I have to fuck her to shut her up. You know, she's hardly my type…"

"She's easy… she's your type."

"She's clingy."

"Not my problem."

"You owe me, son."

"I don't owe you shit. You don't *have* to fuck her. You *choose* to. Maybe she'll leave me alone if she bags the King of Hell. Good luck with that." It was a quick stroke to his ego so he could bask in it while I hung up the phone.

After a scalding hot shower that washed away Aurora's stench, I feel utterly drained and unprepared to delve into the depths of my emotions. Seeking solace, I secure my house with protective wards and relish in the soothing sensation of the cool silk sheets against my skin. With a sigh, I slide my exhausted body onto the expanse of my luxurious king-size bed, allowing myself to sprawl out, finding the calm within its embrace.

Even though I am the Prince of Darkness, my heart, which is as black as soot, is being held hostage by the delicate hands of my little book bee, transforming a fierce lion into a gentle lamb.

Why am I giving into the bond?

Because I don't want to end up like him. How different would he have been if my mom was still here?

Could he have loved her?

Or me?


I sigh, feeling that sharp pain of thinking about what could have been, but will never be, a happy family.

# CHAPTER 4

## HAVEN

I SPENT ALL SUNDAY MORNING UNLOADING THE SHIPMENT THAT Cherry told Levi about. I'm sweaty and exhausted because I'm doing it all by myself. I removed my cardigan to get some air on my soaked skin. Cherry was sitting in the comfort of her office, probably watching some mindless reality TV show. All these beautiful books, but she'd rather watch TV.

"Are you not done yet?!" She came out bellowing.

"It's 25 heavy boxes full of books and me," I emphasize her lack of assistance since she wants to complain.

She scoffed while leaning against the door, filing her nails. "You're the help, and I'm the owner. It's your job; if you want to keep it, I suggest you shut your trap! And by the way, you look gross. No man will want you if you look and smell like a home-less person."

*I bet Levi would. You're just jealous of our chemistry.*

I kept my snarky reply internal while I continued to unload the books my way. She wouldn't help, and I didn't need her useless opinion. I sniff myself, and I don't stink. I smell like my honeysuckle perfume, as always. She always does that! Make me feel insecure. There is nothing wrong with me!

I huffed loudly, seeing she had disappeared back into her

hole. One day, I'm going to tell her how I feel. Luckily, I spent the next few hours alone when she left for a girl's night out. Her friends came barging in like they already drank a few. Loud and belligerent, knocking over the stacks I so carefully put together. They laugh as they pull their sober friend to join in their drunken antics. Good riddance!

Since I didn't get to make up the day I lost coming in, I was up early and opening Monday morning. I needed coffee in the worst way. Even in my silence, I was moody and cranky. I am still going to try to be more social and approachable.

I make my coffee more potent than usual. It's as dark as a black hole and I bring it to the front in my favorite unicorn mug. The first sip is always as warm as a hug from your mom. I remember those hugs because they engulfed me in love, and she always said, "I love you, my sweet girl." What I wouldn't give to hear and feel it once more. To know that my parents are around or that they visit me.

I'm startled by the bell; it's kind of early for a first customer, but we are open. I look to see a man in a lovely blue plaid shirt and dark blue sweater vest. He stands there like he's waiting for me to…oh! My greeting!

"Good morning, welcome to Book Lair of Dragons. Umm, how can I assist you?"

He went from stoic to quite a handsome smile.

"Good morning to you. This is my first time here."

*I know. I would have remembered someone so distinguished.*

"And I'm looking for a rare book on Greek mythology. It's titled *'Greek Myths and Ancient Folklore.'* The first edition, not the eighth edition that's being used for current college courses. I can't recall the author's name." He sounded like he was trying to stump me, but I already had the answer.

"Cyrus McAfee and Brendan Arthur."

He looked so surprised. "Yeah… how did you know?"

I felt the blush happening. "I, uh, read it before."

Now, he leans onto the counter. The space between us lessened in a matter of moments. "No, you seem way too young. Aren't you in high school?"

I laughed. "If I were, I would be at school now." I tapped my wrist, telling him to check the time.

He chuckles, "I suppose you're right. My apologies." He was even closer as he eyed me up and down.

"I'll be back." I squeaked and went to the history section. It was way at the top. Almost out of my reach, even with the library ladder. The moment I felt the ladder shift beneath me, a surge of terror shot through my body, my fingertips trembling on the edge of the leather-bound spine, and I lost my balance! I let out a small yelp instead of a long, horrifying scream and ended up in someone's arms. Well, it's better than ending up on the floor.

He smells fantastic, like an ocean breeze, as he sets me on my feet.

"Are you okay? Sorry, I didn't get your name." He runs his fingers through his hair and fixes his sleeves. I am mesmerized by that small gesture until I see his brow raise because I haven't answered his question.

"It's Haven. I'm okay, you, you saved me. Thanks so much…" I trail off, hoping he'll get the hint.

"Trevor."

Trevor, I like it. Very fitting. I quickly hurry to the counter to ring him up. I was out of my element and feeling anxious. It felt wrong. It's hard to explain. Like he was too friendly, intentionally showing interest.

"That'll be $98.94."

"Do you work here every day?"

"Umm, yeah." I said with an upward inflection because I didn't know where he was going.

"So, if I wanted to, I could come back and make you blush again?"

Stupid blush! I wish I could control it or turn it off!

"I… I guess."

He handed over a hundred-dollar bill and waited for me to give him the change.

"$1.06 is your change." I dropped it in his hand to avoid further contact; landing in his arms was already too much. I wrap his purchase and place it on the counter, sliding it forward. I think he sensed I was trying to avoid any additional contact. "Thanks for your help; hope to see you again… Haven."

I simply nod my head, and he's on his way. I exhale hard, clutching my chest. Probably the most intense interaction with any human being, especially a man. I was proud of my progress but also felt guilty for such an interaction, and I'm unsure why. The sound of the bell and other potential customers distract me from that strange feeling.

# CHAPTER 5

## LEVI

"YOU TOUCHED HER?!" My roar echoed through the room as I forcefully slammed him against the wall. The impact was so intense that the books in the neighboring case were jolted off their shelves. I halt their movement mid-air and carefully return them to their original position, all while maintaining a firm grip around his neck.

He couldn't help but let out a chuckle when he noticed how uneasy I was.; he found my Achilles heel, and it would be in his best interest not to aggravate me further! But knowing Trevor…

"Relax, Levi, nobody wants to steal your boring little mate. I was curious to see the incredible and sexy bombshell that has the son of Satan weak in the knees. She's cute, but not the downfall I expected her to be. To be honest, she's quite plain. Come on, you can be honest with me…this is a pity fuck, isn't it? She'll just be somewhere to empty your seed?"

He smirks, and it reminds me of my dad, further pissing me off. I yank him forward and shove him back into the high-back chair. Leering over him menacingly.

"Pity fuck?! You're dancing on a frayed trip wire, Trevor. I wouldn't expect you to see what I see. You're a whore, and you're not even a dignified one. You wouldn't see the pure beauty in such an angel. If you ever approach her again, I'll shove your dick in a meat grinder and feed it to my hellhounds while you watch."

Apparently, my little threat hadn't worked as he chuckled while fiddling with his hands, "You know...she was quite fond of me...literally falling into my arms. She is awfully cute when she gets that blush across her nose." He points to exactly where her blush appears—the blush I give her.

Not. Anyone. Else!

I quietly step away toward my window that faces the darkness of the forest, no matter the time of day. I can hear him struggling to breathe as I close my fist tighter, shifting from my human form to my demon form. Remembering him referring to Haven as a cum dumpster in not so many words earlier.

"Say. That. Again..." I don't have to turn around; his struggling to gasp is music to my ears.

"Le...vi..." His thrashing was getting worse, but I didn't give a shit.

"What's the matter, Trevor? Don't you have the balls to stand by your smug little statement? Or a cat got your tongue?"

It wasn't a cat, but my phantom grip. I could easily snap his larynx, but his suffering is more satisfying. He thinks I'm getting soft because of love. He should know better; I could incinerate his carcass and reincarnate him as many times as I'd like. Peel his skin off and spit roast him like a suckling luau pig, or perhaps introduce a slow penile acid drip right on the tip that burns from the inside out. Or simply rip his spine out of his mouth.

*Oh, dear...he's gone silent.*

I finally released my grip and heard a deep inhale; I looked back and saw him fall to the floor, wheezing.

I wouldn't allow him to continue talking shit about Haven and decide this was an excellent opportunity for my demon to stretch his wings. I withheld it from Aurora, but she didn't say the inflammatory bullshit he just spat out about Haven, and on top of that, he touched her! His vile fingers touched her precious skin, playing with her innocence and making her feel guilty. He doesn't know I could feel her emotions, which went from intrigue to fear to uneasiness.

I allow my form to expand to the very top of my vaulted ceilings. It still wasn't enough space for my entire being, but it would do. My onyx skin, like polished obsidian shimmered with fiery red veins that snaked across its surface. As I underwent my beastly transition, a noxious smoke billowed from my transformed form, filling the air with an acrid smell that stung the nostrils. The intense heat radiating from my body created an unsettling, prickling sensation, like hot needles grazing against the skin. My horns, black and massive, sweep back and upward, creating an imposing silhouette. I raise my arms and puff out my chest to let out a thunderous roar, then sweep my enormous tail before I see Trevor groveling at my feet. He's terrified as he looks into my fire-filled eyes. I haven't felt this amount of uncontrolled rage in a long time, but when it comes to my mate, it's a trigger. I reign my beast in to gain back control.

*Easy, I think the bastard gets the point.*

My monster doesn't see the light of day much, especially on Earth; now he wants more. He grumbles as he makes his way deep into my subconscious, and I shrink back to human form. I noticed Trevor was still trembling and whimpering.

"Final warning…STAY. AWAY. Got it?!"

"Yes."

"Good. Get the fuck out!" He disappears quickly.

First, my dad, now Trevor, only makes me more nervous about revealing everything and extremely anxious at her response. Unfortunately, I have to go back to Hell to tend to some business. I hope it doesn't take me as long as last time. My lame business trip excuse can only work so many times. I ponder, taking a quick detour to see my heartbeat, but I will delay gratification.

# CHAPTER 6

## HAVEN

I'M INCREDIBLY WORN OUT, TO WHERE I'M CONTEMPLATING sacrificing dinner for sleep. My yawns are so forceful that my eyelids battle to reopen. With my brain operating on autopilot, I quickly warm up a hearty vegetable soup, its aroma calming my unsettled stomach. After that, I dragged myself into the steamy hot shower, which soothed my sore muscles from moving those books on Sunday. I imagine firm hands kneading my aching shoulders, stiff neck, and achy calves. Working the knots out while working me up at the same time. His lips would trace every square inch that he touched. I move quickly to live out my fantasies in my dream with my mystery man. One day, he'll be real. I know it.

Not getting a break and continuing to work long hours caught up with me, and I had to call in on Wednesday. It broke my heart that I would miss Levi's weekly visit. If I hadn't woken up dizzy with a migraine, a sore throat, and a cough, I would have stuck it out for that moment in time, but I couldn't, so I rolled over, defeated, and went back to sleep.

I only got up to use the bathroom and find a snack, but I was feeling much better after taking a cocktail of pills. I fought my cough with some soothing lemon ginger tea, and by nightfall, I was feeling better but also sad I would have to wait that much longer to see Levi again.

The following day, I took my time because I knew, eventually, I'd have to hear her complain about having to work the counter. It's like she was an indentured servant, but even on our busiest day, we'll see like 20 people. It's not like we're in the middle of Times Square. She's not unboxing a shipment or anything, and I guarantee that if an order came in, she would leave it there for me to do alone.

I open the door to the familiar sound of the bell and the sweet smell of old parchment paper. As I head to the counter, I see books on every table and some piled in the chairs! Which means she left this mess for me. If I didn't know any better, she probably made a bigger mess on purpose because no customer has ever been this sloppy, not even the college kids. I cringe to think what the shelves look like. "Lazy bitch." I mumble while gathering some to put away before opening the doors; I had 20 minutes.

*A few hours later:*

I've been running between the counter and finishing the cleanup. I had finally finished when Cherry waltzed in with her typical venti triple cream macchiato. She's in another skin-tight dress, hoping to catch someone's attention. We're a college town with a few lucrative businesses. Anyway, she stopped at the counter, waiting for me to drop everything to give her my undivided attention. I stacked the last five books and went to shelve them instead.

She followed me. "I hope you know how much work I had to do in your absence. I don't do manual labor; I have you for that. A minion to do my bidding, so get to work! Make sure this place is spotless!" She walks away and slams her office door.

Ugh, I'm so sick of her and her bull…

***Ding***

My whole body shuddered while feeling a simultaneous heat

flash. It couldn't be…he was supposed to come yesterday when I was sick.

Then her door opens, "And another thing, you're staying until every item is in its place. I almost canceled a date because of your little runny nose."

It shows how much she paid attention to what I said on the phone. Her response was to complain for five minutes about how I was faking it and that I should try anyway. I told her I would not risk the customers catching whatever I had, and she hung up on me.

"Do you hear me, Haven? You're staying late without pay…" She looks over my shoulder and smiles while hiking up her ridiculous implants and smoothing down her dress.

"Levi, what a surprise after yesterday." Her voice seemed a little clipped.

So, he came in yesterday. Then why was he here today? Surely, she helped him, probably in more ways than one. I cringed at the thought as I turned to see him flash that brilliant smile. He motions for me to come here using his two fingers instead of one, and I obey like he's pulling on invisible strings. At that moment, I questioned what I was wearing. It was a regular cap sleeve floral dress with a boring burgundy sweater coat because I always get cold. Maybe I should wear something more form-fitting, like Cherry. Perhaps he'll notice me more.

"There's my book angel. I hope you feel better than yesterday."

I was definitely starting to. It was almost like he was doting on me. I try my hardest to keep eye contact, but it's so intense that I can't help but look down. "You look very pretty today." He added.

Oh mercy, he said I looked pretty! Internally, I'm giggling like a schoolgirl.

Cherry scoffed behind us, "Yeah, Levi came in and promptly left when I told him you were supposedly sick." She said rudely.

I roll my eyes and let her continue to make herself look bad.

Levi smirks, grabbing my attention again. "I didn't want to miss time with my favorite girl. Besides, Haven knows where everything is. You would have taken forever, and I had time-sensitive matters to attend to rather than watching your incompetence. But today, my whole day is free, and I heard something about you having to stay late?" He tapped his fingers while looking behind me at Cherry for confirmation.

I pipe up to lighten the mood because he sounded upset. "Umm, yeah, but it's no problem. I didn't have any outside plans."

Cherry gasped sarcastically, "Shocking. Anyway, I need the stockroom cleared out before the next shipment in ten days. There are 275 or 575 new books coming in. I don't remember the number, so stock the shelves."

"Okay." That is a drastic difference in numbers. I hope it was the former, but because it was Cherry, she'd vindictively order a metric ton of books, knowing I'd be the only one working on it.

"Good. I'll be in my office. Levi, you can…join me if you want."

He stands from leaning against the counter and unbuttons his suit jacket. I'm entranced by his simplistic yet sexy movement. He slips off the jacket and is now in his burgundy dress shirt and black vest. Today, his raven hair slicked back made him look like he took no-prisoners.

"No thanks, I will help around here before we tackle today's list. Isn't that right, Haven?"

Oh no, a direct question.

It's not like I haven't answered him before, but they were private conversations.

Even though I'm not looking, I can feel her staring daggers at me. Levi steps closer after unbuttoning one sleeve to roll up. His fingers tip my chin up; it's like the entire world disappeared. "I asked you a question."

I felt tears well up, but not sad tears. No, it was exhilarating! It felt like tiny phantom sparks coursed through my body when he touched me. I wanted to show my obedience, like the girl in bondage. "Yes." I finally responded, and he continued unbuttoning the other cuff and rolling it up. It looks just like the man in the same bondage photo. While wearing a power suit, he modified it enough to play with his pet.

What I wouldn't give to be Levi's pet.

"You can leave, Cherry. We'll be fine without you."

# CHAPTER 7

## LEVI

The way Cherry choked after I told her we didn't need her was quite amusing. She's lucky I couldn't interfere, or I would have made her one of my waste demons who clean up after my babies. Perhaps when Haven takes her place, I'll make Cherry her servant.

Haven grabbed a couple of books to put away. I felt tempted to follow her and corner her in the darkest part of the bookstore to have my way with her. I'd also be content wrapping my arms around her as she tried to do inventory. Or I could be like a wild animal marking his territory. I would claim her with gentle, feather-light kisses on her bare shoulder, tracing a path up her delicate neck, savoring the sweet sound of her soft gasps escaping her lips. The intoxicating scent of her skin filled the air, heightening the intensity of the moment. The tension built as we struggled to remain silent, until finally, she whispered to me, her voice a seductive invitation, urging me to take her.

I had to stop fantasizing before I could help her. I shook myself like my hounds do after they get up from belly rubs. After a couple of deep breaths, I grab a stack of books, almost covering my face, before heading in her direction.

"Haven, my little book mouse, where are you?"

"Over here." I follow her siren's call. I turn the corner and see the bottom of her floral dress because she's at the top of the ladder, putting away some science fiction novels.

I'm curious what kind of underwear my little mate wears. She seems innocent, but what if…she isn't? What if beneath that adorable yet demure dress lies a tantalizing fusion of intricate lace and luxurious silk, whispering against the skin with every movement, accompanied by the faint rustle of fabric? Or just maybe, concealed within a hint of a garter belt's seductive allure or a touch of supple leather. Nothing I would expect from such a sweet girl.

I felt the rise again, now mixed with a dull pulsing. I need to submerge myself in ice-cold water, like the Arctic.

*Okay, easy there.*

I stood next to the ladder, getting the slightest hint of her honeysuckle perfume. "Any of these in this section?" She scans the stack, slides two out to put back in their proper place, and grants me some of my sight back now that the stack rests under my chin. "The rest is romance. Follow me."

I'd follow her anywhere. What is this tiny human doing to me?

She stopped in romantic suspense and effortlessly put a few away from my pile. It'd take me forever to put away one book, but she's in her comfort zone. Now, I'll try to get more than one-word answers.

"So, tell me your favorite book."

She looked back, blinking rapidly, and seemed overwhelmed by my request. "Uh, it's not that easy. My entire life is books, and there are so many options."

"Okay, let's break it down then; autobiography?"

"'*The Distinguished Career of Justice Ruth Bader Ginsburg: A Voice for Women Everywhere.*'"

Look at that: an answer. "How about fiction?"

She takes a few more books and casually puts them away. The way her tiny fingers grip the books before pushing them into place had my heart racing. "That's difficult. It's a tie between *'I Just Want to Sing'* and *'Irrevocably Me.'*"

We are deep in the romance section, where her heart lies, and she searches for where the next book belongs.

"Here's a tough one, romance."

She scoffed, and I heard the confidence before she even answered. "Easiest one yet. I live my perfect life in that section. *'He Just Wants to Kiss Me'* piqued my interest in the anti-hero main character. Everyone saw the bad in Evan, but Mary only saw the good. What made him worth loving. It didn't make him a better person, but he knew she would be his good, his saving grace."

It's like someone wrote a story about us. She also didn't realize she gave me a little breadcrumb into her fantasies. "Do I have that book?"

"Hmm, don't believe so."

"Add it to the list. It sounds like a real-life story."

"It was a beautiful tale. What about you? Do you have a favorite book?" She asked as she effortlessly found a copy. I watch how her delicate fingers pull and then wrap around the book.

I loved she was comfortable enough to ask something in return.

I felt the pressure. "You're right, it is a tough question. I hadn't prepared an answer. The first one that comes to mind is *'Dante's Inferno.'*"

*Naturally.*

"Timeless classic. I am impressed, sir." Then she moved the ladder over to place the last two books on an eye-level shelf, which for her is the third row from the bottom, while I could easily reach periodicals on the top shelf. I positioned myself so that I was practically right behind her, inhaling deeply to capture more of her intoxicating scent. The bell rang as I was about to place my hands on her shoulders.

"Oh! Potential customer! Be right back." She smiles sweetly

and greets them, but the two young girls pass by, still enthralled in each other's conversation. Haven sighs, and her shoulders slump in disappointment. Then she grabbed more books and headed back my way. I turned to look like I wasn't watching. I wish my little butterfly were more social or that people could see how amazing she was at being a decent human. I want to keep her to myself, but I can't be selfish.

Well, I mean, I can.

She silently walked past me; her mood now solemn after the unsuccessful encounter. I took the chance. I took her shoulders and spun her to face me, but she didn't. Her focus is on our feet.

"Hey… don't worry about that. Humans can be cruel for no reason. Don't let it get you down." I punch myself for saying human, damn slip of the tongue. She caught on but said nothing; she nodded and walked to the non-fiction section. It's almost a response to the interaction when she stopped shelving her beloved romance for real-world nonfiction—the harsh, bitter truth of life.

I got an idea. "Hey, I'll be right back."

"Okay." It was softer and more muted than before. I couldn't lose the progression of our conversation. I can't let that happen.

# CHAPTER 8

## HAVEN

I DON'T KNOW WHY FEELING IGNORED EMOTIONALLY DRAINS ME. IF I were a battery, I'd be dead and tossed into the trash. I didn't mean to bring the mood down, but I'm sure Levi sensed it because he couldn't wait to get out of here. I don't blame him. I'm just not that interesting. I'm a simple girl who loses herself in books. I'm too boring for someone as worldly as Levi. I don't even know why I thought I ever had a sliver of a chance.

"Ha! You're so boring that he didn't even want to stick around. Did you really think you had a chance with someone like him?"

*My chances are better than yours.*

"A man like that is looking for his equal, not a charity case. He wants a woman who can speak her mind and say what she wants… like me. I'm working on my carefully laid plan; in the end, I'll have him in my bed. He looks loaded, and then I won't have to work again; this store can rot for all I care."

And she thinks I'm delusional…

"Hey! Did you hear what I said?" She's so close she's breathing on me. "Levi is MINE, so the sooner you know to back off, the better. Especially if you want to keep your job. I let you believe he felt anything for you; it was quite pathetic but enter-taining! You look like a fool!"

Her laughter echoed in my ears, a haunting melody that pierced my heart with the bitter taste of defeat. I knew it was a long shot, but I still let my mind wander there.

I feel the lump in my throat as the tears form, but I fight to keep them hidden. The bell rings as I try to pull myself together. There's Levi still in just his shirt and vest. I didn't notice his jacket was still where he had left it. He saw my face and headed my way immediately. I swore his eyes flashed black, but that's crazy! He's not a monster; it must have been a weird angle.

"You're back," I whispered, holding back the relief I felt in his presence, hugging myself for a comforting touch.

He brings his arm around to show me a drink holder with two cups.

"I went to the coffee shop and got us hot chocolate. You didn't need any more coffee to make you jittery." He nods at my empty, oversized mug. He handed me a cup, and I heard her huff behind me.

"What about me?"

There's another flash of irritation in his eyes. It's like he knows how she treats me and how awful she is when he's not here. "Oh, well, you had that huge sugary concoction in your hand earlier, and you're not helping us. Seriously, do you drink that every day? That can cause quite a bit of fat buildup around the gut area; think about cutting back. Anyway, we'll be getting back to work. Come on, sunshine."

In that one statement, he called her insignificant, lazy, and fat. I laugh internally as he touches my shoulder to guide me back to the counter. There's this weird fluttering feeling when he touches me, but it's not off-putting; I like it.

"Thank you."

"I thought you could use a reward for all your hard work."

This is the most exquisite hot chocolate I've ever tasted. Its velvety texture caresses my tongue, its aroma tickling my nose with hints of cocoa and warmth. The rich flavor envelops my senses, far superior to the instant powder I typically settle for at home. Indulging in this decadent treat feels like a luxurious escape. I sigh after my sip. It's the most splendid thing in a cup and pushes me to finish my menial tasks.

"How is it?" A playful smirk behind his cup, his eyes mischievous.

"So good…"

***Ding***

I turn to see a well-dressed man, even more so than Levi, and I hate to say out loud, but…more handsome. He cannot be real like no man of this caliber waltzes in. He must be lost.

Oh, my greeting! I walk forward while saying it. "Welcome to Book Lair of Dragons. How can I help you?" He straightened his cuffs and placed his huge hands on the counter; he looked like a giant leaning forward! He looked me up and down, and I immediately felt judged. Then he scoffed before plastering on this fake smile.

"Oh, you don't even have a nametag. How…insignificant. Even the lowliest of employees should have a nametag." The stranger trailed off. It was such a rude thing to say, but I ignored him.

"Do you need help to find something in particular?" My question clipped in reaction to his attitude.

"Well, I think your other customer over there wouldn't like that I took you away from him. He seems…irritated." He tsks. I turn around to see Levi angrily glaring at the new guy. Did he know him? They both have equally elegant attire. Could they work at the same company? Or competing companies?! That would explain the death stare. If looks could kill, though, I swear that man would be ashes. But Levi locked eyes with me, and the anger dissipated quickly. He even picked up some books and walked back somewhere.

I smile. "Oh, no worries about him. He's one of my faithful regulars."

"Would you call him your favorite?" He raised his brow as if this wasn't a strange question from someone I met 37 seconds ago. "Yeah, he is."

"Interesting. Anyway, I'm looking for *'The Unstoppable Power of the Antichrist.'*"

A chill shot down my back, and I suddenly felt uncomfortable. I looked up and replied, "Be right back with it."

# CHAPTER 9

## LEVI



The way he judged her…infuriates me! But the moment she looked at me, it doused the flames. She doesn't know the unbridled power she has over me. He gave her some book title she'll undoubtedly have to look for, and I took that opportunity.

"Son, I don't see the appeal of being around these vermin."

I looked around to make sure Haven wasn't nearby. "Don't small talk me. What are you trying to pull here?"

"I can't buy a book. Is that your territory now?" His tone is dripping with arrogance. It drives me mad.

"You know damn well this is MY territory! You can pick any store in the world but stroll into this one?! You don't even read! And in your captivating, dark, and brooding meat suit?"

This was his attention-seeking human suit. He put it all together in this package to guarantee he'd bring some poor soul home. I hated feeling her temporary pull and intrigue at my father before he belittled her.

"You can be so territorial. I was curious after Trevor reported she was such a plain Jane, and he didn't see the appeal. And we all know Trevor would fuck a rubber duck if he had to. But I can see how correct he was in his assumption. You're going to stick to this one, huh? Pity…"

"I'm sure you wouldn't say that about mom." I shot back with malice.

His ears went blood red, and his eyes flashed between his demon and himself.

"Watch what you say next, Levi, or I'll blow your cover before you can reveal the truth."

"I heard about how Grandpa felt about Mom! He thought she was just some…thing to satisfy your urges. That she couldn't have been your mate because she was so weak and worse, human! But she loved you! And before you became this shallow shell of a man, you loved her, too. I don't know who convinced you that you were better without her, but they were wrong."

He was a breath away from me and wanted to lash out but couldn't. He may not like it, but he had to abide by the agreed-upon rules. However, he would happily reveal his true form to the masses.

"DON'T you ever speak of her again! She's gone and never coming back! She abandons me and leaves me with HER mistake. I never asked for this! Love is for the brain-dead weak!" He quickly puts space between us, trying to pull himself together. I try not to react to the cold-hearted words toward my mother. There has to be more; he's not telling me the whole story. Why would I expect him to?

"Anyway, I've got an appointment with Aurora." He says, quickly changing the subject while checking his wristwatch.

"I thought she wasn't your type?" I knew he'd add her to the rotation. Any open pussy is better than no pussy to him.

"She has a forked tongue like a snake that wraps around my dick and constricts. It's goddamn magical! Did she not…with you?" He pointed to emphasize his point.

"Guess she was holding out." It did sound interesting, but I was not going back. Besides, who knows what my little book mouse wants to be taught? And the thought of endless possibilities makes me remember my goal.

He snaps his fingers arrogantly to bring me back to the present. "Gotta run. Pay for it, and I'll pay you back."

And with that, he disappears as she rounds the bookshelf. What felt like 30 minutes of banter was mere minutes and enough to elevate my blood pressure into stroke territory if I were the average flesh bag. I looked around to see if anyone saw his exit. It was so goddamn irresponsible, but I'm not surprised. He would enjoy seeing the sheer terror when they realized who he was.

I see her rifle through the pages, and I can feel fear from whatever she had read; then she looks up, "Oh, did I take too long? It was in the religion section. I'm not as familiar with it."

She set the book down and looked slightly upset. "Don't take it personally. I know him so I'll buy it and give it to him. Let's focus on my list." The hell if I give him that book! He didn't even want it. Looking at the illustration on the front cover, I could see why she was uncomfortable. It was a scene from Dante's Inferno, a graphic interpretation of Hell. She held it differently, away from her body instead of nestled against her.

"Alright. You know him? He was mean and…I don't think he liked me."

"Well, he's a pretentious asshole. And irrelevant."

She shrugs, and I follow her back to the romance section. She found the first few quickly, which was my plan. The other four were deep in the erotica section and very obvious. I was trying to make her aware without breaking the set rules.

She hands me books from the ladder, "Here is *'To Love a Black Soul,' 'Take My Breath Away,'* and *'Electric Pulse.'* The others are over here." She goes into the erotica section. Glancing at the list, I see the redness form. "Let's uh, let's start with *'He Wants to Dominate Me.'* That's in the BDSM section. I think *'Tie Me Up, Daddy'* is there, too."

"Mhmm." The way her tone shifted when she spoke those titles. I could practically hear her submissiveness. She climbs the ladder again, but I'm watching her as she uses her fingertips to trace the spines. She hands me the domination one; her touch is fucking torturing me. I want to sit her on the rung and slide into her so deliciously. To claim her where she works and get lost in her dreams and desires.

"Here's the other one. Umm, I can't read this second-to-last one. What is this?"

I laugh internally. I saw an unintentional shudder as I leaned in closer to her. "It's *'Unexplained Sexual Attraction.'*" My eyes met hers; I saw and felt it, the animal attraction. Lost in thoughts, she recalled the nights when she indulged in fantasies of what could be between us. Unaware that I was doing the same.

Another shudder, "I-I think that's in the self-help section."

"Mmm…self-help is good."

"Y-yeah. Umm, it should be right here. Oh, I don't think we have it. This is a first. I'm so sorry, Levi."

"It's not your fault; order it, and I'll come by the day it arrives. I can learn about my attraction another time. Let's locate that last one." I already knew my attraction was fated. My desire to take and please her for eternity was my destiny. To have someone by my side through it all, as above, so below.

"Yes, *'101 of the Greatest Love Stories' is* romantic history." She quickly moves to that section and locates the thick book. She hands me the others while shuffling through the pages as she walks toward the front. She didn't know I was following like a lost puppy. I hear her sigh as I look over her shoulder. She's reading the tale of Cleopatra and Mark Antony.

"Are they your favorite couple?"

"Oh no, that would be John and Abigail Adams."

"Why is that?"

"He penned her countless love letters when they were apart. He adored her and only wanted to hold her again. It's classically romantic. But no one does that anymore. It's not like I would know, anyway. Your total is $255.35."

I would pen her a million letters. She deserves to know she is as beautifully adored as any other woman.

"Thanks for your help today and the cocoa."

"It was my pleasure. Do you realize you had quite a lengthy conversation with me? Entire sentences and opinions. I'm proud of you."

She laughs. "You made me feel comfortable and, I guess, special. It was…nice."

I boldly lifted her chin, and she gasped. She didn't look away; she seemed to make sure she looked me in the eyes. My little book mouse is getting bold.

"You are special to me. Remember that. I'll see you next week."

"Okay." Back to the one-word answer. I'll allow it. I can't wait until she's eager to say 'Yes, Daddy' or even better, 'Yes, sir'.

Fuck! I can feel myself growing. I've got to do something distracting, like a long public torture session, to keep up my reputation as the Prince of Darkness. Instill the fear upon the masses and prove I'm still the demon spawned from the King of Hell. I don't know why I have to prove anything, but they think her presence weakens me. I'll show them as I round up some sinners and spit-roast them medium well for my babies to snack on. They prefer a bit more tender than if I cooked them well.

I snap into my office; the screams are extra loud today. I assume they are trying some new methods on the latest arrivals. I select 20 of the most notorious serial killers and set them on a plateau where everyone can witness what happens next. They look frantic and confused as they look around, trying to see which direction their punishment is coming from. Metal arrows shoot through the flames and pierce them precisely, instantly cooking them from the inside out. Then they fall into the pit for my hounds to devour, and they are not quiet eaters.

Bon appétit.

It doesn't still my thoughts about Haven. The pull gets

stronger, the attraction grows, and my thoughts become more and more intense. Soon I won't be able to resist my desire.

There is one concern: when I reveal the creature within me, will she be able to see past that? Can she look past the monster and love me?

# CHAPTER 10

## HAVEN

THERE'S BEEN A WEIRD INFLUX OF INCREDIBLY HANDSOME PATRONS, and they all have features similar to Levi's—strong jawline, coiffed hair, mesmerizing smile, and exquisitely dressed. Unless the University has commissioned a new batch of professors or I missed the announcement of a new up-and-coming business in town, I'm curious how they ended up here.

It reminds me I don't know what Levi does for a living, but he always has a business meeting or something he has to rush off to. He's definitely essential to whatever it is. But I don't understand why he hangs out at this tiny, no-name bookstore when he could be fine dining in Milan, perusing highly acclaimed French museums, or tanning on a five-star resort beach in Fiji, yet he enjoys this place. It seems odd, but I know so little about him, except his book obsession.

I know he is incredibly handsome and looks slightly older than me. I'm 24, but soon, I will hit my first adult milestone after 21. I wish I had friends nearby to celebrate these moments with. I remember sitting in the middle of my dorm room floor with my first bottle of red wine and a confetti cupcake on my 21st birthday. My roommate Lexi had to go home for an emergency but made it up to me when she returned. She treated me to dinner and a movie.

I decided this year would be different! It's my 25th birthday, and I will do something exciting and follow through. I want to celebrate myself and who I've become. I want to gain that confidence to be okay with doing things myself and for myself.

That's what I'll do! I'll get dolled up and make reservations at Il Primera; it's the hottest spot in town! I'll tell them it's my birthday and maybe they'll sing Happy Birthday. I'll wish to find the one who makes me his #1, who makes my heart flutter. I can't explain this sensation that started about two years ago. It's a feeling, a voice in my head that whispers to me to be patient and that it'll all be worth it. I wonder what that means.

I almost forgot I was at work until I felt a harsh tap on my shoulder, almost like a shove. "Are you hard of hearing? I've been calling you! There are books strewn everywhere, and it's almost closing time. I'm not paying overtime and leaving at 5:00 pm sharp!" She stomps away before I can even reply that, of course, there would be books everywhere. It's a goddamn bookstore! I've spent plenty of non-paid after-hours putting this place back together. It was my peace.

She's only working here because her daddy owned the store. And it's operating because it's a provision in his will. If she closes it, she'll stop getting her inheritance.

Her father was the one who hired me before his retirement and sudden death. He'd say things like, "Haven, you're like the daughter I always thought I'd have and not the one I got." He made me smile as we picked up books and put them in their rightful place. He told me tales of his days as an Air Force pilot. It was so fascinating. I enjoyed every day with Mr. Smith; he was like my second dad.

So, it was very heartbreaking when his wife broke the news to me of his death. She didn't have to; I was just his employee, and now I had to find a job that gave me just as much purpose.

She held my hand and told me he raved about how sweet a girl he thought I was, which warmed my heart. To think anyone else could love me.

"Walt loved you dearly, Haven, and I do, too. That's why I wanted to tell you myself." She spoke softly, her eyes still filled with unshed tears. She'd blot them with her handkerchief that he had embroidered with their initials and wedding anniversary date.

"Thank you, Miss Emma. It means a lot. I'm sad because I'll have to find someplace else to work now."

"Nonsense! The bookstore will stay open, but Cherry will run it." She sighed while patting my hand. "Don't let her ruin her father's legacy. If this place were yours, I know he'd be so proud. You both had this love and passion for the bookstore. Even though it isn't yours, I know you'll keep Walt's love of books alive."

"I-I will, Miss Emma." Sometimes, I forget that I have people who care; I guess I'm too focused on the romantic aspect and forget about familial and platonic love. This reminds me to write Miss Emma a letter. She moved to Paris to live out her remaining days and connect with her side of the family again. I got a letter from her last month. I'll send something out this weekend.

"Miss?" I look to see a petite girl in glasses. She is wrapped up in a cozy sweater. She looks like a younger, even more innocent version of me.

"Yes, how can I help you?"

"I'm, uh…looking for…" I can see she's embarrassed to ask for something in particular. I know that feeling all too well.

I smile. "I won't judge. What's the title?"

She pushed her short, wavy blonde locks behind her ear. "The uh Basics to Bon-Bondage…"

"And BDSM. I know just the book."

"You do?" She seemed relieved, maybe because I looked like an older version of herself.

She followed me to the erotica section, where she started turning even redder. I grabbed the book, but a special edition with a more discrete cover, and handed it over. She presses it against her chest to hide the title and its contents. Thinking about what would happen if her professor saw her clutching such a book! I understand, but lately, I've felt this little flame grow bigger and bigger about my curiosity, not caring who knows what interests me.

"No need to feel embarrassed about your curiosity. Knowing what you like will make your life a lot easier. Even better if you can find someone gentle enough to explore them with you."

I was shocked! Who was this woman talking to this girl about adult situations?

"I, well, my boyfriend isn't curious, but I am. I saw this movie where a secretary enjoyed being restrained and spanked by her boss. When I watched it, I imagined myself in her place and liked it. Especially the spanking. I want to read about it before I bring it up, you know?"

"Totally understand. I'll tell you a secret…" I go behind the counter as she walks around to the front, leaning forward like we were old friends gossiping. "I found myself immersed in that book, too. Imagining myself as a sub for a pretty regular customer here. How he'd teach me every single lesson. And that same day, he came in and bought that book!"

"Talk about coincidence! So have you…?" She made a gesture that I understood.

"Oh no, I'm hardly his type. He probably went to his fancy skyline condo and used it on some tall, statuesque blonde wearing couture lingerie, but I can have him in my fantasies until I find someone. The point is, go for what you want. You only have one life."

"Thanks, that's what I'm going to do. And I hope one day your handsome prince charming whisks you away and teaches you everything you want to learn but also captures your heart. It was nice meeting you…" She offers her hand, and I shake it.

"Haven."

"Claire. I'll see you around."

I wrap her book, and she walks out more confident than when she came in. I'm glad I could help her even when I can't help myself. The obvious question is, what do I want?

# CHAPTER 11

## LEVI

"Go away, Aurora! You said not to summon you again, and I didn't. The rules topside apply down here, too! Besides, you're bedding the old man now. And why didn't you ever use your forked tongue on me? You know what, never mind. Get out!"

She doesn't heed my threat; instead, she sits down smugly, "Your father could give me four orgasms in a row, and I thought I would treat him. You hadn't earned that trick yet. Anyway, word around Hell is that your mate is an unbelievably plain bore of a woman, unfit to sit beside you on the throne, so you should reconsider having me instead. You could have the sexiest demoness as your Queen; what do you say?"

I sigh and rub my eyes. She doesn't get it.

"Aurora…" I lean forward, causing her to lean in further. A sly smile crossed her lips as her eyes flashed yellow before returning to their brown hue.

"My dear, why would I want a sloppy, revolving-door whore to be my Queen? You've fucked my father…consistently. Everyone else may not give in to their mate bond and instead enjoy the carnal paradise, but I am not my father. I know now that I'm more like my mother without even knowing her."

I lost myself in wondering what she looked like. I have no

memories of her. My dad said she left when I was a baby, and he could be telling the truth. But then again…

"Whore?! It wasn't such a problem when you were slamming me against the wall, when I was clawing your back, or when I was swallowing you down my throat! Was I a whore then?!"

"Yes, in fact, that's the very definition! They are only there to fulfill temporary needs. Now you're banging the King of Hell. That's a huge step up for you."

"No, it isn't. Your dad, though capable, is ancient and banging everyone. I even saw him with a few of his male…"

"Unnecessary information!" I scream while trying to wipe my brain clean from that image attempting to manifest.

"The fact is, Levi, you're next in line for the throne, and every succubus is going to shoot their shot, but they all know that I have the best chance." She crawls onto my desk and lies on her back, arching it dangerously. If I had never found Haven and I was delusionally stupid…maybe, but I know my princess exists, nothing will stop me from claiming her.

Seeing I ignored her exploits, she chuckles, "And what if she rejects you because you're a monster? Hmm, ever get out of that perfect fantasy of yours to realize that maybe she doesn't want to be mated to a demon? Not only a demon but THE Prince of Darkness, and she's only seen your human form. Are you going to keep your demon side hidden or risk scaring her to death when you reveal your true self? Then you'll never have her because she won't end up here, not Miss Goody Two Shoes." She said with a bitter laugh, the arrogance in her words. With a quick snap of my fingers, she disappears, but the lingering emotions of frustration and doubt weigh heavily in the air.

Haven's birthday is in two weeks, and I'll have to do the most challenging thing ever: stay away until then. I don't trust the already frayed strings of my control around her. I'm so close I can't risk it!

I plan to bide my time by increasing my torture schedule and extra one-on-one time with my hellhounds. Spoiling them with their favorite treats, double deep-fried pedophiles. They love watching them flail in the oil until they can't move. Did I mention that both times they fry them, the pedophiles are still alive? Those screams are the most satisfying.

I love that I can allow my wings to extend to full span. I plucked some victims from the pit and dangled them high, watching them squirm as I peeled strips of flesh from their bones. I am saving a few to chop up for Abaddon and Amon, who are awaiting their puppies. The next generation of soul-snatching servants will arrive soon.

My other babies wait anxiously below. Their hunger knows no bounds, and neither does mine. I've rubbed myself raw these past few days. I yearn for the gentle brush of her fingertips, the intoxicating aroma of her presence, and the sheer essence of her being enveloping every inch of me.

I almost prayed for relief.

# CHAPTER 12

## HAVEN

Cherry thought it would be great to try extended hours, from 9 am to 9 pm, to be more available for the college kids. Apparently, she's been flooding the campus all week with the same flyer that greeted me on the door this morning, and of course, she decided to tell me the day of. Oh, and it's not US staying late; no, just me. Shocking, right?

We had an influx of people curious to expand their minds about whatever we housed within these walls. I saw a team of basketball players break the stereotype of the dumb jock when they came after their practice. It warmed my heart to see such eagerness from everyone, whether it be books, magazines, or comics. This could be a good idea. I just wish she had talked to me about it. She knows I would do anything to keep her father's dream alive. And she uses that to her advantage.

It's almost closing time, but I'm bombarded by the violent bell jingles and loud cackling voices instead of whispers. Cherry strolled in with some girls; all dressed up to go to a club or the nearest lit street corner. Their dresses are short, tight, and bind-ing. Their heels are sky high to accentuate their long legs. The fur coats and crop jackets they wore were just for decoration; it wasn't to retain heat.

"Glad to see my brilliant idea worked. Maybe we'll do this more often."

WE?! I just stare at her.

"Let me grab some extra cash for the VIP section. We always upgrade, right, girls?!"

They whoop and holler, causing them to become the center of attention and ruffling the feathers of a few patrons.

"Cherry, who's that?" A brunette with a lollipop in her mouth points at me while leering. I feel uneasy as they all turn to stare at me. Cherry scoffs, "That's Haven, my minion. She does anything I tell her to because she's poor and needs this job. Isn't that right, Haven?" Cherry laughs as she enters her office, followed by her friends, except for that rude one.

The way she looks at me makes me feel like I did something wrong to her. But I've never seen her before! I try to look away, but her scowl is hard to ignore. She popped the sweet treat out of her mouth as she stepped forward and leaned over the counter.

"It's amazing how the most incredibly handsome and powerful men fall for the charity cases, the doormats, the down-right…boring. I don't see his appeal…to you." She looked me up and down with such viciousness.

*Was she talking about me?*

"How can he be even the least bit interested in someone like you? Especially when women like me are ready to bend over and accept that amazing dick. But you wouldn't know what to do with a man like him. I bet… you're as innocent as a nun in church. Ha! How stereotypical! He deserves a woman who makes him moan as you choke, trying to swallow him down your throat, saying thank you when he empties into your mouth. Looking innocent when he tells you, 'Good girl.' But no, he wants you…you! This has to be a joke!"

I had no idea what she was talking about. Does someone like me? Apparently, someone she knows, but I don't! She is still judging me, but now she's not silent. She's worse than Cherry, and she is not in the least bit remorseful.

"You don't even know who I'm talking about, do you, Haven?"

I shook my head. For the first time, I'm relieved when Cherry comes out of her office to interrupt this very cryptic conversation.

"I'm sure he can sense your distress, so I'll make this short. You don't have a claim to a man like him. You're mediocre... he deserves a girl like me. Do yourself a favor and don't even consider accepting his proposal...I'll make your life a living Hell."

Cherry squeals, "Alright bitches! Let's party and find some hot, rich guys to spoil us!" She gyrates and dances towards the exit, and her friends follow but not her; she stares daggers at me until she's out of sight.

What was that all about?! She must be crazy because no man has approached me like that. And a proposal? She must be high or something; maybe I look like her ex's current girlfriend. I can tell he dodged a bullet!

I admit I felt a sharp pain when she cut me down. But it also lit a fire within me...she doesn't know me! She's just one of Cherry's easy friends; she had no right to judge when she was going out to find men to screw for the night.

Ooh! She made me so mad! I imagine myself punching her right in her whorish mouth. It'd be hard to suck dick with a dislocated jaw.

My thoughts surprise even me. Violent outbursts, first with Cherry, now this girl whose name I didn't even get. But it felt good, and one day I would verbalize those threats and mean it.

I checked to see if all the customers had left before I closed the store. I smile, knowing I have booked an appointment for tomorrow after work. Some much-needed me time and a present to myself.

Cherry or whoever that girl is will not ruin my birthday! Twenty-five was my year, and I felt something big would change my life forever.

# CHAPTER 13

## LEVI



"Tell your newest conquest; if she approaches Haven again, I'll make sure not even the sex demons touch her!"

"Please, do you really think I can control your old fling? Why don't you tell her? I'm sure she'll still come at your beck and call. She screams your name instead of mine, anyway. Guess this old bull needs to find someone a little less... stuck on you. But can she suck a mean..."

"For fuck's sake... I don't care! You can screw her until your balls fall off. I don't want her. I have Haven."

"Son, you can't think this will go well, right? In the end, she will shatter you, and you'll become...I don't know..."

"Like you? Trying to fuck his feelings away instead of relishing in the woman who loved him enough to bear him a son, an heir? Why don't you talk about her?"

"Nothing to say; it's in the past. It's irrelevant." His passive comments only piss me off more.

"But it isn't irrelevant. She was my mother! Did you ever think that maybe I'd want to know why she isn't here? Is she dead? Did she leave us? What are you hiding?"

He stands up, his eyes flickering. He's trying not to lash out, but his monster grows annoyed with my interrogation.

"Leave it in the past, Levi! She's gone and never coming back. I wouldn't allow her back if she crawled on red-hot coals. It's too much power held by...a woman."

"You're a coward. A monster."

"Call me what you want, but you'll never call me a fool for a woman."

With that, he disappears to cut off the conversation.

He's hiding something, and I feel it's a big piece of me that I'm missing.

*Several days later...*

I've put together a carefully laid plan to put in motion.

Realizing how many of them were skulking around the store, I sent a memo warning that if anyone else was caught at the bookstore without my explicit permission trying to hinder my plans, I would use them for experimentation, for the punishments that live in the dark recesses of my mind. In the last one I implemented; only certain demons were willing to carry out. Or the only ones who could stomach it. How they avoided me when I walked around let me know they got the point.

Aurora has crossed the line, and I will ensure she understands that her actions have dire consequences.

It was agony to skip my weekly visit; I was exceptionally unrelenting that day. Truthfully, I was venting; I wanted to be as calm as possible before professing my love.

"Wow, someone's been lashing out today. Is it because you're skipping your little book fix?"

I look up from my paperwork to see Trevor and our mutual friend Carson. He brought Carson to decrease his chances of being turned into a standing fire pit.

Carson smacks Trevor upside the head, "Shut up, Trevor. The man is about to reveal himself to his mate. You'd be on edge, too, if you weren't such a promiscuous slut. Listen, Levi, I'm one of very few who share your views. I wish you luck because you'll need your Queen to battle all this pandemonium."

I look over. Trevor is smirking like the weasel he was, but I saw the sincerity on Carson's face, and I buckled.

"I'm fucking terrified. What if she runs away from me? It can't be easy being mated to the son of Satan."

"But she's your white light, your grounding. If everyone turned their backs, she'd be the one who would be there no matter what. In that sense, I think I know what's bothering you."

I raise my brow in response.

"You're afraid you'll taint her. Becoming a permanent black stain on the snow-white wings of your angel. She is as pure as it gets, but her place is with you. I bet she knows that, but you wonder if she'll regret her decision. Will she be okay with all this?"

He was spot on. I gain her, but she loses so much. Not only will she be okay with that, but will I also be able to live with the guilt of taking her away from her mortal life?

"Or you could let her find some equally boring guy up there and live a mediocre life until they die."

There's Trevor with his 'wisdom.'

"You're really asking for it. Remember who was curled up like a fetus at my feet, begging me not to separate them from their manhood." He looks away, and that kills his entire conversation. I thought so. I can make sure it never grows back. An eternal eunuch is the perfect punishment for him or anyone who crossed me. Why didn't I think of it sooner?

"Well, either way, it's now or never. Either I return with her or don't return at all."

They both look at me in shock, admitting out loud what I've only been thinking. Carson breaks their silence, "What the hell are you talking about, Levi? Not coming back? You're next up for the throne; it's your birthright as the firstborn."

"And I've watched my dad rule, and as shocking as this seems, it's not my entire life's goal to be the next King of Hell, at least not without her. I'm content with living the rest of my days with the humans if that's what it takes to be with her. If I lay it all out on the line and she says she doesn't want to come down here, we won't. That simple."

"ARE YOU INSANE?! For a human woman?! Does your dad know this bit of information?" I could see him salivating at the gossip he could run back with.

"No, Trevor, but I'm sure you'll go running back the first chance you get to relay the information and suck his dick. Do you usually use knee pads? Or do you …whatever. You can yell it from the sulfuric cascade mountains; it won't sway my decision. If you'll excuse me, I've spent two weeks away and am ready to lay it all out on the line. Carson, thanks. Trevor…I truly hope your balls fall off and you have recurrent uncontrollable discharge and acid fire erupts from your pee hole." I snap them out of my room before I snap myself above ground.

I warded my Earth domicile to keep away unwanted guests, also known as my father. It's still not strong enough. I place candles that strategically lead to every room: the kitchen, the master bath, the bedroom, and the playroom. I want to taint my sheets before we christen the playroom. It would be her choice where we go first, but I plan on marking every square inch of this home with her essence, her moans, and her cries of passion as I feel her tighten around me.

In the dining room, red roses in sleek black vases set the scene, complemented by a few candles on the table. I wanted nothing obstructing my view of my radiant beauty.

I still need to change into my suit. I wear one she's already seen, then snap back to the bookstore around closing time. Or what I thought was closing time, but they're still open and pretty busy. She better not be working my mate too hard because now… all bets are off.

# CHAPTER 14

## HAVEN

*Sigh*

"Well…happy 25th birthday, Haven. Please, world, be kind to me this year."

The weight of loneliness settled heavily on my shoulders, causing my body to sink deeper into the comfort of my bed. The room, once filled with the warmth of hope, now felt cold and desolate. As I lay there, the tears welled up in my eyes, threatening to spill over onto my pillow. I clenched my fists, trying to hold back the flood of emotions that threatened to consume me. The lump in my throat grew larger, making it harder to swallow the bitter taste of disappointment.

I closed my eyes, desperately seeking solace, and whispered my plea to the man upstairs. I desperately sought solace, closed my eyes, and whispered my plea to the man upstairs, infusing each word with a mix of desperation and longing, as if my entire existence depended on the kindness of a higher power. The silence that followed was deafening, leaving me to wonder if my words had fallen on deaf ears.

Birthdays were supposed to be a time of celebration, a reminder of the love and joy shared with those closest to us. But for me, it had become a painful reminder of my isolation.

But a glimmer of hope flickered within me. I refused to surrender to the darkness that threatened to engulf my spirit. I vowed to push through the loneliness, to find strength in myself, and to believe that the world could be kind to me, even if it hadn't been in the past.

I'm in a slightly better mood when walking to the shop. Something is different, but I can't put my finger on it; it's like I'm hypersensitive to my surroundings. My shower felt sensual as the hot water massaged me in all the right places. It only intensified these feelings I couldn't say aloud. I blushed at my highly provocative thoughts of Levi.

I enjoyed the peace while I could before it was interrupted by patrons or, worse, by Cherry and her holier-than-thou attitude.

I stopped at the coffee shop where Levi bought those decadent hot chocolates. Their coffee had to be magical if the hot cocoa was that amazing.

The bells announce my presence. "Good morning, welcome to Craving Coffee Cafe. My name is Nigel. How can I start your morning off, Miss..."

Goodness, he was handsome. His infectious smile lighting up the room, filling it with warmth and happiness. With his strong British accent, blonde hair, and beautiful smile, he was quite the charmer. His white button-up sleeves were neatly rolled up to his forearms. I noticed because it reminded me of the book.

"Haven."

"Haven, what a beautiful name. Don't you...don't you work at the little bookstore not far from here?"

"Yeah."

He pours a coffee but never takes his eyes off me. He smiles with his eyes as he completes the perfect pour. I didn't even give him my order; it's like he read my soul. I drink coffee in all forms, and the way he presented it, I knew it would be delicious.

"I'll have to come in some time. Especially now that I know..."

He trailed off, but I knew what he was implying, and here comes the heat in my cheeks.

Having another regular customer who pays attention to me would be nice, especially since I haven't seen Levi in two weeks. I hoped nothing had happened to him, but I had no way of finding out. I could only hope that, eventually, I would get those familiar tingly feelings again when the bell alerted me of my swoon-worthy shopper.

"What brings you in today, darling?"

I raise my brow. Mainly because of the use of a pet name, but I remember how friendly they are across the pond. He's just being polite.

"What I mean is, I've never seen you in here until today. Treating yourself?"

"It's my birthday," I whispered.

"It is? Well, happy 21st birthday, gorgeous! If you didn't have to work, I'd add a splash of Brandy. But here, let me…"

He takes my coffee, puts it in a larger cup, adds whipped cream and confetti sprinkles. Then he pens my name in a calligraphy style with loops, swirls, a bouquet of balloons, and finally, a 'happy birthday' at the bottom. It looked so festive now, and I couldn't help but smile at his sweet gesture.

"What a pretty smile! Here you go."

"Thank you. Oh, I'm not 21, I'm 25."

"I'm going to need to see some ID. There's no way you're my age. They say those who are blessed look younger. They don't let their circumstances mar their faces. Consider yourself lucky."

If I did, I'd look like a decaying mummy corpse, but I remind myself of one positive thing to be thankful for daily. Even with Cherry's verbal abuse, I'm grateful for my job. I could've been miserable in a menial corporate position, probably making coffee and food runs for a room full of sexist men who think a woman should be at home or taking care of the men in her office in every way imaginable. I suppose I could be in a worse situation than dealing with a loud-mouthed, spoiled, bitch.

I giggle at my honesty about how I feel; in fact, she is the fucking worst! I have held my tongue for far too long. The switch was flipped today.

"Haven, you zoned out there, love."

I snap back into reality, right into his dreamy blue eyes. Gosh, they were pretty.

"Oh, sorry. I, uh, got to go. Don't want to be late to work."

"I understand. Have an amazing birthday. See you soon…"

I send a quick smile his way before rushing out with my special coffee. I can see the shop, but it doesn't look like Cherry beat me here. She'll probably stumble in around 10 am if she didn't spend all night blitzed and on her knees, noonish if she did.

Either way, I was out of here at 2 pm for a much-needed treat to myself. It was a spa appointment and a makeover. I notified her yesterday, but she didn't respond. I made the appointment anyway because I deserved this, especially for all my hard work. It was not like she was giving me the day off or even a half day, so I took it upon myself. She'll have to deal with customers for the last few hours. God forbid!

I'm still in a great mood, and my smile brightens when Claire strolls through. She walks in confidently, not timidly like last time.

"Hi, Haven!"

"Morning Claire, how are you?"

She had a megawatt smile as she rocked side to side before placing her hands on the counter.

"I'm so happy! I wanted to thank you for your help. I went home, told my boyfriend about my curiosity, and showed him the movie with the secretary. He watched how turned on I was and said he would like to try it out. We've been reading the book together."

She paused, causing me to lean forward, waiting for the next juicy detail. "And?! The suspense is killing me!"

She smiles, craning her neck up, and I notice a thin leather strip held together by a metal heart and something etched next to it. I had a guess but wasn't sure.

"Did he?"

"Yes, he collared me. I am his, and he even got a matching bracelet to mark that he is mine. He loves this journey, and I've never been happier!"

"I'm so happy to hear that."

She's so elated that she can hardly stop moving. Then she reaches toward me, turning my cup to see Nigel's sweet message.

"Oh my gosh, Haven, it's your birthday? Happy birthday! What are you going to do to celebrate?"

"Thank you. I have a spa date, and maybe I'll take myself somewhere and have them sing to me. I've always wanted that. Nothing big."

"I hope you enjoy your spa and your birthday to the fullest! Maybe you'll finally get the courage to approach your crush. Have you made any progress?"

I didn't want to frown after not having seen him in weeks. My mind made up endless scenarios that always ended up with him and some painfully beautiful woman who was more his speed, unlike quiet, timid me. I sigh and roll my eyes, "No, like I said, he's out of my league." I hated listening to the words leave my lips. Then I'm reminded of how he smiles at me, how I feel when he's directly behind me when I'm looking for his books, or how he calls me his favorite girl or book mouse. How could such a cute pet name make me want to rip my clothes off and give myself to him?

I'm brought out of my thoughts by Claire's tsks. "He is not out of your league. For all you know, the feeling is mutual. What if he's in love with you? I can see that you are…"

Whoa…love?! No, I think it's more of an innocent high school crush. I couldn't be…could I? The fact that my heart aches because I hadn't seen him is irrelevant. My entire body feels like it could erupt into flames at the mere sight of him. My body was screaming for him, and I don't mean in an innocent way.

What was happening?

I see the hope in Claire's eyes.

"All I'm saying is give it a shot, and if you're wrong... well, he didn't deserve your hot ass, anyway!"

A loud laugh slipped before I covered my mouth and looked around.

"What are you in here for, anyway?"

"Oh! Almost forgot. I wanted to peruse what else you have in the same style as the other book."

A blush starts to appear; hers is totally adorable, unlike mine, which looks like what drunk cartoon characters get: a solid red stripe across the bridge of my nose.

She follows behind me. "Well, we have plenty over here. Might I make a few recommendations? *'The ABCs of BDSM'* is great. Umm, *'Daddy's Good Girl'* over here and..." I crouch down to the bottom shelf and grab a bright red book. I wondered if she would cradle it like last time. "And this one, *'Do You Want a Spanking?'*"

I hand Claire the book, and instead of clutching it against her, she opens it while walking back to the counter.

"Ooh, here's a list of compliments a companion can say to their pet. They have some normal ones like *good girl/boy; you're doing so good, who's my beautiful girl or handsome boy*? If Henry said those, I'd be a pool on the floor. I have to show him this."

I rang her up in silence, thinking about when I replied to Levi with yes, sir. I was waiting in anticipation, on bated breath, for him to lift my chin and whisper, "Good girl."

Claire's right: I'd last like a snowball in front of a hairdryer.

"Ooh, they got some naughty ones, too. *You feel incredible; you can take it,* and *good girl, now ride this dick.* Gosh, is it hot in here? Let's wrap this up. I definitely need to get home now."

I rang her up, feeling like I was sitting in a dry sauna. My entire body flushed. I tucked the bookmark in and tied it up beautifully.

"That's $78.42." She hands over her card, and I hand her the receipt. I smile, "Alright, well, have fun." She squealed in excitement, "Oh, I plan to! Enjoy your birthday. I'll treat you to a decadent dessert and sinful hot chocolate at the French bistro on Blythe Cove by Paradise Park?" Her brows raised, and her tone had an upward inflection, posing it as a question.

"Sure, it's a date."

"See you laters."

"See you."

I smile happily, knowing that I have found a friendship. One I never thought I'd have again.

*Four hours later*

***Ding ding***

"UGH, I'm never drinking again."

Noon on the dot, and like I figured, with her instant verbal confirmation, she spent her night on the stroll.

"I'll be in my office. Don't disturb me."

"Fine with me. Just remember I'm leaving at 2 pm. I have an appointment."

She dragged her huge dark sunglasses off her face to reveal a different look. She came in without full makeup and looked terribly aged, at least 20 years older.

"What?! You can't leave. We're having a late night today!"

A surge of power washed over me, and I turned to face her as she looked at me, trying to intimidate me.

"I told you yesterday, and I won't cancel it. It's bad enough that I'm working on my birthday, but you don't care. I'm doing this for me, and please, let's not go down the 'I'm going to fire you' route because we both know that if I contact your mother, she'll cut you off so quickly you'll end up on the street."

*Sucking pruney old dicks for cash.*

Cherry's eyes bucked, and her mouth fell open. She wasn't expecting her quiet little worker bee to bite back, but today was not the day. I cross my arms and continue the stare down until she huffs.

"Fine, but you have to come back after. I'm not closing this place up by myself again." She scoffed.

"Fair enough. I'll finish upon my return. As for right now, I suggest you put on some makeup."

Once again she looked shocked, but I didn't feel like sugarcoating that she looked like a moldy raisin in the desert sunlight. She'll scare the customers. That's what happens when you're ugly on the inside.

Now that I know I have to return, I'll have to change at the spa for my dinner at Il Primera. I'm excited to taste their menu. I've always thought it was petrifying to go out alone in any sense, but I was going to try.

The hours just zoomed by as 2:00 pm came, and surprisingly, Cherry was already out at about 1:45 pm. She was behind the counter, looking human again with a full face of makeup.

"I'll be back after my appointment to close up." She flips a magazine page and waves me off. I didn't even give her a chance to change her mind as I rushed out and down to my apartment. I called for an Uber, grabbed my dress, and was on my way to Winterfall Springs Spa.

Even the outside was magnificent; waterfalls flanked the entrance, the sound of the water calming your mind before you even stepped foot into the reception area. Everything is basking in a warm white, not that cold, stark white light they use in hospitals.

"Hello, welcome to Winterfall Springs Spa. Name?"

"Hello, the last name is Evers, Haven."

She enters my information dend smiles, "Ah, here you are, Miss Evers. I have you for a deep tissue massage and facial with hair services afterward. Follow me, and I'll take you to your changing bungalow."

Ten minutes later, I'm face down and hesitantly naked under this towel, ready for my massage, hoping it will relax me.

Then it hit me: what if I have a male masseuse? I didn't think to specify gender when I booked it! Then my door opened. "Hello, Miss Evers. My name is Xanon, and I'll be your masseuse. I see that today is your birthday. Happy birthday. I'll tack on my world-famous foot massage. It'll be like walking on clouds."

I giggled because it sounded heavenly, but he also sounded gorgeous. I didn't dare look up unless I wanted to flash him.

"Thank you. I'm excited." I can hear him rub his hands together, then pump something, probably oil, and rub them again. I assume to warm his hands, so I don't scream at icy fingers touching my skin. I take a deep breath and concentrate on the soothing music. He does amazingly as he works the knots out of my neck and lower back. Then I turn over and nod off.

I feel thumbs circling my collarbone. "There she is. Your time is up, Haven. I hope you feel relaxed." He uses a softer voice. I'm amazed at how loose and light I feel. "Wow, you have magical fingers. My toes are tingling." I wiggle them, and they send a pleasant shiver up my spine.

He turned toward me, and I finally saw the literal master-piece that caressed me into a peaceful slumber.

*Aren't there any average-looking guys or guys I have a chance with?*

He had to have been a model in his former life. Knowing that his strong, bronzed arms were all over me, a smirk crossed my lips as I kept myself from biting them.

"I'm glad to make a small part of your day magical. Step out once you are dressed, and I'll escort you to the salon." He leaves me with a wickedly flirty smile.

"Thank you, Xanon." Once he leaves, I fan myself, but it does nothing. I stretch myself one more time before putting my clothes back on.

He hands me a water bottle and leads me to a tiny space. Oh my gosh, my hairdresser has lilac hair! And it's totally adorable.

"Hi, Miss Haven. My name is Taylor, and I'll be your stylist today. Tell me what you're looking for."

First, she gently pulls my hair back, and then she moves it forward. It's long, lifeless, and straight. It's just plain boring. I wanted something fun and whimsical…like hers! I'm not saying it would instantly turn me into a conversational genius or social butterfly, but it would be an icebreaker.

"I want waves and a new color…and chop it off! Shoulder length with bangs. I don't want to recognize the old me."

"Okay, I love your energy! We're going to do something fun. I have a great idea! I'm going to blindfold you for a grand reveal. I have just the look in mind. Can I choose the color?"

I took a deep breath, knowing I would be oblivious until the end. "Yes!" She lowers the blindfold while smiling. "Well, then… goodbye to the old Haven…"

# CHAPTER 15

## LEVI



There are a lot of losers in the store for it to be so late. Then, I noticed the revised hours posted on a piece of paper. Interesting, I'm sure my sweet girl had no say in that decision, but she always does what's best for the bookstore. The only thing I wanted her to love as much as me.

I paced around, waiting for a few of them to leave. My disdain for these creatures is at an all-time high. Honestly, I am not a fan of anyone above or below; the only person who makes me feel least like a monster is Haven. I'm about to gamble it all and possibly live amongst the humans, and the worst thing is having to silence my demon. He's unhappy about the risk of being locked away and has made it known. Keeping him under control has been more of a challenge than usual. I know that the things I love act as his ultimate trigger.

In the history of my existence, there has only been one uncontrollable outburst with him, and that was in my hormonal teenage phase.

Yes, even I had those.

Mix my developing hormones with a dad like mine, and you get an explosive chemical reaction.

That is how I met my demon.

I demanded to know what happened to my mother. It was the first time my father went utterly unhinged.

*"You want to know what happened to your...mother?" He spat so viciously, "She saddled me with a useless burden. She was a worthless cum dumpster, a refuse for my seed! I didn't even think I could breed with such a feeble creature. Another one of their punishments! My life was fine without her or you! I should have hung her on hooks and forced her to drink lava before you were born. Then I could have eliminated both problems!" His demon was unrelenting in his verbal assault against my mother. I knew nothing about her, but I knew deep down that he was fucking lying!*

*In my subconscious, a red light flickered...and it got my attention as it grew and grew while he continued to bash my mother until it resembled a flame. That flame grew out of control almost immediately until it was a wall. Then, a dark figure appeared from behind it. His eyes glowed as red as the flame behind him.*

*And he growled. He just growled.*

*Somehow, his growl came through me. I was shocked, but not scared. It made me feel powerful and assertive against the disrespectful motherfucker who spoke ill of the woman who birthed me, who I loved!*

*I heard a voice whispering for me to let go. I didn't quite understand what that meant, but I complied. I closed my eyes and felt a rush of air. I opened my eyes and was in my subconscious looking down at my father from a towering height. He looked shocked. Judging by the size of the ceiling, I'm at least 20 feet tall. I look down to see my skin that's now charcoal-black, but my veins glow red. This was my first interaction with turning into my demon, except with no control, because he let out a vicious roar and destroyed part of the wall in my father's office with a flick of his arm.*

*After I swept the wall, destroying everything, my dad shifted into his demon, and was pleasantly shocked by his stature compared to mine. He was at least two feet shorter than me and smaller in build, yet he still tried to grab my neck.*

*"Have you lost your mind? All over the incompetent woman who left you? Know your goddamned place! I AM THE KING OF HELL!"*

*He screamed while trying to wrap his hands around me, but he only further pissed me off.*

*The flame behind me was roaring, and my veins grew brighter. I took my father's demon's arm and plucked it off me before tossing him against the nearest wall, causing more structural damage.*

*"She was my mother!" As fire spewed from my horns, I roared, setting his entire wing ablaze. I rampaged through the lair, destroying everything in sight. The only thing that brought me out of my rage was the whimpering of my dogs. I looked down, and they were cowering in fear. I felt myself being pulled forward and shrunk back to my usual size. I sat on the floor panting as their whimpers and comforting licks on my cheek and hands drowned out the screams. After that, my father only interacted on my side of the house, and I didn't venture to his side.*

That was the last time my mom was brought up; now, he ignores any conversation. I gave up long ago trying to seek the truth from the ultimate deceiver himself. I'm not giving up on finding out what happened because she didn't just leave him. I need to figure it out because I don't need an uncontrollable outburst for Haven to witness. I have to ease her into this.

When I check inside again, I see a few people waiting in line to complete their purchases, but Haven isn't at the counter: it's Cherry. She looked uncomfortable servicing customers as a decent person, not a whore.

Where was my mischievous little book mouse? She better not have her slaving in the back on her birthday!

Another person walked out as I walked in.

"Mmm, what did I do to deserve such a special visit from you, Levi? Did you miss me? It's okay to admit it."

"Where's Haven?" I said bluntly.

"She's got some stupid appointment, but she'll be back because closing the place is not my job, but what can I do for you, Levi?" She kept purring and bouncing her tits like it would convince me to fuck her. She'd make all the adulterers below blush in shame; she was scandalously relentless.

"Nothing. Only she can find what I'm looking for. I'll wait for her to come back." She tuts while I sit in one of the leather chairs. She wanders to the back, and I'm frustrated that I can feel Haven but not see where she is so I can sweep her off her feet. I would have to suffer and wait among these helpless Neanderthals.

I'm stuck watching Cherry prance about. She's trying to get me to notice that she pulled her red skirt up to where the lace of her thigh highs starts. She suddenly needed to bend over to grab that stack of magazines to fill the already full display. It fell on deaf ears, and rolled eyes, but I let her put on a show if it made her feel seen.

Maybe I should suggest to Haven that we sentence Cherry to eternal servitude. My choice would be to toss Cherry's carcass to my hellhounds and be done with it, but they don't like the taste of overly used whores. Besides, my book bee isn't a violent being; her heart is 1,000 times larger than mine, if mine even exists. I would free her conscience from any guilt. As a power couple, I would be the hammer, and she would be my shield. She would look down from the throne, her rightful place beside me, my love and Queen.

I don't remember nodding off, but a clinking-type ringing noise awakens me. Unable to decipher it, I open my eyes to see Haven smiling innocently in front of me while doing something so sinful.

In my confusion, I allow it. I've always wanted to take her here in the store. I graze her cheek with my hand while she's on her knees. The innocence in her gaze makes me painfully hard.

"Levi..." She whispers alluringly. I can't look away from her eyes until her hands move from my knee and rest on my upper thigh. I cursed this fabric that kept me from her unyielding touch, but I didn't want to seem too eager if I snapped myself naked.

She sighed as she slowly, torturously slid her hands further up, inch by inch. I couldn't hide my erection if I wanted to. I was expecting the fantasy I'd always dreamed of in my head.

Seducing me with her innocence and then turning into a sex kitten, confidently taking what she wants.

She slowly unzips me, and I feel the relief of being able to stand hard and erect. I could feel the throbbing becoming more intense in anticipation of her touch. I expected her to be surprised and timid about the size, but she just giggled. Not an offensive laugh, but a curious one as her hand stretched out to touch me. Her lips pursed into a circle; they were waiting to be soiled by my seed. For someone so pure, she seemed to know what to do.

I growled. I had no words. I desperately yearned for Haven to touch me. To relieve this pulsing, only her touch combined with our sparks would drive me to climax.

"Levi." She whispered. It was so soft when it caressed my ears. She licks her lips as she stares at my dick. It jumps in anticipation.

Instead of granting me relief, she leans back in her seat, her fingers curling around the edge of her crisp white button-up. I've never been more jealous of a piece of clothing. I became thoroughly intrigued as she revealed more of her flawless skin. She reaches for the last button, a mischievous smirk playing on her lips. It pops open, revealing a tantalizingly seductive red bra, its delicate straps crossing over each other in a desperate attempt to contain her ample bosom.

"Wow." Was all I could conjure up from what I could see. She shifted a bit, and in that distraction, her hands crept back up my thighs until I watched as her fingertips wrapped around me.

FINALLY!

My eyes rolled to the back of my head as I exhaled deeply, relishing in the comforting heat radiating from her gentle touch. She giggled, as her hands slid up and down my shaft.

But it was wrong.

ALL WRONG.

No sparks.

No electricity.

No urge to pin her against the wall and fuck her senseless.

Everything was wrong. I look at Haven once again but notice something is off. Her once innocent face was corrupt, smiling with ill intent behind it. She kept stroking as I tried to get her hands off me. This couldn't be my Haven. I would have felt it. My body would have caved into her very touch, enjoying every single stroke, but I didn't, and it wasn't.

She continues to reach for me, but I fight it and tuck myself back in my pants. I can't stand up, and I don't know why. This is a nightmare!

I need to wake up. Then the imposter tries to straddle me, and I shove her as hard as I can while standing up.

And I'm finally awake…and aware.

I groan, rub my eyes, and realize someone is actually sitting on me. After the blur subsided from rubbing my eyes, they shot up to see Cherry straddling me in her underwear. It's the same underwear I saw Haven wearing in my fantasy-turned-nightmare.

It was a lie! Before I could even throw her off me, I heard a gasp and looked over.

There was this beautifully dressed woman at the door. Her almost calf-length red dress showed off her petite curves, and her heels accentuated her legs.

When my eyes met hers, I immediately felt my body shudder. The sexy woman who stood there with fire in her eyes and over-whelming heartbreak was Haven. My bookworm had turned into a beautiful butterfly. Her once standard brown tresses that covered her face had been chopped short and given deep red highlights. She was stunning, but my awe didn't last long when I saw her lip quiver and the tears form. My stomach twisted into knots. With a heavy sigh and teary eyes, she turned around and fled.

Shit!

# CHAPTER 16

## HAVEN

About an hour later, Taylor finished placing the wispy pieces away from my face. I could feel the fine hairs being moved; it almost tickled! She has the chair turned around, so even after she removed the blindfold to work on my hair, I'm still blind. I'm dying of excitement! She also did my makeup as a birthday gift.

"And you are done! Wow, she looks more confident and ready to take on the world! I'll schedule you six months out for a touch-up and send you a text reminder, but we should also hang out sometime; here's my number."

"Thank you. I'd love to hang out sometime! Can I turn around now?" She takes my shoulders and slowly turns me around. "I'd like to introduce the new Haven to herself. You are worthy of all the happiness a girl can take. It's the ones with the purest heart who reap the biggest rewards. Enjoy your birthday, hon. Here's everything I used to enhance that beautiful face." She hands me a makeup pouch.

I turn around to see a sight I've never seen. A huge smile on my face! "Oh my gosh, I love it! I've never seen myself like this before. My once dull, lifeless hair has been transformed. It's now brightened with lowlights and has bold, attention-seeking red pieces underneath. There are also a few strands framing my face."

I couldn't wait to accent my new hairstyle with my special birthday dress and celebrate at Il Primera.

The dress, a stunning deep red, exuded simplicity, and elegance. It made me step outside my comfort zone with its bold and sexy color captivating my senses. Falling just below the knee, it gracefully flared at the bottom, adding a touch of femininity. To complete the outfit, I slipped on my only pair of black high heels. As I embraced the chilly air, I buttoned up my black pea coat, using its dark tone to balance the brilliance of the dress.

I took a cab to the restaurant, and a charming man approached me, "Good evening, Miss. Welcome to Il Primera. Name?"

"Good evening, reservation under Evers, Haven."

He scans the computer and smiles. "Ah yes, thank you for celebrating your birthday with us. Follow me, please."

"Alright."

He glanced back with a smile as we went deep into the restaurant, passing families and couples laughing and enjoying their time together. I felt that pang, but I shook it off as he stopped at a small table. I noticed the other chair had balloons tied to it. The people around smiled as they finally saw the guest of honor for this table. He pulls my seat out, takes my coat, and opens my menu, setting the tone for a luxurious dining experience.

"Can I start you with a drink?"

I brush my hair behind my ear. "Umm, what do you recommend?"

"A nice bellini is a good starter for a special celebration such as a birthday."

I agree, and he heads back to place my order. I look around to see a smiling woman at the table across from me. I notice she and her husband's hands are together on the table. They look like they've spent most of their lives in love, and now they're celebrating a significant anniversary, like their 45th or even 50th anniversary. They are so darling! I can feel their love from here. She nods to me and mouths a 'Happy birthday'. I smile and thank her. I took a deep breath because I bypassed my anxiety and stepped out into the world. This is my beginning.

"Peach bellini for the madam."

"Thank you."

"Have you had a chance to peruse the menu?"

How fancy! Almost too pretty to drink. "Oh, yes. I'd like the mushroom risotto stuffed chicken, please."

"A superb choice."

As I looked at the dessert menu, someone placed a bright orange tropical-looking drink, complete with a pink umbrella, on my table.

The waiter smiled. It was a different guy than the one who took my order. "From the gentleman at the bar."

I look in the direction he pointed. The mystery man wore a simple all-black suit. He carried himself with confidence, bordering on arrogance. Before I could thank the waiter and relay my appreciation, he was getting up from the bar and heading my way while buttoning up his jacket.

Oh, no! What should I do?! I'm not good at social interaction, especially being flirtatious! EEK! Heaven help me not to be awkward!

He stood in front of me and held out his hand. By instinct, I placed my hand in his. He smiled as his lips touched my hand. The moment he did, it felt inappropriate. I knew I wasn't supposed to.

"I wanted to buy the beautiful birthday girl a drink. Dining alone?" There was an upward inflection in his question.

"Yes, but I'm meeting with my boyfriend later."

*I'm what now?!*

"He must be a fool for letting such beauty dine alone. I would drop everything to be here, never letting go of your delicate hand." He flashed his swoon-worthy smile, hoping I would invite him to join me.

"I did something for myself while he had important business to attend to. I'll be with him soon enough. Thank you for the drink." He shook his head in disbelief that any man would allow his girl to celebrate alone. "Well, it was my pleasure. Enjoy your birthday and your night." He finally took his leave.

I was impressed by the narrative I invented. Truth be told, I would love to spend my birthday with Levi. Whenever he crosses my mind, my body instantly ignites with a fiery heat. I was an untouched inferno, making me want to rip my clothes off at the mere mention of him. In fact, my thoughts were all-consuming and downright indecent. I imagined myself forced to face the wall, with him pulling my hair as he attacked my neck and me trying to catch my breath while he ravaged me. And somehow, it didn't feel like a dream but a premonition, like it would eventually come to pass.

*Now you're letting the drinks give you silly romance fantasies; it's never going to happen, Haven!*

I finished my bellini and brought the tropical drink forward. Disappointed because I would not get a naked and ravenous Levi as a birthday gift, getting drunk was the next best thing.

I was glad the waiter came with my plate to distract me from these intense, heated thoughts.

The restaurant ambiance was elegant, with soft lighting and tasteful decor. The gentle hum of conversation and clinking of cutlery created a pleasant atmosphere. The aroma of the sizzling chicken and aromatic spices filled the air, enticing the senses. The first bite of my perfectly cooked dish brought a burst of flavors, satisfying my taste buds. It was everything I hoped it would be. I was so thankful the night turned out so well.

Feeling more comfortable in my surroundings, I was waiting for the waiter to return to treat myself to dessert when I heard a distant noise, like clapping. It was getting louder, and then I heard whistling and cheering as some staff walked my way.

"Happy birthday to you! Your special day is dear! We want to wish you all the best! Thank you for being here! Happy birthday, Haven! Yay!" The staff presented me with a decadent piece of chocolate ganache cake, which had 'Happy birthday' written in piped icing and a tiny sparkler candle. I couldn't stop smiling if I wanted to; the song and the applause from the restaurant were more than I imagined.

The staff handed me the balloon bouquet after I paid for my tab. I then hailed a taxi to go close up the shop. In my mood, I didn't even care that I had to go back to work. Nothing could wipe the smile off my face.

In the car, I wondered how different my life would be now. I kept glancing at myself in the driver's mirror and caught him glancing a time or two. I looked amazing, and yet I was still so unsure of myself. I was still determining if I could land the person I wanted most. I had to think of something else to avoid the hot flashes.

"Here we are, Miss. And happy birthday." I assume that during one of his glances, he read my balloons.

"Thank you. How much?"

He waved his hand. "No charge, pretty lady."

"Oh, thanks so much." I let the balloons out first, then myself. I straighten out my dress while walking toward the door. I grabbed my keys and then shook my head, remembering our extended hours.

The door was open.

I stepped inside expecting one or two stragglers, but it should be practically empty in this late hour. I bask in the bell, announcing myself, but almost choke at what I see.

Words failed me, but the fury in my eyes spoke volumes as I beheld the sight that left me overwhelmed.

Straddling Levi's lap was Cherry, and he wasn't even fighting it. He stared at her in awe of her lap dance, grinding against him while trying to slip her hands underneath his already unbelted pants. Her face showed triumph while my heart shattered.

She had him.

She got the only person I ever wanted.

And all I saw was red...a virtual crime scene. Her blood splattered over every square inch of the store.

And him… to hell with him.

Instead of reacting, I walked backward out the door.

I'm so confused, shattered, and heartbroken. My heart feels betrayed. As I walked backward, tears welled up in my eyes, longing for Levi's presence to fill the emptiness that surrounded me, but he didn't even run after me. I spin around to gather my thoughts elsewhere because I don't want to be alone right now. I walk in the opposite direction of my apartment.

I wiped the tears away angrily, realizing I had let go of my birthday balloons. I continue to walk down the street until I see a familiar face. Nigel's cleaning up the coffee machines and whistling a merry tune. I tap on the door and watch his smile fall when he comes closer to the door. Once he saw it was me, he put urgency into getting the door open.

"Haven, come in. Come on." He lets me step inside. He closes and locks the door, then guides me to sit down. "Hey, tell me what's wrong." He searched my eyes for clues while I tried to speak.

"He…she…I…" I couldn't even put the agony into words. I collapsed into his arms while he held me tight.

"Shhh, don't cry. Whatever it is, it's not worth the tears." I sniffle and sigh.

*He WASN'T worth my tears. I just thought…*

I don't even know how long he had me cradled, but it didn't feel right, so I separated myself from him. He hands me a fabric napkin to wipe my tears.

"Thank you. I'm sorry for interrupting you from closing up and going home."

He smiles, "It's okay, love. I didn't have any plans. How about some tea, English style? It warms the heart and can even mend it."

"Okay," I muttered sadly as I watched him grab two clear mugs and place the satchels in the cups. He fills an electric kettle with water, and while it heats, he disappears below the counter.

I sigh; each flash of what I saw cuts my heart even deeper, and that he didn't chase after me hurts more. It only proved my point: I would never be good enough.

I felt my lowest until a pink frosted chocolate cupcake appeared before me.

"I know women love chocolate, and it's still your birthday, so we're going to celebrate, no matter the circumstances."

"It's incredible how a single moment can permanently ruin a day," I say with a scoff.

"You want to talk about it?"

I shake my head. I don't think I could without sobbing.

"Okay, we don't have to, but I'm determined to salvage the day. I don't have a candle, but I want you to pretend there is one." He stands behind me. I can feel his breath on my neck. He places his hands in front of my eyes. "Now, close your eyes and imagine what you want the most. Even if you think it's impossible or unattainable. When you're ready…blow out the imaginary candle. I'll get the tea while you think long and hard."

I could hear him moving about as I stared at the sweet treat. The tears welled up because I could never get what I wanted, even if this cupcake had magical candles on it. I sat back. What else could I want?

I close my eyes, take a deep breath…and settle for the next most logical thing. *Please, help me love myself so I can be loved. I don't want to be alone. There is someone in the world who loves me.*

I want them to find me.

# CHAPTER 17

## LEVI

I threw Cherry off my lap. "Oof!" When she fell, it looked painful, but I couldn't give a fuck less, especially when this boisterous and cocky laugh erupted from her lips. She licked her hand, tasting the essence of my dick on her palm.

That'll be the only time she does.

"Hahaha! Aurora said she'd crack like an egg at seeing you all over me."

*ME ALL OVER HER?!*

She said Aurora…that means…

I slowly stalk her like a predator. "You know who I am?"

She scoffed. "No man of this caliber could ever be human. At first, it scared the hell out of me, no pun intended, but now I just wanted to cause a little chaos. Besides, Aurora said, once she's on the throne, I'd be her advisor and reap all the benefits."

I should have known that despite my warning to all, that jaded lot lizard would try to cause a rift in my plans. She should have known this would not end well for her if she failed, but she believed in her plan so much that she didn't give a fuck.

And at this moment, neither do I.

I summon that cum-guzzling bitch right in front of me. Judging by the position she appeared in; she had some random demon dick down her throat. She wasn't the least bit discriminating.

The realization that she was no longer satisfying someone shook her to the core, and she wiped the corners of her mouth before standing up.

She glances down at my undone belt and then at Cherry, who grins fiendishly. "I take it my little spell worked?" She asked Cherry.

"Oh yeah, she was so distraught. If I hadn't negotiated our deal, I would have loved to finish what I started. You taste amazing..." She purred at me.

Aurora laughed, then pointed at me. "I told you she wasn't meant to be at your side if she couldn't handle the competition."

All I could imagine was their bodies being shredded into pieces and blood strewn everywhere. There wouldn't be enough to identify them. They continue to laugh at the pain they caused her.

I felt the moment her heart broke. I still feel it even though I don't know where she is. I wanted to run after her, but had I given my demon half a millisecond of distraction, my wings would have burst out fully engulfed in flames, destroying everything, and revealing myself to Cherry and anyone within city limits.

He's still trying to break free to gut them while they laugh, giggle, and high-five, thinking their little scheme worked.

It did... but not like they expected.

I raise my hand toward the door in a twisting motion, causing the door to mirror my motions, locking with a gentle click. Aurora was the first to realize and quickly snapped her fingers, but nothing happened. I smirk when she takes a few steps back, ending up behind her groupie whore. She's stuck to suffer the consequences of her hare-brained scheme.

My demon gave me the scout's honor salute to abide by the rules if he can exact revenge on the people who caused our mate harm.

*HA! Where'd you learn that from? Nice try.*

I trust him as much as I trust my father. I knew he could relay my disgust better than I could, so I let him step in front of me. I don't completely let go and hold the reins tight but allow him to give them a show.

A low snarl creeps from our throat as our eyes shift black, and razor-sharp claws appear. I was a hybrid of us, my body human except for my horns, soulless eyes, and claws that wanted to rip them open.

Cherry looked petrified, and they kept trying to cower behind one another. I was ready to unleash a verbal tirade before my physical one, but my demon shook his head at me before uttering just one word to them: "Run."

I laughed because I made escaping impossible, and even if Aurora could snap herself to the Underworld, I would hunt her down, destroying everything and everyone in sight until I was satisfied.

Cherry didn't even move. Her body shook uncontrollably in her panic-stricken state. Aurora neglected to mention to Cherry that I could shift, even though she hadn't witnessed it. She couldn't have thought this meat suit was my pure form.

I AM THE GODDAMN DEVIL!

Cherry could finally move, looking around for her partner in this heinous crime who scurried to hide somewhere.

I stepped forward into her space. "Did you know what Haven means to me?"

"What, what do you mean?" Her eyes are still darting around.

Playing ignorant wouldn't work. I conjure a wall of flames that explode behind me, expressing my rage without physical harm. "Did you know she was fated to be with me?"

She flinched as the fire seemingly burned everything in its path. With the company she kept, I already knew the answer. I wanted to see how painful she wanted her afterlife to be.

"DID YOU?!"

"Yes! I'm sorry! Aurora…"

"SHUT UP! She can't even protect herself as she hides like a coward because I voided this place to keep her from disappearing. You have no idea the shit show you put yourself in."

"Am I going to Hell?" She whimpered, realizing the consequences of her actions.

The laugh that erupted from me was loud and deep. "Your indiscretions with married men solidified your place in Hell long before this. Let's review your life, shall we? There were your high school English and gym teachers, the car dealership owner that 'gifted' you that Lexus as a bribe not to expose him, and, for fuck's sake…the pastor at your church! You didn't care about your repercussions, and neither will I."

She began bawling.

Keep that for eternity. My demons relish the fresh tears of sinners. Right now, sign over the bookstore deed to Haven. She deserves it for the pain you caused her. I witnessed her endure your constant nonsense week after week. I couldn't intervene until now, but, Cherry, I have special methods of inflicting pain reserved just for you.

I conjure up the paperwork, then grab her hand and use my claw to slice her finger open. She didn't even physically react as her blood dripped into the pen. "Sign!" I ignored her tears but was kind enough to close her wound. Bleeding out was way too easy an out for the likes of her.

She grasps the pen as best she can, her body shaking so uncontrollably that she has to sign slowly. I took that time to snap Aurora's sorry ass before me.

She appears on her knees as usual. "M-m-my King."

"Tsk tsk tsk Aurora… you had to interfere after I explicitly told everyone to back off. Did you think you could stop me? Or…that my father would save your sorry ass? It's almost entertaining."

She stood up and seemed to have gotten some gall. "Can you blame me? You'll be a laughingstock! She isn't worthy of the title! You think that pathetic, ugly bore of a…oof!"

She clutched her stomach as a pool of blood began seeping from her wretched lips. She let out a scream, but her lips were sealed. I melted her tongue and sealed her mouth shut. You could tell it was one of those ear-piercing screams.

Too bad.

Listening to her gagging on her tongue's molten, vile, noxious-tasting ooze trickling down her throat was very entertaining. I think she was trying not to vomit because there would be nowhere for it to go but back down. What a vicious cycle.

"Despite your dire predicament, you STILL bad-mouth my mate? It'll be hard to suck dick now, won't it? And this... is the tip of the fucking iceberg, Aurora. You and your partner in crime will regret ever crossing me."

I snapped her back to Hell and let her be a walking visual to the rest of them. My demon, temporarily satisfied, allowed me to revert. I smooth my hair and adjust my suit. I snatched the paper and made sure she signed correctly.

"I don't want to die!" Cherry screams out once she knows that this is all real.

Satisfied that Haven was the owner, I folded the papers and put them in my inner jacket pocket.

I leaned into Cherry's space. Before all this, she would have basked in it, but now that she saw what I was, her instincts tell her to back away.

"Death... is only the beginning," I smirked before raising my hand, watching when she fully understood what I meant; then poof, she was ashes on the ground. She will physically feel every bit of pain as she's eternally dismembered until she becomes Haven's property as her servant.

I ensure there's no trace of my actions before leaving the store. While I enjoyed tormenting them, I was being tormented. I could feel her disappointment, and that was a million times worse to know that she was somewhere thinking I didn't care. Besides my mother, she's the only other human I care about.

Frustration boils within me, and an angry groan erupts from

my throat, shattering the silence of the empty street. I can't do anything until tomorrow—another cold and lonely night without her. Tonight was supposed to be day one of our life together, but I messed it up.

Maybe I deserve this.

# CHAPTER 18

I ACTUALLY FELT BETTER BLOWING OUT THE IMAGINARY CANDLE, BUT only by a fraction.

"I can see that beautiful smile wanting to come out. I've made you some delicious tea with a spot of cream and a decadent dessert. What's it going to take to bring it out? How about…" He turns a small radio on that belts out some sort of upbeat rocka-billy tune. Before I could lament, Nigel pulled me to my feet and spun me. I don't know if he's singing horribly on purpose, but it makes me laugh.

Then a slow song comes through. He cradles me, and it's super awkward.

I felt this sting in my heart and my conscience saying, '…he *belongs* to you'. I think I know what that means, so I separate us. "I'm sorry, Nigel, I can't. Thank you for all this. You salvaged my birthday from the awful incident, but it's late, and I have to open up in the morning."

Honestly, I'm not sure I want my job anymore. I may lose it at the sight of Cherry, or worse, them together.

I couldn't deal…I won't.

Then I realized that sometimes, the dream doesn't work out

like you want it to. A new look meant a whole new perspective on my life.

I'm drained physically and emotionally. I fight the tears and give myself a comforting smile. "No matter what, you deserve to be happy, Haven. Do not settle, especially for some man who doesn't know your worth. Tomorrow is a better day."

They were severely empty words and even less emotion. I felt so numb. Tomorrow, I will act like I don't care.

The next day, I woke up late because I forgot to set my alarm —another reason for her to fire me. I got ready and didn't even rush. I'd get there when I got there. She can get off her lazy ass and open up *her* store.

I'm around 30 minutes late and see the store is still dark. A few people are waiting by the door. I hurried and opened the door for them.

"Sorry for being late; come on in. Your first book is on me." Actually, it's on her; she wouldn't be able to tell. I work on the books, too.

They wander in and look around. As I flip the sign from closed to open, I notice a piece of paper taped to the door. I pull it as I remove my jacket and put my stuff away behind the counter. While they're seeking their next adventure, I unfold the paper.

"I hereby transfer Book Lair of Dragons' ownership to Haven Evers… signed Cherry Smith."

I mouthed the words as I read, then gasped as the realization hit me. "No way…" I read it several times, and her signature is in red ink.

*What an odd color to sign in.*

This has to be a sick joke. She's probably back in her office laughing her ass off at me. I make my way to her door, push it open, and as I get ready to let her have it, there's no one there. It completely takes the wind out of my sails.

"Miss! I'm ready to check out."

No time. If it was mine, I needed to keep business going. It wasn't about her. It was about the customers and her father's legacy.

"Thanks for waiting. I see you found a few great choices."

# CHAPTER 19

## LEVI

Last night was a literal fucking nightmare. Now, I've got to have dinner with my father tonight, and I can't get out of it; he said it was essential to the inevitable change of command or lack thereof. No doubt Trevor relished in relaying my ultimatum of ruling Hell *with* her or relinquishing my reign *for* her. In short, this dinner would be a fiasco. If I ignored him, he'd ruin my already botched plan before I could salvage it.

I lie in bed, reluctant to believe the turn of events. I should have been more vigilant. How did I get bested by a pair of slack-mouthed, revolving-door sluts?!

*Attention! Immediate adjustment to Aurora and Cherry's punishment: after you rip out their entrails, set them on fire and shove the ashes down their throat when they regenerate. Do this until I tell you to stop.*

I relay to the lackeys in charge of their eternal punishment. Did I mention they can feel every bit of pain? At this moment, I relish in my evil. My demon is satiated, but I won't be satisfied until I make things right. I should be waking up to my beauty and devouring her to hear her whimper my name, gasping for the tiniest bit of air.

"Levi! Levi, are you up?" I think I hear Carson walking around. I don't think Trevor's that stupid to appear in my home unannounced, not even with Carson. At least, I hoped not. I was not in the mood for his back-handed compliments or smug remarks.

I stroll out of my room in my silk pajama bottoms and see Carson in my kitchen. "What are you doing here?"

"Are you kidding? After what you did to Aurora and that other girl? You've done some dark stuff, Levi, but this has crossed another realm."

I started a pot of coffee. "Is that sympathy for the lot lizard who may have ruined my chances with my mate?"

"No. Not at all, but I assume from the aftermath that last night did not go as planned?"

"Not in the least bit. Haven had gone to an appointment. I waited for her at the store to return and fell asleep. What I thought was a fantasy was Aurora manipulating my dreams to make me think it was Haven trying to seduce me, but it wasn't. I realized Haven was standing there, and Cherry was grinding on my lap. My demon was a millisecond from surfacing and ripping them apart. I didn't want to introduce him to Haven that way, and she ran off before I could explain. I have to go back this morning and try to fix it."

"How? It better be a damn good plan because she saw some girl all over you. Not even some girl, the one that has been making her life miserable. Do you think that felt good?"

"I know it didn't because I felt it, Carson. The moment her heart dropped; it broke into a million pieces; it still lingers at this very moment. It's not as intense, but she's still upset. Whenever I think about it, I find another way to make them suffer. I want the message to ring loud and clear."

"Sealing her mouth shut and now the intestinal burning? Yeah, I think that's ringing crystal fucking clear. Like the Liberty Bell, Notre Dame, or Big Ben!"

"I melted her tongue off, too. Compared to what she may have cost me, I let her off easy. But I'm nowhere near done punishing her, not by a long shot. First, I have to get Haven to my house."

For that, I needed a miracle and a prayer.

# CHAPTER 20

## HAVEN

I CHECKED MYSELF OUT IN MY COMPACT, REMINDING MYSELF I LOVED my new look and would continue putting myself together.

"Wow, you look even prettier than you did last night."

I lower my compact and see Nigel. He held a cup in his hand. "Good morning. I wanted to check on you. I brought you a dark roast blend with two pumps of cinnamon sugar and a splash of almond milk. It's my signature drink."

When it hits my nose, I inhale; it smells so good. "Thank you. I suppose I'm better than yesterday."

"That's good to hear. While I'm here, can you tell me if you have this book I was fond of long ago? It's a collection of poetry titled, 'The Spring of Love Fades'".

Poetry was near the entrance, and he followed behind me. "Let's see...it sounds familiar. I think it has a springy book cover with a swing."

"That's pretty...accurate. How do you know that? Did you read it?"

"No, but I practically stocked this entire store. Doesn't hurt to have a photographic memory."

As I flashed back to last night, I could still feel that painful stab in my heart, as if it had just happened. I pictured them laughing, clutching the sharp dagger that pulled out my heavily bleeding, shattered heart. I wish I could scrub my brain of last night's events. I would go so far as to say I wish I could wipe the memory of Levi Asant altogether. I had no hope or chance, and I needed to set my sights on options within my reach.

Maybe I was looking at one.

"Ahh, here it is." I return to the register and look around while Nigel thumbs through the book. Could this store actually be mine? It would be my absolute dream.

"Ahem." I noticed his hand was close to mine, and I leaned back.

"Sorry, I zoned out. I got some news this morning that I don't know how to deal with."

"I hope after last night it's at least good news."

"It is, really." I unfold the paper and hand it to him. He skims over it. "Haven, you own the store! That's wonderful, love!"

"It is."

"You don't sound excited."

"Because of what I saw last night. There's this guy...and...I thought he liked me. Maybe I was too hopeful because he was out of my league."

He tips my chin. "Nobody is out of your league, I assure you. Maybe he doesn't deserve you."

I feel myself blush and look down at my feet. I realize how close he is to me again; half his body is leaning over the counter.

"So, what happened?"

"The former owner was half naked and in his lap, claiming him as her own. And when I ran out, he didn't even follow. That's how I knew; I was merely someone he relied on for manual labor. To fill his library and nothing more."

Nigel cracks open the book. "I want to read you something. It's a poem titled *Her*.

> She's radiant amongst nature's beauty.
> She's the calm the storm tries to overwhelm.

She's Cupid's greatest work and all within her.
She doesn't know her greatness, her beauty.
She doesn't know she deserves the world.
Love is envious, and so is my heart.
I knew when I saw… It was her.

He spoke it as if he were the original creator and I, his muse. His rendition is beautiful, and it made me feel special and adored.

"It's one of my all-time favorite poems. I thought you'd understand it."

I did. He spoke it beautifully, and I saw the spark in his eye.

"Thank you, Nigel, it's beautiful."

"Just as beautiful as you. Your heart is pure, and you deserve everything you ever hoped for." His hand grazed my face.

Then my body shuddered, and I felt that now cursed feeling. I tried to keep my eyes from rolling to the back of my head because now the object of my desire stood there as he witnessed Nigel's hand on my face. I expected to feel shame, except I didn't. I felt betrayal, a rage I had never felt before as it swept over my body. I stepped back, and Nigel looked at me. He raised his brow, and I reluctantly nodded to confirm his silent inquiry.

"You know where to find me, love." He hands me the exact change. "For the book."

"Thanks for everything."

"Anytime. Remember what I said."

He walks toward Levi and stops to gauge what kind of man he is, looking him up and down, especially after knowing he hurt me emotionally. Levi's casual, nonchalant gaze held a very sinister tone. It looked like he could incinerate Nigel just by his hardened stare. Nigel tuts and walks out unbothered.

A young man sets down his selection as Levi inches closer. He's feeling me out, but I ignore him.

"Hope you found everything that you needed. That'll be $45.50."

"Whoa, that's a great deal!"

"Remember, I said a book is on the house for the late open-ing? I took off your most expensive item. Chemistry books are so overpriced. All college books are. I intend to change that."

"Oh, thank you! Now I can buy extra food to put away this month."

"You're welcome. My name is Haven. See you next time!" I wrap his books and hand them over. He smiles and is out the door.

My nostrils flare…His signature scent gives me goosebumps. He's impeccably dressed in a well-tailored black suit and white button-up with a deep blood-red vest and tie. His hair slicked out of his face. He had one hand in his pocket as he stood before me.

I felt my emotions bubbling up even at the sight of him. Not the good ones either, the ones that wanted to inflict pain and hurt. "What do you want? Your whore isn't here." I felt so confi-dent in spewing my insults toward him.

"Haven, can I explain?"

"Get the fuck out, Levi!"

# CHAPTER 21

## LEVI



Rage consumed her, and I could feel it in every fiber of my being. If her anger wasn't directed towards me, I would find it incredibly sexy. I suppress my anger because of that scrawny guy who was all over her attempting to stake his claim.

I could end that pathetic peon like that! If I see him around her again, I'll snap off his dick!

"I said get out! Whatever game you two are playing, kindly do so without me. I wish you nothing but misery together." She snapped. It was years and years of frustration and anger finally set free.

"My sweet little book bee, it's not like that."

"Don't call me that! Your sweet words won't work today or ever! You're just buttering me up for your sick mind games!" She quickly grabs a stack of books to escape me, but I'm hot on her heels.

She slams the books down violently before placing them in their assigned place. She continues as I watch her mannerisms. I don't need to see the visual display that she's hurt because I can feel it. After the fifth book, she groans, putting her hand on her hip, after running her fingers through her beautifully tousled hair.

"Why are you still following me? I told you that slut bucket isn't here. Why don't you try the local whorehouse!"

"I'm not here for her. I never have been." She rolled her eyes. I stop to really soak in her new look. She didn't have a full face of makeup like last night; what she had on was more natural and incredibly more beautiful. "You look stunning. I'm sorry about last night." I couldn't stop repeating my apology. I would keep saying it until she let me explain. She mumbled something and stormed away.

She went to the front to check out another patron with a big smile, but I knew it was fake. She was overly friendly with him, knowing how to push my buttons by giving her time and attention to someone else. He left her his number, and she slipped it down into her bra; he responded by kissing her hand, and she gave an innocent wave before he left.

The millisecond he was out of view, I snapped my fingers and incinerated him! His ashes scattered in the wind. She'll never know, but that would be anyone's fate for touching her.

Her frown returned when she looked at me. Now, it was just her and I.

"I really am sorry."

"For fuck's sake, stop saying that! You're only sorry you got caught! It's fine. I know my place, and it was never with anyone of your caliber, anyway."

This is the first normal conversation we've had without her shying away, and it's her ripping me a new asshole. I wanted to pull her by her hair, grab her by the neck, and slam her lips onto mine. To feel her quickly intake a breath before I promptly took it away, to see her eyes pool in lust for me…and only me. I wanted to tell her exactly what I did to that walking STD and that she owned the store because I'd do anything to make her happy.

"Haven, I swear it's all a terrible misunderstanding." I quickly check my watch with my meeting looming over me. "I need a favor from you, please. Can you bring these books to my house at 8 pm? I have a meeting in five minutes. I swear I'll explain everything then."

She scoffs and rolls her eyes, "Why don't you get Cherry to do it? She can finish what she started. She looked quite comfortable grinding on your lap; your hands were all over her!"

"I don't want her, Haven! How many times do I have to say it? My house, 8 pm, and I'm not leaving until you agree."

"I thought you said your meeting was so important?" She finger-quoted the important part.

"This is even more important." I lifted my hand to brush her cheek, but her face clearly said fuck off and take that bitch with you. But her heart wanted to believe there was something there. A sliver of a chance. I quickly retracted it before she bit me in spite.

"Whatever. Give me the list, but this doesn't change a thing."

I put the shortlist on the counter, with my address written on the back, and she reluctantly picks it up, obviously annoyed.

"Thank you, my book angel." With that, I walk behind the building and snap myself to the authentic restaurant he picked in a beachside town in East Italy. Of course, he would pick a super inconvenient place.

And he's late—surprise, surprise. I check my watch, 8:07 pm when he finally strolls in.

"You're late."

"I'm the Demon King. I do what I want. Besides, you can't force an orgasm."

I should have known. "Whatever. Why am I here?"

"What's this I hear about relinquishing your title if your human says she doesn't want to live in paradise?"

"It's not paradise. It's Hell for a reason, and if that's too much for her, I have no problem letting you rule for a while longer or forever. And this isn't up for discussion."

He glares at me, but I don't flinch. "Fine. Make your little mistakes. Let's talk about Aurora and that girl who owned the store. She wasn't supposed to check out for another 14 months. What's with the early check-in?"

"That cum magnet and her little human ass kisser interfered in my affairs after I explicitly warned everyone. She didn't listen, so I made an example."

"Sealing her mouth?"

"And melting her tongue, I could've been a real bastard and closed *all* her holes..." I pause, raising my brow so he'd get the hint, "It's still an option the way she pissed me off. If she ruined everything I worked hard to get, I'll make her wish she was human again."

And that's quite extreme for any demon. Why on earth would you want to ditch your powers and freedom just to become a regular human with all these boring rules and restrictions?

"You are the next reigning King! I've done my time and am ready to sit by the sulfur pools while getting a five-star blow job...hell, maybe two. You know I can grow a second dick; DP is insane for them and me; I don't know why everyone doesn't do it! Anyway, you WILL take your place! THAT is not up for discussion!"

"Don't interfere, Father. The same warning I gave everyone else applies to you as well!"

"The fuck it does! I'm allowing you to pursue her, entertaining this bullshit and all so you can rule!"

"This conversation is utterly useless! Are you done?"

A waiter stops by our table. "Buongiorno. What can I get you to drink?"

"Son?"

"I told you I had more important matters."

"Okay, but they have a wonderful 1927 Chateau that pairs well with their famous spicy fettuccine alfredo."

"I know what you're doing. Stop wasting my time."

He ignores me and faces the waiter. "I'll have the Chateau and Alfredo, thank you."

I hear the distinct doorbell to my place in my ear. It's now or never. "I got to go."

# CHAPTER 22

## HAVEN

"I'm sorry, my little book bee...bLAh bLAh bLAh... whatever." I mocked Levi.

What a load of bullshit.

Now that I could speak my piece towards him, it was a mix of fury and longing, my brows furrowing in frustration. It was a conflicting torrent of emotions, as if my heart waged a battle against itself. Yet, even in my anger, I couldn't deny the impact he had on me. He had the power to make me feel alive, even in moments of infuriation.

At that moment, I realized the complexity of human emotions. We can feel both extremes simultaneously, our hearts capable of loving and despising with equal intensity. It was a bittersweet realization, for it meant that even in my anger, a part of me still longed for his presence, yearning for the connection we once shared.

I reluctantly looked for the books that he requested. I stand in the romance section because they'll all be there. Now that I've had some time to think, I realize that some titles he's chosen in the past seem to have underlying meanings. I know that *'Take My Breath Away'* and *'Electric Pulse'* are opposites-attract romances, much like us. We come from different walks of life.

I'm the poor little orphan, and he is the suave, rich businessman.

But he also bought books that held my curiosity. Could he have seen me reading that BDSM book before he walked in? I was so lost in my thoughts of being dominated that I wasn't paying much attention to my surroundings. And he bought the book. He had to have seen me! Oh my God!

Then, on the next visit, he bought 'He Wants to Dominate Me'… and 'Tie Me Up, Daddy'.

Was he subtly flirting? Did he find my innermost curiosities and tailor his list?

After finding out it was my favorite, he bought 'He Just Wants to Kiss Me' and asked all these questions about what I liked. He was trying to find out about me! But I didn't get it; he could have any woman.

Maybe it was my imagination running wild.

Now, I peer down at the books he listed. 'From the Desk of Love,' 'Her Innocent Soul,' 'Love Takes Time,' and 'Fantasies of the Heart.' I recognized two were second-chance romances, and one had a very tragic and heartbreaking ending. Like the ugly cry type. Is he expressing how he feels after I caught him with Cherry?

Was I too hard on him? Or was I just conjuring up my hopes and dreams for nothing? I didn't want to come out looking like a fool again. I promised to stand by my opposition and not listen to his lies when I dropped these off at his place.

But first, I need to go home and change. I like the confidence I've gained and have ventured into the side of my closet from which I shied away. My roommate would add clothing to my closet without my knowledge. Eventually, I would notice; to be fair, she knew not to go too extreme. She called it casually sexy. I was lucky enough to end up with a handful of friends. They would say, "Haven, you're such a pretty girl; you just have to tell yourself and believe. We always tell you, but it's more important if you think that. You ARE beautiful." I should look them up on social media, especially so they can see my new attitude and look.

I wrap up his order and head home. After a quick shower, I slip into a midi-length black dress and chunky sweater coat. I changed my lipstick to a deeper red and added more mascara. I recall how his eyes raked over me and the momentary weakness before I could assess the situation. Instead of heels, I pick some comfortable, strappy black wedges.

I look in the mirror, "Well, this is it, Haven. This is when you find out IF you have a chance. But do you even want it?"

Did I want the affection of the man who sends my senses into overdrive? Yes! But it would destroy me if I were wrong, and he wasn't interested. I felt the ball hit the pit of my stomach, making me momentarily queasy.

What if…what if?

Fighting the urge to wrap myself in a blanket cocoon and watch Titanic because it seems fitting, I shake off these nerves and look at myself one more time. I take a deep breath; it causes a pulse to shoot from my heart to my core, and my knees almost buckle.

"Steady…we're going because we love this store, and he's a loyal customer. It's good customer service! Oh, who am I kidding…" I close my eyes, making a spiritual connection to say a quick prayer. "I know you have made my life the way it is for a reason, and I never questioned it before. You knew I was strong enough to withstand all this, but... now I'm terrified. My heart and this little voice in my head say he's mine. I want to think that the voice is you. If he isn't for me, please keep me from getting there, and that's how I'll know to move on."

Even the slightest hesitation would solidify my greatest fear, but those were the rules.

I called for an Uber and grabbed my keys.

*Keep your mind open.* The little voice whispered.

That's an unusual statement, but okay.

I waited a few minutes out in the chilly air, causing me to

clutch my sweater tighter. I stepped into the car once I confirmed the license plate.

"Evening, love."

I was shocked when I looked up, "Nigel? What are you doing? Wait, my driver is supposed to be Dillon." I confirm on my app.

He extended his gaze in the rearview, especially after my sweater fell off my shoulder on one side.

"Dillon is my middle name, and I try to separate my job personalities. Nigel is a handsome, friendly barista with a friendly smile."

"And Dillon?"

"Same charisma, just named Dillon." I laughed so hard and shook my head. "Smooth."

"I thought you'd appreciate my witty British humor." Then there was this awkward silence before he cleared his throat.

"So, uh, your destination is deep in Mulhoney forest. It's certainly secluded. I didn't even know people lived out there."

"Yeah, apparently." He saw the books in my hand, and I assumed he knew I was making a delivery. And I left it at that. He took the hint and pulled away from my apartment.

We hit the outskirts of town and immediately made a right on Mulhoney Drive, named after the forest. Because they were trying to preserve the natural environment, only a few street-lights dotted the eerily dark road.

Nigel is leaning forward as if it helps him to see better. We finally pass a beautiful house that seems ill-fitted with its sand color paint against the dark landscape.

"I guess people do live out here." He said while driving slowly as we passed another beautiful but out-of-place home: a red brick cabin-style house. It had two sports cars parked out front. You had to have money to live out here, to pay a pretty penny for absolute privacy. I guess Levi likes his solitude.

Nigel slows down and turns into this beautiful home, but this one differs from the others because the outside completely matches the landscape. The ink-colored paint job gave the illusion that nothing was there but the beautiful red wooden door. The two luxury cars also gave away that someone lived there.

Nigel pulled up as far as he could. "Alright, here you go." He hands me a card. "Call me, and I'll pick you up at no charge."

"Umm, thanks."

I step out with Levi's books in hand, smooth out my dress, and walk behind Nigel's car. I stand at the door and take a deep breath. I realized Nigel was watching me, so I waved, and he nodded before pulling away. I remember the terrifying look Levi gave Nigel after he saw him touching me. Another clue he might be interested is that insanely jealous gene men often carry. I admit a little possessiveness never hurt anyone—nothing like an Alpha male claiming what he wants.

I shake my head out of my dream and remember I'm supposed to be upset because of the painful flashbacks that plague me. The thought alone triggers a defensive reaction in my heart. I'm only here to deliver his order and hear his sorry excuse about why a half-naked slut was straddling his lap.

I was so mad I screamed into the sleeve of my sweater before pressing the doorbell.

You're sorry? Oh, you will be!

# CHAPTER 23

## LEVI

The second my doorbell rang, I snapped home and switched to the suit I planned to wear when I revealed my true intentions. The outfit of choice was a stylish, custom-made black suit accompanied by a sleek black vest and a bold red button-up shirt. I brushed my hair to one side and checked my reflection once more in the foyer mirror.

I take a deep breath before opening the door to the most beautiful sight of her casually sexy in a tight black dress but surrounded by the comfort of her well-worn sweater coat. If she was going for a sexy librarian/bookworm, she nailed it. As my eyes met hers, my lip involuntarily curled upwards, only to be met with a lack of response.

I could feel it, too; she was fighting her boiling anger and loving adoration.

I try to break the ice. "Haven, please come in."

She holds the stack of books out in front of her to put as much space between us as possible. She grabs her sweater to pull it tighter against her, but part of it has fallen off her shoulder, giving an innocence about her. "I'm only here to drop off your stupid order."

Peering into the shadows of the deserted street. "Where are you going to go? "You were dropped off," I say, looking past her.

"I'd rather walk home."

She is painfully stubborn. "Will you let me explain? I told you, what you saw wasn't what you saw!"

That sounded astonishingly stupid.

And her face confirmed how stupid I sounded. "Oh, so I didn't see Cherry's slutty ass grinding against you? She didn't look like she was one button away from screwing you right there in the place where I work and love? Where... never mind, I don't want to hear your excuse! I'm tired of being a joke or plaything. I have genuine feelings! You don't get to..."

I lean against the door as she rambles on. I know she's pissed, frustrated, and upset, but how can I replace that with unending pleasure if she won't let me grovel and beg for her forgiveness?

That's it. I was tired of being nice and coddling her.

"Haven, inside now! I won't ask you again. Next time I'll throw your sweet little ass over my shoulder, and I promise you, I'll enjoy it."

Her jaw dropped; a faint gasp escaped her lips. A hint of anticipation lingered as she stood there momentarily before her feet carried her through my door, her steps echoing softly against the wooden floor, and I shut it.

That's my good girl.

With a slight quiver in her lips, she looked at me and asked, "Levi, why did you ask for these books? Or the others? You're not just collecting them, are you?"

I give her a deep chuckle, "I think you know why..." I signal her to set the books down by tapping the console table. "Follow me."

She took my nonverbal cue and set them down.

"Wh-Where are we going?"

"I wanted to show you how well your hard work has paid off. "But first," I forget about my superhuman speed and swiftly spin around. Startled, she lets out a yelp as I come to a halt.

Standing just centimeters from me, I can clearly observe her labored breathing. I wanted to slam her against me in the worst way. I take that moment of awe to present her with the rose I had conjured behind my back. It was a small gesture, but I knew the little things that mattered to her.

"Oh, thank you." She said in my attempt to short-circuit her anger.

"You're welcome. And happy belated birthday." She looked so surprised.

"How did you know?" Her breathing hitched, and I backed away, noticing her disappointment in my actions. I open a door and motion for her to step inside.

"My love, soon you will know everything, but first, I want you to see my most cherished possession, and I am indebted to you for it."

She steps into the library. A fraction of all I've collected over the millennia. Where most of the romance lived, her labor of love.

She twirls around to immerse herself fully in my collection. Her smile is absolutely radiant. "Levi…it's breathtaking! If I had a library, it would look exactly like this."

Little did she know she WAS standing in her library. What's mine is now hers.

While she is in awe, I take my place behind her. Her scent mesmerizes me as she freezes and feels me tower behind her.

"Why have you tensed up, my sweet book butterfly? Does my ever-close presence make you nervous? No, that's not nervousness; it's lust, right?" She didn't have to answer because her whole body flushed, sending an intense shiver.

"You may have been furious with me, but now these intrusive thoughts taint your innocence. If everything had gone to plan yesterday, today would have marked our day one…the day after."

Another shudder, the air thick in her want.

"What, what do you mean the day after?" She gathered the

courage to turn around and look out from under her bangs, and I saw a twinkle in her eye; it was hope—more than she had yesterday.

"Oh, darlin', why the day after I fucked you into complete submission, of course. The night after you moan my name so wildly, begging me… not… to stop. When all your most wanted desires come true, now follow me."

With her jaw on the floor, she followed me into my kitchen, where I had a chilled bottle of wine waiting. She tries to maneuver herself up onto the barstool. I would have helped but enjoyed the jiggle of her breasts as she straightened herself out.

"Ahem." She broke me out of my staring but didn't wrap the sweater back. I pop the cork and pour two glasses of bubbly. She pretends to be unbothered. "What are we even toasting to? I'm still mad at you; this changes nothing, Levi."

Like an aggressive chihuahua, she was insistent about being mad. But if you present the right…reward, the little yapper becomes quite submissive, especially with the right touch.

"It doesn't? Well," I set my glass down and approached her, sliding the barstool toward me, away from the kitchen island. I ensured not to touch her skin because it would instantly give it away. I slowly, methodically, bunched up the fabric of her dress and slid it up her legs. Not once did she stop me; she watched to see how far I would push. Once I got it past her knees, I slowed until it was back far enough for me to step in between her legs. I leaned forward, caging her between my arms with her back against the island. I had her exactly where I wanted her.

"We are toasting to my groveling and begging for mercy and forgiveness. For a second chance."

"You think you deserve one after what I saw? You didn't even chase after me!" Her voice cracked, and she crossed her arms in protest. It's the one thing I regret not doing. My demon is upset that he let his emotions keep us from making it right. Then he perks up when he catches a whiff of her arousal.

Fuck me. I just wanted to move her panties to the side and

slide my fingers in. To watch her gasp in shock and then melt into a puddle at my fingertips before tasting her.

"I assure you, after I tell my side, you can stay or go. Is that alright?"

"Mhmm." She squeaks out quickly as she takes in the proximity between us. Her lips pouted perfectly for the taking, but there was no verbal answer.

"Use your words, Haven."

"Yes, umm, I mean, yes, sir."

She's so fucking perfect. Her submission will be my weakness.

"That's my good girl." I groaned when I saw her give me a smile of contentment.

Basking in her actions and keeping my demon at bay is an exhaustive struggle.

"I know what you were thinking. You thought you were never in my league, that a timid little book mouse like you could never attract someone like me. Darlin', how could you ever think I would be more suited to someone like Cherry? When I need the light to my darkness, a beauty that can tame her beast, a kind, caring soul who understands that I may not show it to everyone, but I have a heart. I need you, Haven. I only need you."

# CHAPTER 24

## HAVEN

"...I ONLY NEED YOU." THOSE WERE HIS EXACT WORDS, AND MY heart exploded! He wants me! He needs me! Deep down, the voice in my head knew that, but I was so angry, frustrated, and tired of coming up short.

I couldn't wait to be claimed. "I'm yours." I needily whimpered, which caused him to chuckle.

"I wish it were that simple, but we have to discuss a few things first."

I rocked against the chair; all I wanted were those hands all over me. I held my hand out, reaching for his hand, but he avoided my touch.

I didn't understand. "Why won't you touch or kiss me?" I asked. His hand brushes my hair out of my face, but still doesn't make contact.

"I will. I promise you, Haven, I'll have you drunk in our lovemaking, but only after this one important thing I should mention." His eyes held something I couldn't put my finger on.

My brain was malfunctioning. "I'm sorry, but if you want me to understand, step back. I'm only having impure thoughts right now."

"I know." He points to the bridge of his nose. "Your blush, remember?"

Damn it! How could I forget? And now I know he knows.

He continued, "I wanted to celebrate your birthday together because it has a special meaning for me."

My birthday? Special meaning to him? How?

"It's only my 25th birthday. Doesn't seem special. Hmm, it is a quarter of a century. Wow, that sounds old." I saw him raise his brow because, judging by his reaction, he was older than me, not that I could tell. It can't be by much. Could it?

"Levi, umm, how old are you?" He couldn't be older than his mid-thirties. Forty?

I saw hesitation before he sighed, "That's the thing, Haven. I'm immortal."

"Hahahaha! You're funny." When I calm down and wipe the tears away, I realize… he's not laughing.

At all.

***Gasp***

His hands shoot up, "Hear me out… It sounds crazy, but that's not even the big reveal."

"THAT'S not the big reveal? That you're immortal?! That you don't die…you don't die, you live forever!" I slapped my hand over my mouth to stop the perpetual word vomit spewing from my lips, but it was still going in my head.

*He doesn't die, doesn't die, forever, forever…*

"It's okay. I expected a worse reaction than that."

I hopped down and walked around the island to lean against the stove. I had to put space between us. I run my fingers through my hair. "I need a second to breathe…because I swear you told me you want me, the very words I've been dying to hear since I laid eyes on you almost three years ago. But then you slip in casually that you're immortal? Like a vampire or werewolf? Well, they can be killed, so not like them. Wait, are you serious? You're kidding, right?"

I'm still rambling because my brain is short-circuiting, trying to comprehend that one word that keeps echoing…immortal. I know what it means. I just can't understand it right now.

He stands up straight and walks around the island toward me with his hands up. "I'm not. I am immortal. I can never die, and I waited an eternity to find and be with you. You are destined for me, and I can prove it."

Like a vampire, he was on top of me at lightning speed, but that couldn't be; he always came around during the day and wasn't pale, quite the opposite with his warm, sun-kissed skin.

He stands there as if waiting for my permission, much like werewolves when they want to mark their mate. I elongate my neck, tracing it with my fingertips. "Prove it."

His eyes widened, and then he laughed. "Sorry, not a werewolf or a vampire, but we share similarities when we find our mate. And for the last few months, I've been able to feel you, Haven. Your feelings and emotions, how you questioned your purpose in life every day, but most importantly, how you felt when you knew I was in your presence. It drove me insane not to claim you in the bookstore where we met. When you turned 18, I knew you were my mate, but I couldn't reveal it until your 25th birthday. If I had tried before that, they would have taken you from me, so I chose certain books as context clues, hoping you would notice. I was happy I was around you."

"By stalking me at my job?" I blurted out.

"Call it what you like. Just being in your presence kept me going, and now I'm going to claim you and finally make you mine. First, you need to know who I am."

Why does that sound wildly ominous? Somehow, I still feel confident in wanting the man who stood before me.

"Okay. Tell me…rip the Band-Aid off! You said you're not a vampire or a werewolf. On a scale from evil to good, where would you fall?"

I saw his Adam's apple bob, and he stepped back.

Uh oh.

It can only mean one thing, "You're a demon, aren't you?!"

"Kind of, hear me out…"

"Oh, God!"

Whoops!

"Sorry." I winced as he glared at me. I mean, what else could I say?

His face softened. "It's fine. I'm not the cursed angel expelled from paradise. My father is bitter. I just am. Besides, I was born down there. I didn't fall from grace."

Wait.

Cursed angel?

Down there.

I know that story… could that mean…

"Satan…your dad is…S…atan." It looks like I was sounding out an unfamiliar word I heard while asking a question and making a statement. My breathing stammered. I was feeling a little woozy.

Levi looked concerned. "Haven, you look awfully pale. You need to calm down, or you'll pass out."

"Or die of shock, Levi! You just told me that your dad is Satan!" He steps closer; my hand shoots up to stop him, and I step back. He seemed to flinch at my gesture. I tried to reconcile.

"Listen, it was a knee-jerk reaction. I'm not running away; it's a lot to take in. A lot…" I realized how tense I was by how much my shoulders dropped after exhaling so hard.

Levi shoved his hands in his pockets. His once dominant posture changed. He appeared defeated and almost sad, like he had given up.

He turned his back to me, peeking over his shoulder. "You think I'm a monster! My mate thinks I'm a monster." He shifted and looked at me again. I noticed his eyes flashed a golden color. I gasped, "What was that?"

He rested his hands on the counter and sighed. "I knew this wouldn't work. Everyone was right." He slammed his hands down, which startled me a bit. "Who would want to be mated to someone like me?"

Despite feeling overwhelmed, I am confident about what I desire. I stand beside him and take his hand. When I do, it's like the jolt of a thousand electric pulses coursing through my body. It's the most beautiful feeling I could never explain. The electricity creates these tears of excitement and joy as we stare at each other. His hand gently wipes them away.

Whenever you touched me, Haven, I experienced this sensation. It was a beautiful kind of torture, and I longed for you to embrace it." Then his eyes flash once more, suggesting he was wrestling with something.

"Why do your eyes keep flashing to this gold color?"

"I don't know how much more you can take, Haven."

I squeeze his hand. "Tell me."

# CHAPTER 25

## LEVI



SHE DOESN'T KNOW HOW REASSURING THAT SQUEEZE IS, BUT I'M still hesitant.

"Levi…please." She begs me.

I didn't respond immediately, so she sat back on the stool, slid her dress up around her thighs, and guided me between her legs. This time, I placed my hands on her soft skin, and the pulses coursed immediately. So much so her eyes closed, and a moan slipped from her lips. Now, I was fighting my demon and a raging erection.

She opens her eyes with a smile, pointing at me. "See, you're struggling."

"Well, I'm in between the legs of the woman I've been pining for. I can smell your perfume, but your arousal is even stronger. Let's not forget that not-so-innocent little moan that left those beautiful lips moments ago."

She blushed as she rocked from side to side. I look down, hoping to catch a glimpse of her underwear, or lack thereof. Then her hand lifts my chin to eye level.

Nothing more needed to be said. I temporarily give up on my carnal quest to answer her question.

"When you see my eyes flash, my demon is trying to get

loose. I have to reel him in like a dog on a retractable leash. He's a mean and vicious bastard, but I think he's genuinely curious about you and eager to touch, much like I am. Flashing gold means curiosity, but black or red means to stay far away."

"Oh. Wow." She struggled to express those two words. I can only imagine what's going on in her head.

"You sure you don't want to run screaming into the night?"

Her laugh eases me. "No. I was thinking about how I saw them flash before when you were in the store. I thought it was just crazy lighting angles."

"When was this?"

"No, wait, it was two times. One time with Cherry and the other…with Nigel. And both times were black as night." I growl as she points at me. "See! Just at the mention of them."

"I wanted to rip her apart every goddamned day."

"And Nigel?"

"That maggot food was trying to claim what's mine. Break it off with him." I said sternly.

"Break what off? There's nothing there. Every time he tried, it felt wrong. Besides, he was only trying to cheer me up. He was a good friend."

He was doing more than trying to cheer her up, but if she says it's nothing, I'll leave it alone, but if he tries again…I'll turn him into a live autopsy!

"So, do I get to meet him? Your demon? He is a part of you, and I should know everything about you."

I sigh because it's an awfully sweet gesture. He's lying in the corner making heart-shaped flames with a creepy grin on his face. He looks scarier, trying to smile. We should use that.

"Not yet, darling. One, my house is barely big enough to contain him, and two, his only purpose is to torture the wicked and damned."

"In Hell?" She adds.

"Yes, in Hell. He is not a pet."

"Isn't that your dad's job, to torture and whatnot?"

"It's a family business. Speaking of my dad, I need you to understand that if he's Satan, then that makes me…" I imply I want her to answer.

"That makes you…" I can see her trying to figure it out, but it's best if I'm completely transparent with her. "The Devil, Haven." Her eyes went super wide with a gulp. "The Devil! I thought those names were interchangeable with the same entity! Lucifer, Satan, the Devil. I thought he was one person!"

She's taking this well.

"Think of it as the unholy trinity. My grandfather is Lucifer; my dad is Satan, and me."

"This is too much! I think the room might be spinning." She closes her eyes and rubs her temples.

"Okay, maybe we should stop." Yes, I wanted her to know everything, but I can't risk scaring her to literal death.

She grabs my arm. "NO! I mean, not yet. I have so many questions! It's all so fascinating!" It's like she was attending a lecture.

"O… kay. Understand, my curious book mouse, that I'm surprised by your intrigue."

"Because you thought I would run away."

"Yes, screaming into the night. My father is counting on my failure."

Haven grabs me by my lapels. Her lips are close. Dangerously close.

"Kiss me."

My resolve snaps as I slam my lips onto hers. The sparks course between us, and she whines needily. Her hands slip underneath my jacket, which I just unbuttoned, and it drops to the floor. I pull her forward enough to slip her sweater off, but then stop. "Wait. Tell me you want this before we go any further."

I needed her to think logically because this was a critical moment in her life, in both of our lives. I backed away so she wouldn't be distracted. I could feel her emotions ranging from shock to lust to want to uncertainty.

She bit her lip while looking at me. "Fuck, please don't look at me like that. I'm trying to be on my best behavior, darlin'."

She smiled; it was not her usual innocent one either. This held an underlying mischief. This tiny human knew she had absolute control over me.

She hopped off the stool, ran her hands down to smooth the dress's fabric, and held out her hand. "Show me the rest of your house."

"That's not an answer." She grabbed my hand and pulled me. "Patience, now come on. You'll get your answer soon. Besides, I always wondered what your place looked like. Not the color scheme I had in mind." She chuckled as we left our discarded clothing behind, heading back toward the living room.

"Everything is so ominously dark." She stated bluntly.

I pass by, whispering even more directly in her ear, "I'm the Devil." My demon senses tuned into her arousal, which became a tad bit stronger.

"It's an eerie yet sexy type of beauty."

I led her down the guest hall, showing the bedrooms and bathroom. Not that I would ever have anyone else here for more than a few hours except her. Now we stood in front of double doors on the other side of the house at the end of the hallway.

"Open them."

She reaches forward, turns the brass handles, and pushes the doors in before gasping at the sight of my oversized master bedroom—a king-size poster bed with luxurious red silks wrapped around the bedposts. My black duvet folded back to reveal those same sensuous silk sheets. The fireplace was to the left, the flames a dull roar, so I snapped my fingers to light the surrounding candles, adding to the ambiance.

I growl in her ear. "You have no idea how many fantasies I dreamt about claiming you here. To hear my name echoing off these walls and to feel you shatter all over me."

Her body shook, and her knees slightly buckled, her back now against my chest. "Yes." Was all she could whisper—a sweet and innocent plea from my little mate.

"Not yet. There's one more room; come." I pull her by the hand, back toward the front of the hallway.

We both stand at the door I bypassed earlier. "The day you lost yourself in those submissive fantasies of that book, touching yourself so innocently while imagining yourself across my lap while I spanked you to orgasm, is the day I made this room for you. Open it."

# CHAPTER 26

## HAVEN

Open it, he says. Meanwhile, I'm still mentally in his bedroom, the epitome of sexy and enticing, fantasizing about our bodies entwined in those silk sheets. But I was also still trying to digest everything he told me.

I open the door with a click to reveal a playroom. I step in, and I first notice a wall of toys. So many… floggers, tassel whips, handcuffs, and chains are hanging from the hooks at different lengths. There was a queen-sized bed with all-black bedding, not as romantic as his bedroom—more of a down-and-dirty feeling, especially with the strategically placed hooks to hold the chains. I feel my cheeks heat up. He had everything imaginable and some I know nothing about. Only what I've read.

And then I realized how much I didn't know about sex because I'm pure. Now I'm nervous; the man I want wants me; he wants to claim every inch of my body, and I wouldn't even know what to do.

I've never even been kissed before tonight.

There is no better time than now to breach the delicate subject.

"Levi, I, uh…I'm a…a…"

"I know," he says, his voice filled with a smug confidence. His hand slips into the depths of his pocket as he leans against the cool, textured wall beside the door. The faint scent of musty wood lingers in the air, mingling with the subtle hint of his cologne.

There's no way he knows what I'm about to say. "You know what?" My brow raises in disbelief, challenging his claim. There's a certain arrogance in the way he speaks, mirrored by the subtle upward curve at the corners of his mouth. It's not quite a smile, nor a smirk, but it ignites a fiery frustration within me.

"Well, it's no surprise that you are my complete opposite. The warm, radiating light to my darkness. Why wouldn't my precious little book angel be as pure as the winter snow? Untouched...both her pussy and heart begging to be filled." I stand there, frozen in shock, as his gaze remains fixed upon me, a silent challenge in his eyes.

I wouldn't have said it like that, but he was right.

He pushes himself off the wall. "Is that what you wanted to tell me? Is that your BIG secret that isn't?" I only nodded as he walked to the opposite side of the room.

"There's so much more we need to discuss, but perhaps another time. That's... if you say yes, Haven. Yes to being mated to the Devil, yes to being my Queen and to sit on the throne beside me as I rule, and yes, for me to fuck you and make you immortal."

I cringed. "Must you say it like that?" It sounded so emotionless.

"How do you want me to say it? You want me to make mad, passionate love to you, hmm? To steal your innocence while whispering in your ear everything you want to hear? My darlin'... it's the same thing, except one is a raw, primal, almost animalistic desire. Don't you feel it between us?"

His voice, now behind me, startles me so much that I jump, but he wraps his arm across my collarbone. The electricity coursing straight to my...

"I can feel your pussy vibrating at the very thought of intertwining our bodies and souls. Tell me, would my fingers be soaked in your desire if I were to slip my hand down into your panties and in between the warmth of your sweetness? Would you shatter at the mere touch of me?"

His chuckles were deep and arrogant. He didn't need an answer; he knew. Knew I would shamefully orgasm around him, whether it be his fingers, tongue, or his…

"You still haven't given me an answer, Haven. Will you be my Queen?"

Queen. Queen of Hell…immortal…could I live forever? What do I have forever to live for? Then, I gaze into his eyes, and although he is inherently evil, that's not what I see. I see a man who waited until the very moment he could tell me I was his. It was a twisted fairy tale.

So many thoughts were going through my head, and I knew he could feel my hesitation, and he broke the silence. "I understand. It's a lot to take in. I don't want to take you from your family. You don't have to sacrifice everything you have…for me."

"Everything I have? Really? What do I have, Levi? A tiny studio apartment, no car, no family, and no friends nearby? Have you ever seen someone around me who wasn't a customer? I'm a social misfit and an orphan. I have my dream job, but with a boss whose eyes I'd like to gouge out with my fingernails. I didn't have much to begin with. You can give me the one thing I always dreamed of…to feel wanted."

# CHAPTER 27

## LEVI

Eye gouging, I can make that happen. That's pretty creative; I'm impressed. Then I refocus back on the rest of her words. I knew little about her life before her 18th birthday. By then, she was starting college. I never understood human logic in finishing school and attending another, more expensive school to find a mediocre job that barely gets you by and leaves you in eternal debt.

"What happened to your parents?"

"Shouldn't you know everything about me?"

"Well, I didn't get a replay of your life after connecting to you, if that's what you mean."

"Well, that's a relief. No offense."

"None taken." I could see the pain in her face and feel it before she uttered her next words.

"My parents died in a car accident when I was a kid, so I ended up in an orphanage. From orphanage to college to current circumstances. Nothing exciting, just surviving the day-to-day."

I tilt her chin, brushing her cheek, and she basks in my touch. "The only reason I tolerate coming up to this repulsive place is because of you."

Her eyes well up, and then she breaks our contact when she

walks to the bed and sits down, crossing her legs. "Now, who knew the Devil could be sweet and caring?"

The very thought makes my stomach churn like the treacherous waters of the Drake Passage to Antarctica. I swallow the imaginary bile. "No one needs to know."

She leans back on her hands, "You have an image to uphold; I get it." She winked and chuckled.

"Laugh now, my little book bee, but you still haven't answered my life-altering question." I watch her watch me stalk her.

"To be your Queen. Well, after that shocking info dump, I think it's fair that you give me time to think through all this. I know you want an immediate yes, but I can't give you that. It'd be based on sexual desire alone."

"All the more reason to agree...the sexual tension is palpable."

"Levi..." She huffs in frustration.

She's right. My rational girl, I owe her that. I swear my dick is going to implode if I don't feel her soon. I sigh, hard in more ways than one, "Alright."

"So, Mr. Asant, am I allowed to stay over? If not, I have Nigel's number, so he can pick me up and take me home. He seemed quite eager to do so. Wasn't even going to charge me." She giggles as she holds up his business card.

Great, now the bastard knows where I live. I snatch it and burn it to cinders right in my hand. "Not funny. You're definitely staying right here."

"Maybe I shouldn't. I have to open up in the morning. I need time to go home and get ready."

"I'll snap you there."

She raised her brow. "Is that how you get there? Just snap your fingers?" She snapped, but of course, nothing happened. She wouldn't get that power until after that sweet little pussy was mine.

I lean down for a quick kiss to stop her from thinking any

further, "Company secret, darlin'. I'm afraid you don't yet have clearance to divulge that information. Perhaps I'll drive you in until I get my answer. I have a Ferrari; it goes from zero to 60 in 4.5 seconds."

"Ooh, how exhilarating!" I led her out of the playroom.

We stand at the threshold of my room, and the ambiance is the same. She's facing me; I wrap her arms around me and mine around her. Now, she's looking up because of her shorter stature. I can see her wheels turning; she wants to say or ask something because she looks anywhere but directly at me.

There's her arousal again.

I step back and separate us to lift her chin. "Say it."

"I, uh, have nothing to wear. Honestly, I'm barely wearing anything under this." She twists side to side with her dress in her hands. I'm actually praying her mischievous side's intrusive thoughts win, and she flashes me. But she lets go and continues swaying.

I'm not sure if she's genuinely being innocent or if she wants to torture me. "For fuck's sake…" I wipe my hand down my face as I go into my walk-in closet and grab one of my lighter sleep-shirt button-downs. I hold it out, and she takes it. "Thank you."

"The bathroom is over there."

With an uptick in her lips, "You don't want to watch me undress?" I knew now she was torturing me, but I was calling her bluff. "Careful, you may not be safe tonight if you keep it up…" And that's all I say as I unbutton my shirt. Any thoughts of hers went out the window as she watched my movement. Instead of rolling up my sleeves to play with my pet, I slide it off my shoulders, allowing it to fall to the floor. Then she gasped, and I watched her blush intensify as if someone was increasing the saturation on the TV.

"There it is," I said smugly.

"Shut up! I've never seen a half-naked man before, except on TV. I'm…nervous."

"I assure you; you have no reason to be nervous. You're my

mate, and you're always safe with me." I pat her ass. "Go change in the bathroom." I didn't want her to be overwhelmed more than she already was. I need her to be okay with this, and I can't rush her. It'll happen on her terms and time, not mine.

I could feel her calm down while she was in the bathroom, then she tensed up again. The light turned off, and she stepped out. Her cute little legs peek out from under my black shirt. My shirt was a dress on her tiny frame, and her hands didn't even reach the end of the sleeves. She flaps her arms, and I'm trying not to laugh.

"I'm so small! Your shirt swallows me up!"

"It won't be the only thing..."

"What?"

"Nothing, come here. You look adorable in my shirt."

"Don't patronize me! I look like a little girl in her daddy's clothes."

My good girl, that's exactly what she was, but I won't taint her.

Yet.

I led her to her side of the bed. She pulled the comforter back and climbed in. She didn't slide in like normal; she hopped up on her knees, which gave me a bird's-eye view of her ass in sheer pink panties. Then she turns and slides into the sheets.

I walk to my side, sit, and sigh while shaking my head. I couldn't help but laugh at the whole situation.

"What's so funny?"

I look back and feel my heart thump in my chest. It wasn't going to grow three sizes, but I was content with its meddling pulsing, signaling its attachment to my mate.

"I can't believe I finally got you in my bed."

"Oh. I expected you to be disappointed because I didn't give you an answer and we weren't having sex.

"Mmm, as much as my demon and I would love to be balls deep and wrapped up in you, it's only fair that I allow you to think this through. Everything is going to change once you agree. Technically, it already has."

"How so?"

I slip off my pants and lie next to her in my boxers. I look over, and she's lying on her side, purposefully only looking at me from the chest up.

"You being the new owner of the bookstore, for starters." Her eyes narrowed. "Levi...what did you do? What happened after I left that night?"

I tried to soften the blow. "To be fair, she ruined my plan to romance you and reveal everything. I had no choice."

"You killed her?"

"Oh, I vaporized her! She sealed her fate long ago when she blackmailed married men, but to go along with her buddy and cross me after I explicitly told everyone not to interfere. No regrets. Besides, you should have always been the rightful owner, with your genuine love of books and the store. Not even the angels above would disagree."

She looks shocked and not in a good way. "I'm not sure how to feel. I'm excited to own it, but not at the cost of her life." I could see her fall into her thoughts, and a worry crease appeared between her brows. She's starting to feel guilty.

I press my thumb to smooth out the crease and rub in small circular motions. "Don't. Whether or not I snuffed her out, her life was already ending. Her decision to botch my plan sped up the timeline. She had a year, and some change left, and her death would have been gruesome. Also, you would have lost the place you loved when it shut down. Technically, it was an easier way out."

She waved her hand. "Alright, that's enough of that conversation."

I can see I'm not swaying her in the right direction. I stop and lay there looking at the ceiling, hoping I didn't turn her off from this morbid conversation.

# CHAPTER 28

## HAVEN

He looks so tense and uncomfortable. I think it's the way I stopped the conversation about Cherry. Not because he got rid of her. He was protecting me. I know I shouldn't think like this, but good riddance! She was my Hell on Earth! I took the abuse because I loved her dad and that store, but I didn't deserve it!

I see his arms behind his head and eyes closed. His body is nothing short of amazing, and I want to touch him. I wanted him to know that I was still interested. I slide the blanket away from me and scoot over to lay half my body on his. It feels super awkward, but I push through. I rub my leg against him, and before my next breath, his hand is on my butt! I froze and looked over to see an intense gaze—a man who boldly acted on his need to touch me, too. I rested my head under his chin and my hand on his chest.

"You're so warm."

"Raging hormones." He said boldly as he moved his hand to scratch my head. I could let him for hours. My eyes automatically close as I enjoy his touch.

"Looks like I found someone's spot."

"How do you know?"

"Arousal, remember. Your body will reveal everything to me

without a single word, and I mean everything." He snaps his fingers, and all the candles blow out. Only the light and roar of the fireplace remain. I feel him pull my hair back... to kiss my forehead.

It's the beloved forehead kiss! The one that connects to your heart, a moment that gives you security and reassurance. I smiled from ear to ear.

After a few moments basking in bliss, I curiously asked, "Are you asleep?"

"Obviously not, since I just kissed you. I'm enjoying your warmth, your scent, that you're even here." Another swoon-worthy compliment. How did I ever get so lucky? However, I guess there's another way you could look at this. I get lost in my thoughts, comparing and contrasting. The good has to outweigh the bad.

I cleared my throat, trying to continue the conversation. "Why does your dad want you to fail?" His whole body tensed up, and he groaned. Obviously, it's a touchy subject.

"My father wants me to be like him. To indulge in the endless paradise of promiscuity and reject my mate pull. He thinks having a mate is a giant middle finger from above."

"Does he have a mate?"

"Did. My mother. I concluded she had to have been, given she was the only woman he allowed to bear him a child. I remember little about her, but he never misses a chance to bash her like he didn't love her. She sacrificed her body to have me."

"Did she die during childbirth?"

"No, he said she just left. She walked away from us, but I am sure he's not telling the entire truth. His entire existence is to lie, trick, and deceive. Like when he said he would cover me for that book at the store. Once I get us settled, I will find out what happened to her. I deserve to know the truth."

I don't know what's worse: his dad berating his mother and giving up or that Levi doesn't know what happened to her.

Hold up...

"Book from the store? Are you kidding me? That mean man asking me about you was your dad?! Satan! Satan was in my store?!" I'm freaking out a bit, especially realizing, "He hates me! He was so...condescending. He'll never accept me!" I tried not to tear up, but it was a sobering reality.

"First, what he thinks is not my concern, and it shouldn't be yours either. Second, he hates everyone, including me; if he liked you, then I'd be concerned he was trying to seduce you. And lastly," He tips my chin toward him, and his lips cover mine. His lips coerce mine open until he slips his tongue in. I can't believe he was my first kiss and now my first French kiss. He's driving me wild. I almost can't breathe, then he leans back, "You're mine. Now, if that's settled, since I can't dive between your legs and taste you all over me tonight, how about we get some rest?" He stares as he kisses my fingertips.

Oh my!

"Okay. Good night."

"Night, my adorable book bee." And with another forehead kiss, I fell asleep happier than I had been. I pray this is real and not a dream.

*Two hours later...*

I can't sleep. I close my eyes but open them to make sure he's still here. I touch him to feel the sparks; it's like a high-performance drug. I never want to grow old of the magical feeling, so I back away, but I still smile so hard my jaw is sore. His hair became slightly disheveled from rubbing against me and the pillow. He has a permanent scowl when he sleeps; it can't be easy. I wonder what a typical day is like down there. The picture often painted does not make it sound like a tourist destination. I wonder how much I could stomach. I also must admit a tiny dark part of me wants to see; knowing that Cherry's suffering down there makes me want to watch...maybe even cause her pain.

Focusing back on Levi, I lean forward and touch his cheek, and the frown disappears. He leans toward my touch, and his scowl is gone. Then his eyes open, he grabs me, and pulls me into his grasp.

"What were you doing? Why aren't you asleep?"

"Can't sleep, too excited and scared that it's all a dream. A perfect dream I don't want to wake up from."

"You have work tomorrow. Well, technically, you don't have to work." He wiggled his brow.

"And who would open the store? You want me to do what? Sit on a throne all day in Hell?! No, thank you."

"I have lackeys to do everything for me."

I snuggle up to him. "Good for you. That doesn't work for me. Now, go to sleep. I've got work in the morning." Emphasizing my eagerness to open MY store.

# CHAPTER 29

## LEVI

It's not surprising that she doesn't look forward to reigning down there.[4] Now, I have to be okay with the possibility of commuting between worlds.

"Levi! Wake up." I hop out of bed and try to head toward the sound of her voice; she was a soulful siren, luring me in. Then I smelled deliciousness and headed into the kitchen. There she was, making breakfast, still wearing my shirt. I wrapped her up in my arms so fast she almost dropped the skillet full of eggs. "Stop it! Let go before you make me spill it." I smother her neck in kisses before finally letting go. "Fine."

"Go sit down."

She fiddles around the stove before she sets a plate in front of me. Then she brings another plate and sits down. I grab two glasses and the orange juice, pouring both of us a glass.

"Thank you." She smiles before popping the bacon into her mouth.

"I should be thanking you. I should have made breakfast; it is my place. Well… it's our place now."

I heard her physically swallow the bacon while trying not to choke on it. "Ours?"

"Of course, everything I own is yours: the library, the playroom, and especially the bedroom. My house now belongs to you. I want you here with me to make it a home. I know staying below will take some time to warm up to." She continued eating in silence, which was her answer. I leave it at that.

We ate, and then I showered and dressed. I tried to coax her to join me, but she replied she had no clothes here. "But," she countered, "I'll give you my key, and you can pack them up." I agreed—any step toward a definitive answer and her permanent presence.

I park in front of her boringly brown-bricked building and follow her up the stairs down the moldy hallway to her apartment. It's like a glorified coat closet. I think my pantry is bigger.

I'm afraid to even touch the walls. How could she stay in such shambles? "There's no way you're staying here another night. You deserve better."

"Well, this was all I could afford. I'm going to take a shower and get dressed. Stay here." Emphasizing the staying part.

I walk around, assessing everything. I can get all her essential things in my car. She had no visible pictures of anyone, not even of herself. There was one photo album; it was an heirloom by the obvious fire-damage cover. It must have been in the car with them. I touch the original rich burgundy color on the inside. In it was a picture of Haven as a baby. It was the first sign of her earlier years. They were chronological, each a few to several years after the prior. At the end was an album-sized family portrait of her as a toddler with her parents. There was no doubt about it; she had her mom's nose, smile, and chin; otherwise, she looked like her dad. Then, underneath that was the funeral program for their double funeral.

"I miss them every day." She startles me. I see she's dressed and towel-drying her hair.

"They loved you so much. I'm sure they're so proud of the woman you've become."

"Yeah? How would they feel knowing that she was mated to the King of Hell? I knew it wasn't malicious, but I, too, wondered what they would think of me if they were alive. I was the man who was supposed to take care of their only daughter.

I spin on my heel. "Prince of Darkness. My dad is the King of Hell."

She shakes her head and grabs her bag and keys. "Semantics. Let's go, Mr. Prince of Darkness." She opens the door and waits for me to exit so she can lock up. I reach up and grab the door frame, leaning forward and towering over her. The classic bad boy pose that makes women want to rip off their clothes and skip work.

If only.

She squeaked, followed by this nervous laugh.

"That's sir to you. Got it?" I should have wrapped my hand around her throat.

*Baby steps.*

She stares with wide eyes, "Y-yes, sir." I reward her with a kiss. "Let's go."

Watching her open the door with excitement, knowing the store was legally hers, was one of those feel-good human emotions. I felt happy and violently nauseous at the same time.

What is she doing to me?

She heads straight to her office. I figured she was going through her new morning ritual. I'm sure she knew the business aspect of this place, along with the layout.

I stay out front and see a few people gathering, waiting patiently outside.

I'm not letting them in. I said I'd live amongst them, not... help them. My entire body shudders at the mere thought.

***Several hours later...***

She's in her element, and her smile while tending to customers is radiant. That once shy bookworm has blossomed into her own, and I'd like to think I helped. Maybe she realized she was worth everything she ever wanted, and all it took was patience and dare I say... prayer.

"Hey." She sits on the arm of the chair, placing her arm

behind me and leaning toward me. I deeply inhale her sweet perfume. I love how she's getting comfortable being so close.

"Yes?"

"You want to go pack up my clothes? I don't want or need anything else but those. Here…" She holds out her keys. "By the time you return, it should be close to closing."

"Are you trying to get rid of me?"

"I'm trying to keep you busy that doesn't involve helping people. You don't like the human population, and your vibe makes my customers uneasy."

I scoff. Who needs them? "I could get rid of them. Say the word, and I'll scorch this miserable world to ashes for you."

She slapped her hand over her mouth and squeaked, kicking her feet before her radiant smile appeared. "That's what every villain or anti-hero says…" Her fingers graze her pouty lips. I want to taste and make them appetizers with her as my main course.

"Says?"

"Says to the one that they love." She grabs my hands, igniting our bond, and places it on her heart. Her heart is racing, and her breathing almost matches. She wants to hear it, but I also realize I'm touching her breast. I squeeze, and she pushes my hand off and tuts. I ruined her perfect moment. Again, it's the sin of lust, but also the mate bond. I love that it fits my hand perfectly.

I know what she wants to hear, and she knows what I want to hear. I'm merely letting the anticipation build.

She goes back to ring up a couple who set down several books. She quickly scans them. "Enjoy your purchase and thank you." She tells them. The guy kisses the girl's temple, and I see the blush on Haven. She's swooning. The bell marks their departure, and she sighs out loud.

I immediately cage her behind the counter. She didn't cower or look down or away; she stood taller and smiled. Someone's getting bolder.

"Levi, what are you doing?"

"I'm not doing anything." I lean in closer.

"You're 'nothing' is very suspicious. I know who you are." She says confidently. Even closer, I can smell the peppermint on her breath. I can see she wants it as bad as I want to give it to her. I just need her to agree.

"Levi…"

My lips are a hair away as I whisper, "Haven… be my Queen."

And then her eyes shifted, and her brow furrowed. "You want to lock me away and be your Persephone? Fated we may be, but I will not be your prisoner!" Then she walked into her office, slamming the door.

What the hell just happened?

# CHAPTER 30

## HAVEN

I KNOW IT SEEMED LIKE MY OUTBURST CAME OUT OF NOWHERE, BUT IT didn't, I swear! I remembered what that girl said, and it all clicked! She was talking about Levi, and I panicked!

*...You're mediocre...he deserves a girl like me. Do yourself a favor and don't even consider accepting his proposal...I'll make your life a living hell.*

I remember her vicious rant. Once I realized, her cruel words played repeatedly like a broken record, getting louder and louder. The doubt hung over me like a cloud; then it burst open like a torrential storm. Whenever I feel like my dreams are coming true, negativity always seems to find me. The way she spoke with brazen cockiness, I'm almost sure she's slept with him. It makes me wonder how many there were. How many is he going to compare me to? What if I'm not enough? He said it was a carnal paradise.

I can't compete.

I try to inhale hard to swallow the lump in my throat and stop the tears.

This can't work.

Then my door burst open, and he looked...mad. Okay, he looked pissed because his eyes flashed again. I don't move but follow his movement as he paces in front of my desk. Literally feeling me out because he is tuned in to my emotions.

"If you think I can't feel your doubt and second-guessing, you're wrong, my beautiful little book bee. What was that outburst about? Huh?"

I feel the tears pool, and my lip quiver before I can stop them. Now I'm bawling. Quicker than lightning, he has me in his lap while sitting in my chair.

When I finally calmed down, I looked at him and saw his concern. I could feel it, and with the sparks, it made me feel silly. It was fate that brought us together; how could I doubt it?

"Hey." He said while his thumb rubbed my hand. It sounded so innocent and wholesome. "Hi." I countered.

"You want to tell me why you think I'd treat you like my great great great-great-grandfather treated his wife?"

"No way, you're related?"

"Hades, God of the Underworld. The Underworld is Hell."

"Levi, how am I supposed to make this feel normal? It's not! What you do, who you are, where you go, the other women…"

"Whoa. Other women? What are you talking about?"

"One day, Cherry's drunk friends came by to go clubbing, but this one mean girl approached me. Saying she didn't understand why he would pick me over her. I didn't know what she was talking about until earlier when it clicked! She told me not to accept your proposal, or she'd make my life a living hell!"

I watched his jaw tighten so hard it had to be painful. "Is that right?" He said calmly, way too calmly. He closed his eyes briefly; then, there was a knock.

"Come in." He spoke. A college-aged-looking boy walks in. He bowed his head. "Yes, sir?"

His breathing was very slow. He was breathing through his nose while rubbing his fingers together. I think it's a way to diffuse his anger.

"I want Aurora and her puppet caged and warded to my bedroom NOW, understand?"

"The acid-laced cages?"

"No, regular is fine. They expect something excruciating. Let them let their guard down before I deal with them personally."

"Yes, sir." He replied with a disturbing smirk that twisted and contorted his face until he resembled one of those jack-o'-lanterns. Then I realized he was a demon from the depths of the abyss.

Now I'm intrigued, and a little creeped out. Ooh, he probably had a sinister name, like Azrael or Kali. Names that make your skin crawl.

"That'll be all, Clifford."

***Snort***

"Clifford?!" I slap my hand over my mouth. I didn't even look at Levi.

"Clifford, this is my mate, Haven. You are officially the first to meet your future Queen.

"It is an honor and my pleasure to meet you, my Queen." He bowed.

"Nice to meet you." I sound like I'm asking a question. I don't know the proper protocol for Hell.

"Dismissed." Levi waved his hand in an away motion. Clifford disappeared right in front of me in a puff of black smoke, and I screamed, burying myself into him.

He laughed. "That's why I told him to knock on the door so he wouldn't scare you to death. Then I'd lose you forever."

"What do you mean?" He looked so worried as he rubbed my knee; he was slowly working his way upward and not ashamed. "If you were to perish before we sealed our bond, you, my angel, would become an actual angel in Heaven and not with me."

Oh. That would be unfortunate. Still, that doesn't resolve my issue about that girl. "I need you to be honest with me. You seem to know who I am talking about. Her name is Aurora. Who is she to Cherry? And who is she to you?"

# CHAPTER 31

## LEVI

Fuck me. I was hoping to mark her before I had to discuss my past. Now, I have an even slimmer chance of success.

It pains me because I can see how much she needs to know this. To be reassured that the past is just that.

"First, she doesn't mean shit to me. Aurora was a place-holder, someone to satisfy my urges and nothing more. It's the only sin I can't avoid. I did my best but had…experiences with other women. Then, I trimmed it down to just her. That was clearly a mistake." I huffed.

"She seems to think differently about her place."

Aurora's place was choking on my dick, as she tried to keep my cum from shooting down the wrong pipe.

"Something like that. She assumes she's best for the throne and has been openly adamant, almost campaign-like. Most down there choose to ignore the mate bond, but I don't. I am not mated to her. You are, which means YOU are my best choice. The person to make me whole, and by having that, I can successfully reign with you by my side, but…"

I squeeze her hand. "If you don't want to reign down there with me, I'll give up my title and live here with you. And because of that bit of breaking news, the masses just had to see the lamb that had the big bad wolf ready to give it all up. You probably saw a lot of new people in the store lately..."

"You mean all those handsome guys? Chiseled jawlines, piercing eyes, and incredibly dressed?" She didn't even stumble on her words and sounded too enthused about it.

I growled because I was going to torture and maim every nosey asshole who visited her. My demon let out a vicious inner roar; he was where my jealousy lay.

"So," she takes her fingertips and traces the buttons on my shirt. I wanted her to grab me with both hands and rip my shirt open, the buttons flying everywhere in the heat of the moment and scratching me up like a cat in heat. "You're going to risk living up here and suffer if I say I don't want to live down there? But you hate people, like really despise our existence."

She's got a point.

"Yes, *their* existence ...but you, I love you, and no matter how evil I'm portrayed, I know you'll always see the good in me. I need to know that one perfect soul in this world loves me as I am. And that soul... is you."

There were those pools in her eyes, but she was smiling, not bawling. Her hand brushes against my face. I grab it and place it where my heart would be. There's so much silence that it's deafening. She has the cutest little lip quiver that keeps her from smiling.

"You said you love me."

"Is it so hard to believe?"

"Well, no, but you're supposed to be this master of evil and all things bad, a plague upon this world."

I mean...I am.

"According to the high and mighty word of man, I'm also supposed to be small-horned, cloven-hooved like a goat, and cherry red with a pitchfork. I suppose I can look like that if you want me to." I hold my hand up, ready to snap my fingers to look like a demonic clown with tiny horns and claws.

Man really is stupid.

"God, no!" She grabbed my hand to prevent me from doing so, then she stiffened. "Sorry. For the record, it's just an expression."

"I know that."

The silence wraps us up again, and she lays her head on my shoulder. I slide my fingers in between hers.

"This still doesn't solve the other woman problem."

"There is no other woman problem because there is no other woman. I've done nothing but torture that slut since the day she set me up for you to find me like that. I underestimated her powers; she cast a spell that made me fall asleep and then made Cherry resemble you. However, I knew it was wrong the moment she touched me, and I didn't feel the sparks. I waited too long not to feel them. I never wanted you to witness something like that, and I never wanted to see that look of hurt on your face again. Besides, I have a foolproof plan to help you decide."

Her eyes narrowed. "What are you up to?"

I look at my watch. "Nothing to worry about, yet. I'm in the planning phase. Anyway, it's closing time, and there will be no extended hours for you. Let's grab your things so I can lock you away." She stared daggers at me. "Kidding. But I will let you in on something. Grandma Persephone was not as 'locked away' as you think and held great power over Hades. In fact, she was the true ruler of the Underworld, not him."

"So you'd be okay if I took over ruling Hell?"

I laughed because it sounded so absurd, but Grandma Persephone made this place what it was. Hades wasn't as sick and sadistic as she was. He met his match and suffered. We always assumed she was releasing her resentment of being held against her will in the beginning.

"Absolutely not."

"Sounds like somebody's scared of my abilities!" Her confidence might write a check her ass can't cash.

"What does that even mean?"

"It means that I could probably handle business better than you could. She did!"

"My sweet girl, I don't think you could stomach the day-to-day. I'm not risking losing you…not until I make you cum repeatedly all over my cock and turn you immortal. Then and only then will we make our first visit down there, but…"

I saw her shudder at the thought of me stealing her innocence but rewarding her with endless orgasms.

I kiss her temple and walk ahead. "Not until you answer me."

# CHAPTER 32

## HAVEN

 think she is a threat.

If I was going to be down there, I needed to confront her and Cherry to let them know I won't tolerate their bullshit, especially not for eternity. Besides, I'll be their Queen. They'll have to bow down to me!

I feel this power surge, knowing they couldn't torture me anymore. In fact, I can torture them! I have been contemplating everything since Levi revealed his true intentions. Am I okay with what he is and what he does? Not entirely, but I've dreamed of Levi since I met him.

My fantasies overflowed with him and everything I saw in that book every night. Then, I realized that if I agreed, eventually, I'd want to recreate that moment in the book. I want to give myself to him...I want to submit to my mate.

"My book butterfly, are you ready to go?" He brings me out of my fantasy. He held out his hand, and I took it eagerly as he escorted me out. I remembered I had a cute lingerie set that I bought back in college with my roommate, Lexi. This is when she was trying to get me to do stuff girls do, like shopping. Her first stop? Victoria's Secret. I had second, third, and fourth-hand embarrassment.

*"Havie, you're redder than a fire engine! It's only underwear!"*

*"I've never bought this type of underwear before, Lexi!" I whisper-yelled.*

*She picks up a tiny red lace thong, twirling it on her finger and making weird sounds, bringing attention to us.*

*"Does this make you uncomfortable? Ooooh...." She chuckles, which makes me laugh nervously.*

*"Yes! Now put it away!" I instantly look around.*

*She throws a few pairs in her basket while perusing. "My mom always said a woman should have at least two pairs of underwear sets for those sexy moments, like a date with a guy, an anniversary, or even for yourself. Just one set for you today; we'll get the other at another time before you pass out. Come on...for me, Havie?"*

*Lexi was genuine about making me feel confident, so I gave in. "Fine, but not in red. That's like level 10. I need baby steps." I look around and see a classic and simple black lace set—a quick fix to shut her up and get out of there.*

I bought it almost four years ago, and it still has the tags. I don't know any occasion more special than this. I also have a black silk robe she bought me for my birthday. I'll have to pack that drawer while he packs stuff from my closet.

When we get to my place, I grab a medium-sized pink suitcase. "Here, you take the closet, and I'll pack my dresser drawers." I grab my black duffel bag.

"Are you trying to hide naughty, vibrating toys you don't want me to discover? I promise I won't get jealous. Because you'll know soon enough, no battery-operated plastic dick will ever...come close."

He has me pushed up against the dresser. I lean up for him to kiss my breath away, but when I open my eyes, he's smirking. "I bet... the simplest touch will bring you to your knees. You'd shamelessly cum all over my fingers." He licks his lips, backs off, and my knees buckle. I didn't even hide my reaction because he was connected to me. No way I could deny it. He'd have his way soon.

"You have no idea how much I want to feel you tighten around me." He continues to taunt me. Looking back, he's browsing through my clothes while I quickly stuff my bag.

"You know what I was thinking?" His question caused me to stop pulling from my pajama drawer.

"What?"

"I can just buy you new clothes. Anything you want."

"That's nice, but I need clothes in the meantime. I can't walk around naked." I realized my faux pas when his lip curled upward, and he rubbed his chin. "Don't! Say anything, just a few sets of clothing, and I'll let you buy me a whole new wardrobe. I need to embrace my new look, anyway." I tap my chin while looking ahead and not at him when I say, "I loved that skin-tight red dress I wore for my birthday. It's in there, by the way. Do you remember? I'll get a few similar ones. They work my curves so well. Don't you think so?" I slid my hands down my waist, and his gaze followed, licking his lips. He snaps his fingers like he is bringing himself out of a trance. Then, he adjusted himself and coughed. He couldn't reply and I loved it. I love having this effect on him.

After grabbing a few pairs of shoes, I take a final look back at my place and smile, saying a secret prayer of thanks even though it is kind of weird to say thanks when my mate is who he is, but there's always a reason. I may not know now, but eventually, it'll make sense.

"Come on. I can't wait to get you settled in. Let's go home." He said it nonchalantly, but my heart burst when I heard it. We were going home together.

The man of my dreams was taking me home.

He took my bag and carried everything while I locked up. He placed everything in the backseat while I got comfortable up front. I had no solid plan for tonight. I was going to follow my heart...or was it my hormones?

He slipped in the driver's seat, lacing our fingers together after pressing the push start button and putting it in gear. I cross my legs toward him and stare. This handsome devil was mine. He lifted our hands for a kiss, and I laughed.

"What's so funny?"

"You're the Devil."

"That I am."

"But you're being so sweet and romantic..."

"Only to you."

"It's ironic, I guess."

He nodded, and I watched this man navigate the roads deep into the haunting forest.

"Now it makes sense why you live out here. It, too, is dark and ominous. Mysterious, like you." I said, while leaning over as he parked. I surprised him by how close I was when he looked back.

"H-haven."

Could I have the Devil himself tongue-tied? Knowing he wants me as much as I want him because our bond was sealed long ago makes this surge of confidence eye-opening.

"Hmm?" I smile so wide my jaw hurts. He's on a hair trigger, teetering on the edge. I wanted to see him fumble like he made me.

"How about I stage the house like I had it for your birthday... to reclaim the moment?"

Oh, he had set up his place for me?! I was fuming mad that I didn't really pay attention to the surroundings and let's not forget the bombshell reveal of who he was. Of course, I wanted to see it!

"Yes, please."

He raised his brow, and I immediately corrected, "Yes...sir, please." And he snapped his fingers.

"What was that?"

"That, my darling, is the recreation of your birthday, and this *snap* is to put all your stuff from the car into our bedroom."

I look back, and indeed, it is all gone.

"Whoa!" He gives me a look before getting out, an unspoken understanding for me to wait so he can open my door.

He holds his hand out after opening it. We walk up to the front door, and he presents me with keys. "To the house and cars. What's mine is yours, now and forever."

I take them, and he steps back to allow me to unlock the door with my keys. The sound they make clinking against each other as I turn them to unlock it makes me so happy! I'm unlocking a part of my dream.

I step in and see the endless number of candles and flowers in the entryway.

He strolls past, and I get a whiff of his cologne. "I may have exaggerated the number of candles and flowers this time. Come, dinner awaits."

"How could dinner possibly be..." **Snap** I exhaled loudly, "Showoff."

"That I am." He stepped closer, making me step back, but he followed me until I was against the door. His scent suffocated me once more, but this time, there was an underlying tone of his masculinity, the feral hormones that wanted him to take me here and now, like a werewolf in heat.

"Levi..." I whispered and saw mischief in his eyes. "I should get ready. I can't wear what I wore to work. It's a special occasion, and I want...I want to look nice."

He doesn't know how worth it the wait's going to be. "Promise me you won't come in."

"But...I'm the Devil..." His mischievous smirk appeared.

"And you said you'd do anything for me." I looked at him and could conjure up some pity tears. "Please... sir?"

His eyes flashed gold before he leaned forward, resting his arm above me on the door. "You're such a fucking tease. Just you wait. Go before we decide not to listen."

I smiled because I knew I would fulfill his wish and mine tonight. I see that not only did the clothes go into the house, but in the closet. I wonder if I'll gain the snapping magic once we… you know.

I took inventory and saw he grabbed everything on the side of the closet where my birthday dress was, basically all the stuff Lexi bought me. He also tossed in a few of my sweaters, sweater coats, and not a single pair of pants. I also noticed a bunch of dresses with tags that I didn't buy, and I think back and realize that the snap in my apartment wasn't to bring himself out of a trance but to fill my side of the wardrobe. I grabbed a simple A-line red velvet dress. I figured it would now be my signature color.

I find the drawer with my underwear and grab the set. I also have some silky lace thigh highs that would enhance the experience. I take the quickest shower of my life.

I'm ready.

# CHAPTER 33

## LEVI

The shrimp carbonara was piping hot, along with the garlic bread. I went to the cellar and grabbed a light, slightly dry Chenin Blanc to accompany our meal. Once poured, I changed my suit to a red vest and black button-up combo with no jacket. I mean, I was in the comfort of my home.

Our home.

Haven was here, and now she is a permanent resident. But I can't relish in it; I feel an impending doom, and he is my sperm donor. Haven's going to have to develop some mighty thick skin. I could try to avoid him, but who are we kidding? Any chance he can have to ruin my life, he will take it.

I heard the doors open down the hall. I took a few steps back into the hallway and saw her in the sexiest red dress. I think it's velvet. She steps forward, and I notice she's barefoot but with lace stockings. She steps on the balls of her feet, conveying a sinful innocence. Even on her tiptoes, she was deliciously petite compared to my towering stature. She stops in front of me with her hands behind her back. The perfect position for restraining her with one hand. She looks up; the scent of her honeysuckle perfume drives me wild. I presented her with a red rose. "Happy birthday, my love."

"Thank you." She sniffs the air, moving around me, keeping me from slamming her onto the nearest countertop. "It smells wonderful. Come on, I'm starving." She takes my hand and pulls me back into the kitchen.

She huffed when she didn't see the food there and looked at me curiously.

"Dinner…" I lean in, and she closes her eyes, awaiting a kiss. Although I love teasing her, it's also torture for me. I gave her two quick kisses because any longer, there would be no dinner. "Is in the dining room."

"Ohhh." She whispered. I don't know how much more of this innocent role I could take. I am going to mark her, defile her, smear her lipstick, and stain her lips. I let her walk in front of me after I pointed her in the right direction. Instead of walking normally, she lifts back off the balls of her feet to balance on her tiptoes again, swaying from side to side this time.

That did it. I hear my composure snap, and my demon rushes forward. I throw the mental barrier up before my horns and claws appear, possibly scaring her to death. I remind him she's not immortal yet, and we can't lose her. I would be inconsolable and destructible at the same time.

I pick her up and storm into the dining room, slamming her onto an empty part of the table. I growl in her ear before nibbling her neck. Her hands on my chest try to put distance between us, but I refuse. I'm a wild, feral beast at this point. I slide my hands up her legs, and she yelps, grabbing my hands. Somehow, that breaks the intensity. I look down and see the lace top of her thigh-highs. Her dress pooled between her legs, keeping what was underneath a secret for now.

"Sorry, my book butterfly. I lost control there." I let her hop down and slid her chair out. She sits and pats the chair next to her, which is not my usual place at the head of the table. I concede and grab my plate and glass. I toss my arm over her chair, leaning in.

I think she was still processing my reaction to her teasing; she looked anywhere but directly at me. "You look handsome. I mean, you always do! I'm not saying you don't. I'm saying..." She's babbling, and her blush is very prominent. I take my fork and dig into the pasta, twirling it around. "Open." Her soft lips open slowly, enough to take the bite, sauce in the corner of her lips, but her tongue slips out to retrieve it.

"Mmm, it's delicious. Thank you." That gesture calmed her down enough to grab her fork and start eating. It was a quiet meal for a while. I catch her taking bites and sips of the wine. She was sipping way faster than I was. I think it was her nerves.

"Delicious?"

"Hmm? Yes. Tell me, is there dessert? To celebrate my birthday?"

I snap my fingers. "There is now, and if I remember from my stalking, as you like to call it, a certain good girl loves strawberry cheesecake. Is that true?"

She nods furiously, "It is, it is!" Then she kisses my cheek, "Thank you!"

I nod, snap my fingers, and it's before us. She licked her lips, wanting to indulge in it like I wanted to devour her. She eagerly cuts a piece, wiggling happily in her chair, and plates it. I await her reaction to the first bite. She pierces it, and a strawberry lifts it, and surprisingly, it's before my lips instead of hers.

"Darlin', the dessert is for you."

"I know, but I wanted to feed you the first bite like you fed me. Besides, I'd love to lick cheesecake off of you."

"What?"

"Nothing."

She put it closer, so I took a bite.

"How is it?" She swipes a bit with her finger and pops it in her mouth. Seeing her finger slide slowly from between her stained lips, she didn't know I was a half second from replacing that finger with my dick. I tried to focus on replying while she gave me this sly smile.

"For lack of a better word, heavenly."

Then she drops the fork. It hits the plate, and the clang distracts me while she straddles me, kissing me fervently. My hands gripped her ass instantly. Her whimpers get louder as she rocks against me. I reach behind her neck and grab her by the hair to separate us.

"Haven?" My voice wavers as I phrase her name as the question I desperately want answered.

"Yesss…I'll be your Queen. Promise to love and protect me forever. I want to try if it'll make you happy. Please…don't hurt me. I'm giving everything to you."

I take her hand and kiss it. "You make me happy. I'm your protector and won't allow anyone to hurt you anymore."

I sweep my tongue across her lips, causing her to gasp as I slam our lips together. She rocks against me in the tiny space between my lap and the table. She's terrified of the unknown but assures me she wants this. I wrap her arms around my neck. "Hold tight." As I stood up with her wrapped around me, I realized I had two places I wanted to mark at the moment, but I would let her decide.

"Playroom or bedroom? Each is a different version of myself. Both will make your first time special. What do you want?"

Her wheels were turning hard; this was a critical and pivotal moment in her life. She would lose her virginity and gain immortality.

"Bedroom." One word, and I understood what she was looking for. My innocent bookworm exposed herself to many fantasies, and I suppose I did, too, while pursuing her. It reflected in her cheeks, from the super spicy to the stereotypical sappy ones. She was looking for an experience filled with romance.

I sat her down on the bed. Her legs never touched the floor, causing her dress to rise and show the top of her thigh highs again. I growled, and she giggled. "You sound feral."

I flip her on her stomach. I let go, and she crossed her legs in the air, and I could see the bottom of her underwear. She looks back and smiles. I could see every curve of her I craved.

I pushed her legs down, straddled her, and ran my hand down the center of her back. "Ooh." I leaned forward, placing kisses from one shoulder blade to the other. I pull the straps of her dress down; she maneuvers her arms out. "When you're ready," I told her as I slipped off her to remove my vest and shirt, unbuckling my pants. She turned around, holding the dress up, and stood before me. I get a whiff of her excitement but notice her physically shaking and looking at our feet. I lift her chin and kiss her. As I grab her face with both my hands, I feel her hands on my chest. Then, there was the instant realization in her eyes when she knew her dress was now pooled at her feet. She bit her lip as she stood in a black set and her flesh-colored thigh highs.

She was the most beautifully sinful sight. It was the only time I would ever thank the man above and acknowledge the blessing before me.

She wrapped her arms around herself in discomfort, so I tossed her on the bed, pulling her forward until her legs hung off. Before she could fully climb out from the luscious, thick comforter, I fell to my knees before her, my breath warming her before I placed butterfly kisses on her lightly flushed skin while I spread her legs apart. She jumped at the initial touch, then sighed as I reached the apex of her pussy. I was kneeling in front of her, my altar, to worship in every way, stilling myself, breathing on it to warm up my dessert. I lift one leg to perch on the bed and gaze at every inch of her.

# CHAPTER 34

## HAVEN

I'm on full display in front of him, and my gut reaction is to cover up, but he won't let me. He wants me to see how much he hungers for me. Once one leg was out of the way, he placed his lips on my covered innocence. The feeling felt so good that a moan slipped.

"Exactly what I want to hear." He chuckled, "I am going to enjoy taking your innocence…let me show you how much you belong to me." He slipped his fingers underneath the sides of my underwear.

I sat up on my elbows; this was the next step. I lift myself so he can remove the only barrier between us. He tossed them aside and didn't hesitate to dive face-first, his tongue exploring me and making me feel like I was going to explode. It feels so good that my hands automatically bury themselves in his hair, like in my fantasies.

"Ohhh! Leviiii…" I finally understood the metaphor 'knot in the pit of your stomach' because I was unraveling as he devoured me.

"Tell me what you want. Tell me…" His fingers explored me while he watched me squirm.

"M-more, please." Even though I've never had an orgasm, I read enough explicit scenes to know the signs of one. He resumed his position. I locked my legs against his head as I tried to hold him there while simultaneously pushing him away until he sent my body crashing over. I felt so amazing, wanted, and beautiful at the same time.

"Ahhh!" I screamed until I was breathing hard, and I saw the smirk on his face between the rise and fall of my breasts. He lies beside me, bringing my lips to his as I taste myself for the first time.

"You almost drowned me with your sweet orgasm. I have a feeling that with the right combination, you might be a squirter."

I read enough to know what that is. I cover my face, but he removes my hands and kisses them. Then he looks at me, watching me intently as he takes my hand and slowly traces down his warm, damp chest. I watch his chest as his breathing picks up, then his eyes roll to the back of his head. When I look down, my hand is in his pants and on his dick! He knew my knee-jerk reaction would be to pull away, so his hand clutched mine tighter. He let out one of those manly grunts of pleasure. It was so hot.

"Take them off, now." He said bluntly. I sat in front of him on my knees and slid his pants off, and when I thought I'd see another layer of fabric with his underwear, I saw nothing at all! He wore boxers last night to make me more comfortable sleeping in the same bed.

Now, it stood up completely stiff. He sighed in relief to be free from the confines.

It was huge! Excuse my French, but there's no fucking way.

"Do you know what to do?"

Absolutely not! I look at him beyond this massive thing and shake my head; I know what I read, but now that it's in front of me...

"Spit in your hands, then wrap them around me. Slowly

move up and down." I did as I was told and was rewarded with his deep groan as he slid to lie flat on his back, occasionally lifting his head.

"Oh fuck… yes, just like that…" I sped up, and he started panting. I loved the way he sounded. It's so intense. I feel this pulsing between my legs. I squeeze them together for quick relief but continue to focus on his moans and groans.

I sat up further on my knees and positioned my mouth over it while twisting. It was a bold move for me to try, but I was curious. I knew he would guide me. Levi finally opened his eyes, and I stuck out my tongue. I lowered my mouth over him, taking him as far as possible. I got about halfway down. I'm unsure if that's good, but it was my limit before my gag reflex kicked in.

He slammed his hands down on the bed, gripping the sheets tightly while growling as he stared at me, "Mmm, look at that pretty little mouth swallowing me whole. Fuuuuuck…"

Then he sat up to stop me. "I want to feel you shatter all over me." He laid me on the bed, kissing me all over; it felt so good, but I was scared. I think he noticed my hesitation.

"Look at me. You will always control how this goes. We don't have to, Haven. Whenever you are ready, okay?"

I knew I was in safe hands and didn't want to wait anymore, even if I was nervous. I straddled him, and his hands slid up to my breasts. He squeezed and pinched until he got the reaction he wanted out of me as a whimper.

"Oh, my sweet book bee, you sound so needy; whine for me. Say it, say you want me, that you want this."

I suppose he was still gauging my willingness to proceed. He needed verbal confirmation. I rock against him and run my fingernails down his chest. "Yes, I want you to take me."

He sat up, his face level with my breasts. I can feel his warm breath sending shivers down my spine. Combined with the bond, the sparks, and the pulsing, I'm going to explode.

"I belong to you, Levi…my heart, love, and purity…because I

love you. I should have said it when you did. I was so over-whelmed to hear those words come from you I thought I had died. Even though it hasn't been easy, and it will take some getting used to, I know my place is beside you to support you and be that listening ear when you get frustrated and remind you to leave work at the doorstep of our home. It starts here…"

# CHAPTER 35

## LEVI



SSHE'S NEVER BEEN SO SURE IN HER LIFE, AND HER GROWING confidence makes me proud. I lay her down and position myself between her legs, holding one against my chest and letting the other fall to the side. This is the easiest position for the first time, with me sliding into her and not her trying to fit me in.

"Last chance…" Letting her know she was still in control.

"Well, since you put it that way…" I pulled away, but she pulled me back; now, our lips are so close. "I'm ready…I know the action will hurt, but I know you won't hurt me."

I lean down to kiss her and simultaneously distract her as I line up against her. I look down to see her visibly soaked as I slide up and down against her.

I can see and feel her apprehension. She looks away, bracing for that initial sharp pain. I ease in slowly, listening to her breathing pick up.

"You okay?" Watching tears fill her eyes.

"Bi-b-big." She said between short, labored breaths.

"You have to relax. Can you feel me at the wall? I have to break the barrier."

"I know."

I lean down, cradling her into me. "I'll never hurt you more than at this moment. You gave me your purity, and I'm giving you my love for all eternity."

I didn't even give her a moment to comprehend as I pressed forward, feeling the warmth of her pristine walls squeeze me in shock but not pleasure. She screamed out her agony, buried her head, and dug her nails into my triceps. She broke the skin, but my pain is nothing in comparison. I wish I could take her pain away, but pain is an affliction given to humans to humble them. I am fortunate enough to heal myself.

I try my damndest not to cum from the feeling alone. A few moments later, she exhales hard while loosening her grip both inside and out. I look down and see the tears falling from her eyes. I kiss them.

"I'm sorry."

"It's..it's fine. I'm fine."

"Are you sure? Can I move?"

"Mhmm. Slow…please."

I rock back and forth and try to concentrate on anything other than the overwhelming feeling of her.

"Levi." She whispered. I didn't know if it was in pain or pleasure, so I stopped.

"No. More…" She confirmed and began rocking against me, asserting herself, finding pleasure in the rhythm and pulsing between us. I'm not moving because I'll force myself to bottom out against her, to slam into her until I feel myself coat her walls. I didn't want to ruin the tightness just yet.

I'm struggling, and she notices, "What's wrong? Why aren't you moving?"

"I'm trying not to cum, baby. You feel…" I shudder uncontrollably before I answer. Fuck…

Then she looked at me with a slight smile. "It's not like we can't do it again." She shrugs. I start again, and the intensity is almost instant. Her moans were so soft and innocent, but she was holding back. I needed to hear her beg. I finessed her clit while I stroked faster and deeper.

"Oh!" Her head fell back, and that caused her tits to bounce. I used my free hand to pinch each nipple. Her walls are tightening, and her breathing is labored between her gasps and moans.

"Levi, gonna...gonna..." I stroke harder, and I feel the signs. Her walls squeeze me. Back arches off the bed, and she takes a deep breath before letting out a scream.

"Mmmpffgh!"

"Oh...baby! Ughhh!"

I collapsed beside her before shifting to my side. I looked over, and she was still breathing hard with her arm on her head, gazing at the ceiling.

She looks at me and smiles, which turns into a chuckle.

"What's so funny, my love?"

She rubs her arms while sighing. "I don't know. I feel different, tingly." Then, a glow began to form and engulf her whole body; it was blinding. I had to shield my eyes from it. I'd heard about it but never actually seen it.

"Levi!" She shrieked as I peeked through my hand. Soon, the bright light faded, and she lay there with a shocked look on her face.

"Wh-what just happened?" She looked at her body, examining it to make sure everything was the same, then she looked at me.

How do I break it to her gently? "Well, you just became immortal. The end of one life into the next." I didn't know how to sugarcoat the fact that...

"I just died!"

"I say it's a hell of a way to go. Pun very much intended. Nobody will know the difference, but now you can alternate between the worlds."

"Ooh...can I do the snappy thing?" She closes her eyes and then snaps her fingers, and the cheesecake from dinner appears on the nightstand. "That's so awesome." She swipes it with her finger and pops it in her mouth. "Mmmm." She falls on her back. This time, the sheet slides off her breasts, giving me a bird's-eye view. She catches me staring. "Ready for round two?"

"Aren't you sore?"

She shrugs her shoulders. "Pretty sure it's going to take a long time to get used to the size of...that." She runs her hand across my Adonis belt, causing my dick to jump. "Careful, my book bee, I am taking it easy. I still have not put you on your knees in our playroom."

She just stared, trying to figure out what to say in response. "Maybe I should get some sleep to open the store." She leaned over for a kiss. I knew her mind was racing at her new possibilities. I ran my fingers across her soft skin, and she shuddered. "Goodnight, my love. By the way, you can snap yourself to work or drive." I lay on my back, allowing my body to air cool. What are you going to do tomorrow?" She inquired. I sigh at the inevitable: "I'm going to talk to my father."

# CHAPTER 36

## HAVEN

Nope! No way am I meeting his father again. The first interaction was a nightmare! And that's when I thought he was a regular person, not evil incarnate!

Getting ready for work, I decided on a simple black racer back dress, along with my cozy green sweater coat. I was a sexier, more confident version of myself. I'm surprised he packed any of my coats, but I suppose it plays into his sexy bookworm fantasies about me.

I thought about snapping into my office, but I also wanted the adrenaline since I had never driven a car. I decided on the 718 Boxster while encouraging Levi that he could deal with his dad. He was hesitant to go, but I bribed him with the promise of a good night later. He was gone in a literal flash.

It's halfway through the day, and my regulars notice the change in my demeanor. They say nothing, but I noticed the longer glances. They're also more talkative now, with awkward attempts at extending the conversation. Would I call it flirting? I think they are just more aware.

It's too little too late, boys.

While I was jotting down some expenses, someone placed a

cup with my name in my view. I knew the distinct smell of hazelnut and vanilla.

"Nigel."

"Hey, I, uh, was just stopping by. Hadn't heard from you since I dropped you off last night. Wanted to be sure you were okay."

I smile, reflecting on last night. "Everything is great. I couldn't be happier."

"Oh. I can see that." He points at my hand, and I now have a diamond band on my ring finger. I internally roll my eyes while screaming my frustration at the top of my lungs, all while maintaining a neutral face.

He's supposed to be talking with his dad.

"Yeah, it was a bunch of misunderstandings. Thank you for cheering me up and making sure I was okay. It was really sweet of you."

"It was nothing. I'm glad you're happy. Congratulations. "

"I am." I ignore the last part on purpose.

"I better get back to the shop. I'm training a new employee. She reminds me a lot of you, shy and sweet."

"She'll be just fine under your leadership. Just keep motivating her like you did me." He nods and waves before the door closes.

I groan loudly, releasing my anger in tiny spurts like a tea kettle releasing its steam. "I'm going to kill him."

"You can't kill me, darlin'. I'm immortal, and so are you. You're stuck with me." He leaned forward against the counter and smirked. That only ticked me off more.

I held up my hand. "Was this necessary? Nigel is a friend, a friend! He has done nothing to make me think I'd ever want him over you, but your jealousy makes you overreact, like putting a ring on my finger! Because you think he could take me away from you? Seriously?!" I pulled it off and slammed it on the counter. "If you really loved me, you wouldn't think any man, especially a mortal one, could ever take me from you. I would marry you in a heartbeat; it's my dream, but…not if you act like this."

Luckily, the day was over, and I could snap the store closed; all the books were back in place, the ledger filled, and the lights out. I grab my keys. "I'll see you at home." I slammed my office door so he would take the hint.

THE BEST DAY OF MY LIFE WAS FOLLOWED BY A REALITY CHECK. I GOT a crew to start constructing our place while my father hounded me for hours about my action plan. He kept saying he wouldn't hand over the reign without a solid plan. I gave an A-1 presentation, and his response was, "It's adequate." I don't know why I continue to try. I fight through another hour of his complaining and 30 minutes of why I should pause Aurora and Cherry's punishment. I am sure it is to fulfill some sick dream threesome. He tried to go into detail, but I left immediately. Their punishments continue until Haven tells me to stop, and I don't think she will.

Speaking of, I went to the shop near closing and saw her talking to that scrawny guy who kept popping up. Annoying little gnat he is. Instead of breaking every bone in his body and boiling him from the inside out, I placed a ring on her hand. It was a subtle fuck off.

That did not go well, as my love is currently locked in her office.

***Knock knock***
"Haven, love, open the door. I'm sorry."
"You're the Devil and full of shit!"

Well, I tried. I appear in her office, leaning against the file cabinet by the door. She growled in frustration. "Ugh! Go away! I can't believe you would ruin a moment that hadn't even happened. The moment I long for, a genuine proposal. That ring means nothing, Levi! It was a sick joke! I'm so...pissed at you, but what should I expect?" I saw her wince as she looked away from me, and now I feel like shit, a disappointment to her as my father is to me.

"Come here, darlin'. I'm sorry. I know I'm the personification of evil, but not with you. You are my guiding light, and I never want to hurt you." I finally feel her against me; the sparks remind me of how important she is and how I need to be considerate. She sacrificed her life for me, her purity, and, in return, gave me her heart.

I kiss her forehead, and she chuckles, "You're a pea-brained asshole."

Pea-brained? Ouch.

"But I'm your asshole. Let's go home."

She stared and then rolled her eyes. "Can I grab a ride with my special girl? I promise to be good in the car. I'll even wear my seat belt."

"Under one condition."

"Which is?"

"You take me down… there… tomorrow." She pointed.

"Why would you want to go down there voluntarily? I am fine keeping you up here. I can commute. I don't want to taint you with the depravity that lives down there."

"But I'm your Queen, which means I should be involved in all aspects, including being in the one place I was taught to fear. I'm not afraid because I know you'll protect me. It would be different if you were just a regular demon, but you are next in line for the throne."

Look at my little firecracker. "Alright, but the moment you feel uncomfortable, we're coming back. You realize there is a 100% chance of seeing my father?"

"I'm aware."

I shrug my shoulders and relent. The next day was Sunday, and the store was closed. She came out in an even tighter form-fitting black dress that hit her at the knee and matching heels. She had to have added that little number recently. I watched as she paid extra attention to her hair and makeup. I swear she was gearing up for a night out on the town.

She didn't even slip on the comfort of one of her sweater coats. She definitely had a plan. "Okay, I'm ready."

"To do what? Go to the nearest club?"

"If I'm going to be seen, I'm going to make a statement. Especially when I have a little chat with Cherry and your ex-play toy." She looks at me in the mirror, then pulls out a deep, almost crimson red lipstick. She applies it and then purses her lips together. I swear a vixen of a woman stands before me. Not the timid little book mouse, but my confident and sexy bookworm.

"If you're ready, I'll snap us into my office."

# CHAPTER 38

## HAVEN

 He says. The images I have of this never-ending vast wasteland filled with fire, molten lava, and the torturous screams of millions of lost souls have me second-guessing myself. It's a good thing I already died; the shock alone probably would have killed me.

I take his hand. "Ready as I'll ever be."

I can't describe how it felt to whoosh into this cavernous office. I can hear the roar of the flames outside and the ear-piercing screams that shatter your sanity. I expected it, but not to this degree.

"How do you deal with the screaming?" I see he's already seated in his chair, looking at some blueprints as if the world isn't burning on the other side.

"They must be new. They'll stop screaming once they know it is useless or their vocal cords snap. Guess I never noticed. It's white noise to me."

I walk around feeling uneasy. I rub my arms as I find myself in front of a wall of books. I recognize most of them; not only did he fill his space above, he did so below. I look back at him, but he's still nose-deep in papers.

"Wow, you really were obsessed with me, weren't you? It's like your own…"

"Library of Congress."

I froze when I realized it wasn't Levi who replied. I fixed my eyes on Levi, who had a sour expression on his face.

"Father."

"Well, well, well…one good fucking from my son, and you think you can keep him interested in this mediocre transformation?"

Even his laugh is condescending. I turn to face the bastard who has done nothing but bad mouth me and make me feel like I was worthless. He was impeccably dressed but didn't look the same when he belittled me in the store. He now has green eyes and tan skin but can't change that asshole-toned voice.

Levi storms towards us, ready to unleash his fury, but I stop him when I take his hands, the sparks sending him into bliss. He looked at me instead of glaring at his father.

"I have to do this."

I gather my strength and step forward, attempting to look confident and not wobble in my heels, getting into his personal space. He's enormous, but I press on, "Satan, is it? Hmm, that's not such a friendly-sounding name, now is it? And since we're going to be the best of friends…I'm going to call you Petey. So, Petey, I know how you feel about the mate bond and how your son should be like you and screw his emotions away. If you don't like me, that's fine. I'm not here for you. I'm here for Levi, to be that love and support he needs, something he never got from you." I pace in front of him, "Oh, and I don't believe for one second that his mother left him, especially to be raised by the likes of you." I could see his anger raging on the inside from my blatant disrespect, but I pushed through. If I don't, he'll walk over me for eternity. "I will not let you push me around. You or any of your minions, got it? Petey?"

"Is that so?" He quirks his brow and looks behind me to Levi.

"Huh…" He turned around and walked away. My knees buckled immediately, but Levi caught me in his arms and turned me around.

"You okay?"

"I, I think so."

I went toe to toe with Satan himself. You know, he's more arrogant and cocky than terrifying, like a college frat boy douchebag, but with an ungodly amount of power.

Suddenly, Levi chuckled, "Petey?"

I shrugged, "It short circuits the brain. You see, it worked."

"I'm impressed, my book bee. You stood up to my father and didn't flinch until the end. That was incredibly sexy." He dipped me, connecting his lips to mine, then pulling me back to standing, and I saw the mischief in his eye. I slide by him to perch myself on his desk, letting my legs spread a bit as I pull myself up before crossing them. "Want to christen your office, for lack of a better word?"

He approached, loosening his tie, and placing his hands on my knees. "How about marking my office or, better yet, defiling my office in the dirtiest, filthiest of ways?"

"Sounds promising." I open my legs and pull my dress up enough to give him space to stand in between. I should have worn a skirt. He steps forward, and I pull him closer by his tie. My lips are dangerously close to his, making him wait. I think he's about to…

***Whimpers***

"What was that?" I asked, hearing the clinking of something approaching. The doors open, and three giant beasts walk in. They were literally the stuff of nightmares! They were fully engulfed in red-orange flames, with horns and huge chunks of their flesh missing. I could see their ribs through their tattered skin!

Levi holds his hands up. "Before you hop up on my desk and start screaming like a banshee, these are my babies, my pets."

Of course! Why would I expect normal dogs or anything normal down here?

They slowly approach and don't look friendly, the low growling a great indicator not to move a muscle. I'm barely breathing. I know what hellhounds are; they are as bloodthirsty as I imagined. I didn't think he kept them as pets! They lower their heads as they predatorily approach me, baring their teeth. I look like their next meal!

"*Prohibere! Sedeo!* (Stop! Sit!) Ok!" He snapped, and they froze, sitting on their hind legs.

"Is that Latin?"

"They already know English, so I'm teaching them multiple languages. They are the smartest blood thirsty creatures, aren't you?" He sounds like a proud parent while I try not to get ripped apart.

I see they are obediently sitting, waiting for their master's next order.

"Abaddon, Amon, and Axel, this is your mommy. This is Daddy's mate, and you will obey her. Understand?"

They whimpered and bowed their heads before he gave them each a treat.

He smiles at me, calming me a bit. "Abaddon and Amon will be new mommies, and Axel is the daddy."

He hands me three treats and whistles. They approach me as I hop down from the desk and sit. I'm terrified, but I have to try. They're cute in a demonic, soul-snatching sort of way.

They sit, laser-focused on my hand, knowing he handed me something for them.

I can do this. "Hi, babies. Aren't you…precious. My name is Haven. I'm going to be down here with your Daddy. I hope you learn to love me; I want us to be best friends." Meaning it this time, unlike with his dad.

I hold out the treat, and each one sniffs my hand before taking it, hopefully remembering my scent as friendly and not tasty. Then one jumps up on their hind legs, front paws on my shoulders, and licks my face! I only laugh as the other two get their licks in, too. You'd think the flames would have burned, but they turn blue and shift when near my skin, giving off a cooling sensation, not the searing burn I expected.

"I knew they'd love you." I stood up before they knocked me all the way over. Levi snapped his fingers to get their attention, "Alright, let Mama breathe. I think you have earned a trip to your favorite place. Do you want to play in the maze? You earned it; go on." And like that, they leave for this maze thing.

"What's the maze?"

"Oh, it's where they hunt their victims down in a huge maze structure. It's exercise and torment at the same time. Saves me many man hours."

I think he could tell that my stomach had dropped. I clutch my stomach and lean against the desk.

"Haven, you look sick."

"I'll be fine. I just got a visual."

"These are not innocent souls. They are abusers, rapists, murderers, child predators, and sex offenders. They deserve none of your sympathy. There are no good souls here, well, except you."

"I don't know how innocent I can claim to be now that I've fucked the Devil, as your dad so eloquently put it."

He rolled his eyes. "Enough about him. Let's talk about our place together down here. Look at these plans and see if I covered everything you could want."

"I want a library."

"You think that wasn't one of the must-haves?"

After a few questions and plotting, I wondered, "So, where is your bedroom in this huge cave mansion?"

"Down the hall. Why?"

"Didn't you mention that Aurora and Cherry were in your room?""

"Yes?"

I wiggle my dress down from sitting in his lap. "Good, let's go."

"What are you up to?"

"Absolutely nothing...just would like to have a few words with my...friends."

# CHAPTER 39

## LEVI

WHY DO I HAVE THIS FOREBODING FEELING OF DOOM? IT WASN'T from Haven meeting my father. It was whatever she had planned for her two favorite people. I always said to be careful of the quiet ones, and Haven had been quiet her whole life.

The sound of her heels down the hallway makes me adjust myself, so walking is less tortuous. I let her lead the way, since my room was the only door at the end of the hall.

I noticed an extra sway in her hips. Tease.

She pushed the heavy double doors forward, and they creaked loudly to signal our presence. As ordered, Cherry and Aurora were in individual cages across from my bed. Aurora was lying on her side, completely unbothered. While Haven looked around my office, I restored her tongue and unsealed her lips earlier. I didn't want the sight to fuel her nightmares.

Cherry was looking…rough, to say the least. She had not adapted to death or eternal punishment well. I was a millisecond from feeling bad for her until I remembered what she almost cost me. I sit back and think about new torture methods as I let my mate say her piece.

Haven stares at them. I can't see her expression since I'm behind her.

"Hello Cherry...uh, Aurora, is it? I should have known that anyone who hangs out with the likes of Cherry is no good."

Aurora laughs and rolls her eyes. "Looks like the baby got Daddy to bring her down here to see how the adults play. Is that why you restored me, so your little plaything here wouldn't be traumatized? You don't belong here. You don't belong with him, and the sooner you're gone, the sooner I can convince him to open his eyes and see that some feeble human bitch could never compare to a demoness like me."

I wanted to inflict insurmountable pain for her blatant disrespect, but Haven held her hand up. She knew I wouldn't hesitate to disembowel her or shove flesh eaters down her throat and sew up all her holes this time.

Haven paces a bit. "You're right, Aurora. I could never be like you. I could never be so blind about a man who clearly doesn't want you. But you won't listen to me, not me! I'm, what'd you call me? A charity case, a doormat, mediocre. Both of you made it your goal to tear me down, even when I had no clue what you were talking about, and I never met you a day before in my life. And you, Cherry, stating so boldly that Levi was yours. Even if I weren't in the picture, you would have had to deal with your little partner in crime. You wouldn't be so, buddy, then."

Aurora scoffs loudly, "Cherry is just a promiscuous cum dumpster who fucks for money. It's easy to get those types to do what you want."

The goddamned irony of her name-calling.

"Excuse you?! You fuck the same night, too. You're no better than me."

"Oh, sweetie, I am. Because I'm the only one that HAS fucked him." She pointed at me, and Haven went deathly silent.

Should I say something? I stepped forward, but she walked up to Aurora's cage, to which Aurora boldly stood on the other side.

"Haven..."

"I'm fine. Aurora will always hold on to the fact that she has fucked you many times before I came into the picture and a few times after. That's fine. You had your fun and fill because we all know the one thing you are not is his mate. He doesn't…crave you, pine for you, moan your name in his sleep."

I didn't even know I did that.

It felt like the room temperature dropped twenty degrees when I noticed Haven's hands turn into fists. Then she grabbed onto the cage bars and leaned in close.

"Isn't that unfortunate?" She tsked, and Aurora sneered.

"Why are you even here? I won't lower myself to the level of a weak human."

"Aurora, that's enough!" I roared. She didn't realize her attempt to hurt Haven was futile.

"What? Can she not handle the fact that you fucked me so good only weeks ago?"

"It was six months ago I used you like a fleshlight. You sucked me off weeks ago, and I sent you home packing. That was the night my father fucked you to shut you up, remember?"

"Call it what you want, but she needs to know I'll always be in the back of your mind, just like you were hitting the back of my throat and pussy."

Haven paced very close to the cage. "You're right. I would love to hear about your escapades. You see, now I'm curious. How much of him could you get down your throat?"

"Haven!" I felt shocked by her manner of question. I didn't want her to hear about my desperate times.

"Hush. Just a little girl talk. Maybe Cherry's curious too since we haven't had the honor of hopping on your dick, as Aurora so passionately stated." Haven cut her eyes at me before returning her attention to Aurora.

"So, how big is he, huh?" Haven licked her lips, showing her curiosity.

She's up to something.

Aurora was trying to figure out the bottom line but stayed quiet.

"Oh, don't be shy now. You were so adamant about telling me what you've done with him. Perhaps you were bluffing?" Haven glances at me.

Unfortunately, Aurora wasn't bluffing, and I couldn't figure out why Haven wanted all the sordid details.

Aurora stepped forward with confidence and arrogance. "You want to live out your fantasies through me? Fine. He was so big that I could barely get a quarter down my throat. I worked the rest with my hands until I tasted him."

"Hmm, only a quarter of the way? He must really be huge."

"Mmm, he is, and he felt so good when my walls squeezed him while he pounded into me."

"Uh-huh. How interesting." Haven makes her way to my bed and sits down, crossing her legs. "Tell me, Aurora," She uncrosses and leaves them slightly open enough to see her underwear. I got a whiff of her arousal, enough to stir my demon. My sweet book mouse was up to something. She snapped her fingers, and I moved toward her. "I know you were eager to get on your knees and do what you do best, but did Levi ever reciprocate?"

I'd rather be sitting in a pool of kerosene-lit holy water.

"No, we skipped right to the point. I didn't need it; I was always soaking wet and ready."

I stood before Haven; my eyes met hers in an unspoken request, and I fell to my knees. I removed her heels as one foot slid over my shoulder, and she leaned further back onto her forearms. I'm now staring at barely there underwear. She relaxed her other leg to bare it all, and I growled.

If I didn't know any better, she sprayed that enticing perfume on her ankles for when they're on my shoulders. As I ran my nose across it and inhaled, I realized it had a highly concentrated scent. I was working my way down, anyway.

She sighed and looked behind me. "Is that right? Well, you missed an amazing opportunity for him to worship you until you were shaking all over him, telling you how delicious you taste, and that initial gasp you feel when he rips your underwear off, and he's staring and breathing on you at the same time."

I took that as my cue to obey my mate, stretching my fingers to the top of her underwear as she lifted her hips to allow them to slide down until they were in my hand. I could have ripped them off, but I knew it would irritate Aurora more, watching me take the time, unlike with her when I was rushing to get off so she could leave. Now, I inhale the delicate fabric. "Mmm, you smell divine, but you taste even better." I placed them in my pocket, holding her leg down while the other stayed over my shoulder. I peppered her pussy in kisses, spreading her to get my tongue as deep as possible.

I watch her stare at them, and what I can only assume is shock on their faces. Although she's proving a point, I still crave her all over me. She looked at me quickly before her eyes rolled to the back of her head.

Found her spot.

She slid flat, her hands in my hair.

"Mmm…you tr-truly missed out on such a magical…magical feeling. Oh god. It's like his tongue knows exactly where to go."

Who knew she could be so vindictive?

"Levi…please." As my princess wants. With the help of my fingers, I sped up, and before I knew it, I was drowning in her. After a few pants, she smiled as she sat back on her elbows.

"You really don't know what you're missing, not that you'll ever find out." She eyed me. I licked my lips as I stood up. She flashed me occasionally as her leg rocked back and forth. She should know that once isn't enough. It's never enough, and I'll have my fill later.

I could tell her knees were still weak as she stood tall and approached me. She grabbed me by the lapels, her lips dangerously close, but then leaned over. "A quarter of the way down, right?" Her eyesight went back to me as she smirked. Her hands slid down my chest to land on my belt buckle.

She wouldn't…would she?

# CHAPTER 40

## HAVEN

I could argue with Aurora until I was blue in the face, but that wouldn't keep her from continuing to usurp me. She's a pit bull in heels; she would try to wear me down until I gave up. Well, that would have worked on the old me. The timid me who could barely utter a word in his presence, let alone take on this vicious woman.

Today's a different story, and I was going to make my point.

With my hands on his belt, I felt him stiffen as I loosened it enough to unbutton the top clasp. "Let's place a little bet, Aurora. If I can't match your distance, I'll hand Levi over to you; he'll make you his Queen, and you'll never see me again. Deal?"

Aurora looked stunned. "There's no way. I was made to take a huge dick like that. You could never."

"Don't flatter yourself, Aurora. I'm usually semi-soft when you start." Levi added his two cents, and she wasn't too appreciative.

"Whatever state you were in, you always finished with me! I tasted you more than anyone else!"

Well, that stung a bit, but I trudged on. I pulled his zipper down and let his trousers fall to his ankles. "Well, you're definitely not soft at all, are you? That changes things, now doesn't it?" I lick my lips, smirking at Levi because she missed my potshot at her having to work extra to get him hard, and I only needed to give him my attention.

Aurora sucks her teeth loudly behind me. "A quarter is a quarter. The rules don't change. Hahaha, this is hilarious! The other demons are going to love hearing about your pathetic attempt and failure! Enjoy what you can because I will finish what you started and show how a real demoness does it!"

I ignored her, knelt, and grabbed it. "Fuck, baby…" He whispered. The sparks coursed from my hands to his dick and throughout his body. I haven't even moved yet. "Haven…"

My handsome Devil.

"Patience. I want to make sure I mark it properly." I wrap my finger a quarter of the way down from the tip. I laughed internally at her pathetic reach, but she was so proud. She would probably gag on a pen cap! And be fucking overly dramatic, too, choking and slurping loudly, believing she was rocking his world. A vacuum could do the same.

I digress…

"Does that look about right?"

"Yup, you got to fit all that in your tiny little human mouth. I bet your jaw aches looking at it."

I play into her taunt and rub my jaw, looking at Levi. Judging by his stern gaze, I hadn't thought about all the repercussions of my teasing until now.

Hmmm…I look forward to it.

I sighed, sitting back on my legs. "I don't know what you're up to, my raven-haired beauty, but if you don't do something soon, I will take you in front of them." He aggressively whispered with a dominant tone. He meant business.

I bring my lips close enough that they graze the tip. I shrug my shoulders, "Well, here goes nothing."

I let him part my lips. As he sighed in relief, I relaxed my throat and passed my marker finger until I was halfway down, like last night. I pulled back a bit; then I felt Levi's hands in my hair as he slid me up and down. He didn't care that we had an audience; he sought relief.

"Fuck, baby. Right there…damn, you fit me so fucking perfectly."

I decided I teased him enough, and he made me cum, so it's only fair. I started humming against him while he slammed into me.

"Ahh, take it, baby! Oh fu…fuckkkk…"

I felt a final thrust and the warmth of him down my throat. It was a bit salty, but not overpowering. He pulled his dick away, but I kept my lips tight with suction for a final tease.

He looked down at me. "That's my good girl."

I felt my whole body shiver as I forgot about them being there until I looked over, wiping my mouth.

"Looks like I won…and do you know why? Because I'm his mate! Only I fit him so perfectly, in more ways than one." I raise my brow, and she scoffs, looking away. Cherry was shocked by what she witnessed, thinking I wouldn't give them a show. I gave them the full IMAX theater experience.

Levi buttons himself up, and I stand in front of their cages. "The timid girl you harassed long ago is dead…quite literally." I snapped a fireball into my hand to prove my point. "What I would love to do is incinerate your overly used carcass for eternity."

Cherry seemed confused and scared, but Aurora knew. "No! Why would he fuck someone like you?"

I tap my head like I'm knocking. "Because I'm his mate, you stupid bitch! I've had endless thoughts of how I can torture you alongside your partner in crime here, but you know what? Any sign of affection he makes towards me makes you miserable, and that's more than enough for me. I don't even have to go further with my plan to let him take me in front of you. My happiness will always be your eternal torture. Maybe we'll keep you in these cages as pets. I hope you're housebroken." Aurora's eyes flashed black, and it made me uneasy. I don't know how powerful she is.

Levi stepped forward. "Excuse me, my love, but I have other plans. She's tried repeatedly to interfere, and now that you're by my side, I'll be damned if she breathes the same air as you. Remember when you said you wanted to see him?"

I felt confused for a second, but then I understood what he meant. I nod and then look up to see his insanely vaulted ceilings carved out of the mountains. He tips my chin up for a sweet kiss.

"So be it. Step back." I take several rushed steps back.

As he spins around, he faces them and declares, "I warned you, and Cherry, well, you're collateral damage..."

"What?! I don't want to continue to be punished because Aurora couldn't keep her fucking mouth shut! I'm sorry, Haven! I was horrible and cruel. You're right; you didn't deserve it. I was jealous of how my father loved you and spent time with you and not with me. When he died and left me the store, I knew if he had time to change his will, he would have left it to you. You were the daughter he wanted, and I just wanted to hurt you."

Well, that was unexpected, but it was also a last-ditch confessional to save her ass from whatever punishment he had for them. I hope she knew I would not step in to save her. Compassionate Haven is long gone.

Levi stepped back, and his eyes turned black. They seemed even darker than Aurora's, the blackest of black. I could see when he allowed his demon to step forward; the growl was low and echoed off the cavern walls. Then, a roar erupted as he shifted into a jaw-dropping black beast with horns and a tail! I crane my neck up as I notice his horns curve back, not straight up like they depict in the book, and they are massive! They match his 20-foot frame. He's right; he would never have fit in the house above ground! His veins glowed red and pulsed with every breath. He fixed his now red eyes on the trembling excuses for women whom he snapped out of their cages and chained to the floor.

He points at them. "Aurora and Cherry…I sentence you to Tartarus!"

I don't know what or where that is, but it caused all the color to drain from Aurora's face—a crack in her arrogance.

He raised his razor-sharp claws and swiftly brought it down where I thought was past them, but it was through them! The claws cut through their bodies, causing them to vanish into a puff of greenish-black smoke.

I felt my stomach heave violently, but sighed in relief when there were barely any signs of the carnage. Then I realized I was alone with his demon and his blood-soaked claws.

It turned around and looked down at me.

What should I do?!

He leans down and is only a few feet away from me. His breath forces me to close my eyes each time he exhales. He tilts his head like a curious puppy who could draw and quarter me in a single swipe. I literally just saw it happen!

"H-hi." I wave my hand. He huffs, inching closer. "Do you know who I am?"

He exhales and nods, bringing his massive hand up. His finger approaches my face. His claw bypasses, so the pad of his finger brushes my cheek. His roar is calmer and not at all intimidating. He seems to be curious, as Levi said.

"It's nice to meet you. I know you'll protect me. Know that I love you as equally as Levi."

A creepy grin appeared, and his eyes were that beautiful gold color of curiosity. I think he approved, but that smile is nightmare fuel. I promised to love all of him, including the beast.

"Can I name you? How about Ares, after the god of war? I know you'll battle the world, so no harm comes to me."

He nods again, not a demon of many words.

"Okay, Ares, we'll hang out again, but can I get my man back, please? His mate has needs." I smile and wink.

I watch him shrink back to average size and color. He slicks his hair back.

"Needs, huh? What could my beautiful little book mouse want?" I blink. Now, he's behind me. "I love it when your whole body shudders to my presence."

I glance over my shoulder. "You feed on what you do to me. Thank you for introducing me to Ares."

"Ares, huh? I like it. He's overly excited. I'll need a long torture session to remind him of his duties. In the meantime, why don't you strip for me?" He pulled up a chair.

I blush as I snap my fingers to remove my dress, but then he snaps it back on.

"No. I said…strip for me." I saw the intensity in his gaze. I don't break the stare as I zip down the side, which loosens it enough for the straps to slide down. I wiggle it down until it hits the floor. I step out and stand there in my heels.

# CHAPTER 41

## LEVI

Even though I saw it when she snapped her dress off, nothing is better than watching the fabric slide down her curves before it pooled at her feet, so she was in just lingerie and those high heels.

"LEVI!" He bellowed.

You cannot be serious?! Before I could even stop him, he waltzed into my room.

"Why the hell did you send them to…" His words slowed down and then stopped as he eyed Haven.

"Whoa. Nice."

"Stop gawking at my woman! What the hell do you want barging in here when I was busy? I'm sorry, darlin'." I thought she'd be upset and cover up, but she didn't. She slowly sits down on the bed and crosses her legs.

"It's okay, love. Petey obviously had something critical to discuss with you. I can wait, but not too long." She kicks off her heels, turns, and crawls towards the head of the bed, giving us both a bird's-eye view of her ass before she slips underneath the sheets. I blocked his view, so he returned his attention to me. "Can you tell her not to call me that?"

I point behind me. "She's right there. You tell her."

He exhaled out his frustration, "Whatever. You want to tell me why you sent them to Tartarus, and since when did you sentence people there? That's my job; only I send people there!"

Just because I don't know where it is doesn't mean I'm going to miss an opportunity to get rid of the people who tortured Haven so she can live in peace. I damn sure would not reincarnate them. They could start the apocalypse. Then I'd never have time for my beautiful girl.

"You weren't going to do anything! My Queen should not have to worry about my past or their attempt to undermine her. Aurora is irrelevant and insubordinate. You want to fuck her and her whore-in-training? Go down there since you know where it is!"

"Remember your place, son! I am still the ruler of Hell. What I say goes, but since you want to impress your little mate, I won't reverse your decision." He glances at Haven, who yawns before huffing. Then she takes her thumb and licks it before it disappears under the sheets.

She sighs and then winks. Her boldness to do it in front of my father shocked me. My father, too, became silent.

"If you boys are done, I've been on edge since earlier when he devoured me so deliciously. You should have been there, Petey; you would have gotten quite the show. Maybe not. Anyway, you can finish this precious father/son moment tomorrow."

He looked at me, and I shrugged. He can deny it, but I know my mom had him wrapped around her finger. Whether it be the King of Hell or the Prince of Darkness, we both fall to a woman's will.

"We're not done here. Ugh, damn woman!" He mumbled on his way out. I appear beside her, completely naked, pulling her against me.

"Were you touching yourself without my permission?"

Her eyes went wide, then shifted back and forth. "Umm. Nooo…"

I take her hand and taste her on her fingers, raising my brow to her blatant lie. "Bad girls get punished." She giggled as I positioned her on her back.

"How so?" She was confident I didn't have it in me. Truth be told, unless I'm in my playroom, I don't, but I push through.

"Bad girls get punished by withholding. Maybe I shouldn't allow you to cum right now. Perhaps I'll work you into such a frenzy, a hair away from total bliss, then…back…off." My fingers roamed her body, touching each of her spots until I slid down toward her pussy, then retracted my hand. She looked devastated.

"What? No, I need it." She whimpered. She thinks her soft voice and sweet, innocent routine will work, but not after the sinful things she did in front of an audience.

No, I wanted to see more of that Haven.

"And what are you going to do about it? I want a replay from earlier, you choking on my dick and the way you hummed while taking me? I fucking lost it. I've been throbbing ever since."

She sat on her knees on the bed, and I stood in front of her. "But…it's so big. I don't think I'll be able to fit it…anywhere." Her sarcasm was cute, but I needed action, not words.

I reached down and grabbed her aggressively by her hair. "I am going to enjoy fucking breaking you, Haven."

She looked worried for a moment before reaching up, and the cool air caused a shiver down my spine. I lean her forward, rubbing her lips across my dick, smearing her lipstick all over it and her.

She's going to be my dirty girl.

"Take me down that pretty throat. Claim this dick like you did earlier in front of your enemies." She let my dick part her lips once again, and I felt her with every inch sliding down; then she swallowed and constricted me further. When I look down, she winks. Why does everything she does drive me insane? I bury my hands deep in her hair; the red highlights pop as I grab tightly. I guide her more forcefully, then pull her off of me to allow her to breathe.

See, I can be compassionate.

"Don't choke."

She gasped, then smirked, grabbing my hips, and pulling me against her until I felt her breath on my skin from her breathing through her nose.

"Fuck me, princess!" I tried to pull her away, but she gripped tighter and started humming while bobbing.

I had no fucking chance.

The way my orgasm raced forward like a tsunami wave, I could only roar out my pleasure, and right before I shot down her throat, she popped me out of her mouth and laid my dick on her lips as she stroked me until I soiled those delectable lips with my cum.

I buckled and collapsed.

She brought me to my knees and chuckled, "I read that in a book somewhere."

Such a dirty book whore.

No one has ever done that before…she had complete control of me.

I grab her legs and turn them, so I am kneeling between her. "Naked…now." She didn't hesitate as she snapped her lingerie away. I swiped my two fingers across her pussy. She tried to close her legs in response, but I kept them spread. I know the breeze was torturing her. I would warm her up as I devoured her.

I watch her watch me, "Well played, princess, but…now it's my turn." I slip my tongue in, tasting while diving as deep as I can. She struggles between grabbing my hair or the sheets while screaming out her emotions. The same sparks that coursed around my dick while she sucked me dry were coursing through the sensitive nerves of her pussy. She was writhing around to get away, but I locked my arms around her legs and dove even deeper.

"Mmm! Sh-shit, it feels so good. So fucking good, please, please!" She couldn't even tell me what she wanted, but it was simple: to climax like never before.

I ensured there was always some contact, whether my tongue, fingers, or both. Her moans increased, and it signaled her close to climax. I stop immediately. "Get the fuck over here and get on top of me." I growled before she quickly scrambled to obey my request. I watch her as I lay on my back with her straddling my chest.

"Ride me until that pretty little pussy belongs to me. Harder, faster, until my name is the last thing on your lips."

I pulled her forward and helped line me up. She took her time to slide down; this was her first time in this position, so the pressure was much different. She grunted, and I put my hands behind my head. When she finally bottomed out, she sighed in relief, and so did I. She closed her eyes, and I took that moment to smack her ass. "You want it? Earn it! Got it?"

She slowly rocked, trying to get used to the feeling of being filled at this angle. She may have lost her purity, but she was still a virgin to so many positions.

"Ye-yes, sir. Ooh…" She moaned as she picked up speed. The faster she rocked, the wetter she got. "Le-Le-Levi!"

"That's it. Work yourself up until you explode. You feel me pulsing?"

"Uh-huh." She replied quickly as she sped up, furiously chasing her climax. She placed her hands on my stomach to push further back on me. Her walls are tightening as I stroke her deep from the inside. "Oh, there! Right there!" She screamed and shuddered, breathing hard. We both look down; there's a pool on my stomach. I knew she was a squirter, but not a soft one. It's gentle, not forceful.

I learned something new.

She looked at me, shocked yet horrified. "I'm sorry, I didn't know I could do that!"

"Shhh, it's okay. There's no need to be embarrassed. That is the sexiest thing ever. I knew you could; it takes the right angle, and now that I know, I will make it my goal every time to drown in you."

She rushes into the bathroom. I thought she might lock herself inside. Instead, she came back with a hand towel. She stops in her tracks when she sees me swipe the liquid and taste her essence.

"Oh my god!"

"What? You taste divine."

"That's gross."

"You just took my load with a smile; what's the difference?"

"That's fair. You taste salty and sweet." After wiping off my stomach, I signal her to come to bed. She happily returns and sighs. "You're so warm."

"Fire in my blood, mind-blowing sex, having the love of my life snuggled up to me. Life is good."

"Don't say that too loudly. Someone will hear the son of Satan happy." She giggled, and I cradled her against me, falling asleep peacefully. Who cares what they think?

# CHAPTER 42
## HAVEN

Now that I have spent time above ground and below, they are pretty much the same except for the horrible landscape of eternal, tortured souls. I can hear Levi and his dad screaming at the top of their lungs as if they weren't in the same damn space. I have an eternity of that, so I followed Abaddon, Axel, and Amon outside to see this maze.

Despite their terrifying appearance, they're like any other lovable pet; they sniff, lick, and want all your attention, especially the soon-to-be mommies.

They happily walk to the entrance of the behemoth after one of their caretakers opens the gate. Not three seconds later, I heard the screams of the damned. I still felt empathy and clutched my stomach as I walked away.

Punishment was being doled out on every square inch of the land. I felt dizzy and made my way inside. I went into the kitchen to prepare lunch. It was the only normal thing I could do at the moment. Something that requires extensive concentration, like lasagna. I walk into the pantry to gather all the dry ingredients. While I'm in there, I hear someone clear their voice. I walk out to see the same guy from the bookstore.

Just how many of them were demons?

"Don't you think it's pretentious to wear white in Hell?"

I look down at my flowy sundress with wispy sleeves. "And you are?" Undermining his arrogance.

I met you topside when I came in with my charm, my A-game. It's Trevor." He held his hand out.

I stare at it, making no effort to shake it. "Oh yeah, the guy who tried way too hard."

His cocky smile changed in a snap. "A good fucking will turn a lamb into a lion, I see?"

Why does everyone keep saying that?

Annoyed, I go into the fridge and grab everything else I need. "What is it you want, Trevor? I'm sure you don't think I can handle all this either."

"And you are correct. Women are only good for one thing. It's only a matter of time before Levi becomes his father. It's inevitable, and you'll end up like Lillith."

"Who is Lillith?"

"His mother." He states so nonchalantly.

I put my hand over my mouth. No way.

"How do you know so much about his mother, but he doesn't?"

"Despite this stunningly handsome meat suit, I'm much older than Levi and apparently wiser. I saw what having a mate does to a man...you're all nothing but trouble." He stares at me momentarily, standing up, "Welp, don't end up in the Darkness..." This evil smirk formed as he turned around, "But if you do, tell Lillith I said hi!"

I stood there because I was trying to process it all.

Is he saying his mother is alive? What if she is alive?! That would change everything!

I wanted to run to Levi and tell him what I heard, but then I stopped.

What if I'm wrong or Trevor was lying? He wasn't down here for his honesty and charm. I so wanted it to be true, but I needed proof. I can't take the word of a demon. I needed to know what or where this Darkness was.

"Well, isn't this a lovely surprise? Playing Suzy Homemaker already?" I turn to see Levi leaning against the door frame. "Why are you cooking so early? It's barely breakfast time."

"Honestly, I don't know the time or day."

"It's around 6 a.m. on Monday up there."

"Oh wow, I was way off. Well, I can still open up the shop. I was going to make an excuse, but judging by your screaming match with your dad, I'd rather enjoy the company of my customers."

He pulls me to him, kissing my temple. "Sorry, it's always been this way since I can remember. I don't think it'll ever change."

"Ever?"

"Highly unlikely. But that's okay; you're all I need."

I try not to cringe now that I know about Lillith—the first Eve, the Queen Mother of demons, and, most importantly, his mother. I know the general backstory taught in bible school, but could she be the actual entity? I needed to do some research.

I distract my thoughts with a kiss. "In five or six hours, pop this in the oven at 350 degrees for 75 minutes. Maybe offer some to old Petey as a peace offering."

He chuckles, "I don't know how you're getting away with calling him that. I think he's intrigued by your sassiness."

"Being reincarnated can do that to a girl. I'm headed topside. See you later?"

"Absolutely. Want to spend tonight up there?"

"Yes, please!" As much as I loved marking his room, it had an 'I still live with my parents' vibe. God forbid Petey walks in on us. He's already come so close. Touching myself under the cover was a way to distract me from my worst fear coming true. He is the King of Hell and, unfortunately, my future father-in-law.

Lucky me.

I opened the store and immediately headed to the history section. There's a book titled *'How Many Wives Did Adam Have?'*

It is a very controversial subject, but I know there was information there.

Between transactions and surfing the web on my phone, I put together a rough bio on Lillith and what may have happened. Allegedly, she was Adam's first wife and was cast from the Garden of Eden after 'disobeying' Adam. As a woman, I'm skeptical it was that simple. Back then, until not too long ago, society considered women as property or beneath men. He didn't like that, so he cast her down. The only person who knows the truth is Lillith. I also researched the seven circles of Hell; none of them were called the Darkness. I would need to do some additional snooping.

It was getting late, and Levi still wasn't home. After the Trevor confrontation, I didn't want to go back down there.

I changed into one of his button-ups and boy shorts. I fastened only one strategically placed button to keep me decent...but barely. I threw on some knee-high socks and returned to the kitchen to prepare our plates.

"Whew! What a long day. I let Ares out for most of the day. I think he may have broken his torture record. I much prefer torturing people instead of sending them to the Darkness. My dad always takes the lazy way out …"

"What did you say?"

"The Darkness, that's what we call Tartarus. I don't know where it is, but my dad does. I know it's a way to never see Aurora and Cherry again. I hope he divulges that bit of information after transferring power. Knowing him, he'll keep it for blackmailing purposes, I'm sure. No matter: I have no reason to go down there, anyway."

But I do!

It's all coming together! I didn't want to seem too eager, so I quickly changed the subject, whatever popped up off the top of my head.

"Do you want kids?"

WHAT?! I facepalm internally because where did that come from? I didn't even know if I wanted kids when I was human.

He raised his brow. His gaze darkened while staring at me.

UH OH.

"What an odd question, my book bee. Where did that come from?" I shrug my shoulders. He's still observing me. "I suppose I wouldn't be against it. Every man, beast, or demon needs a legacy. Truth be told, I never thought about it, but I guess I should. The real question is, do you want kids?"

"I mean, I'm not against it. I never thought someone could love me, so I never thought about what follows."

Now that I think about it, would I become the next Mother of Demons? Will the baby come out as a *cambion*, half human and half demon? Or entirely demon? Am I a demon now? The thought makes my blood run cold, but then I focus on the present moment.

He has me caged against the kitchen island. His gaze turns my insides to lava, and I'm panting. He sees his effect on me. "I love you."

"I know." I whispered, feeling the tingle of my blush rise from the ashes. Hadn't felt this way in a while.

"So," He tips my chin, "know I want whatever you want. We have an eternity for that; there's no rush."

I exhale a sigh of relief. "Okay."

"I'm starving. What's for dinner, and how was the shop today?"

It was almost like we were an average couple talking about their day, minus the damnation.

I told him about my day in the store and how one kid almost killed himself when he reached for a book on the top shelf, and a few others came with it. He looked so embarrassed that I suggested he use a ladder or step stool next time. Levi tells me about dipping someone in a vat of poisonous snakes. He deemed it slow torture but preferred it when the hounds chased them through the maze. I asked if the souls would return if they died in Hell, and he said they would go to Tartarus. He said the only way there is to die in Hell, most of the time, by his pets.

Does that mean if Lillith is down there, someone might have fed her to her son's pets? I pray that isn't the case. Could his dad be that cruel?

"Hey."

"Hmm?"

"You zoned out there. Something seems to be bothering you. Remember, I can feel it."

"I know. I don't want you to worry; I'm just getting used to this. It still makes me queasy."

He watches me momentarily; my eyes follow his movement as he shifts from left to right. "Are you sure that's it?"

I nod, trying not to feel guilty for lying. I have to see this through before I tell him.

# CHAPTER 43

## LEVI

The way Haven's face paled when I talked about my day. I'm glad I didn't go into detail about how Ares tore through one pit, ripping all his victims in half and bathing in their blood. My sweet girl can't handle it. I know she's trying to be that cold, heartless sort of Queen, but that isn't her; it's my job to hate and punish the damn.

The only person she needs to take care of is me. Like right now, I have her in my lap, that lone shirt button teasing me with flashes of her abdomen and part of her breast. I run my hand across her thigh as she rambles on. I'm hyper-focused on how smooth her skin feels.

"Levi! You're not even listening. You're just groping me." Her eyes knitted in frustration.

I concede because I know she'll understand, "I've had a very rough day, my love. Everything is coming down all at once, and I don't feel like I'm in control of anything."

Having an extended full-blown pissing match with my father got to me today. I lost my appetite, so I didn't heat the lasagna she so lovingly prepared, so I put it back in the freezer. I didn't even visit my babies or their pups. My mind was racing with doubt. Could I even do this? Rule Hell? The only reprieve I get is the sparks from touching her sweet skin and scent. But suddenly, she stood up, grabbing my hand, "Levi, do you trust me?" I thought it an odd question, because why would I doubt my sweet book mouse?

"Of course."

Now, I'm curious.

"I'll be right back. I'm going to make you feel better."

I sit back and wipe my face, wishing I could exhale, and my problems would disappear. I can't let my father win. I deserve to be happy with my beautiful girl.

I look at my half-eaten plate and exhale again.

"Haven?" It's been a bit. I wondered what she could be doing. Perhaps running a hot bath to soothe my muscles while she joins me, massaging my cares away. I unbutton my shirt in anticipation. Even the thought has me feeling better. I am grateful to have such a beautiful soul willing to care for me.

I felt my entire body shudder and knew it would be some-thing good.

"Levi...." She said just loud enough for me to hear. As I walked toward the hallway, about to head to the ensuite in our bedroom. I noticed that the playroom door was cracked open.

*I usually kept that closed.*

I ran my hand down my chest as the door creaked open from my push.

My my my...

Nothing could prepare me for what I see. Her obediently on her knees.

For me.

"Haven..." There's something classically sexy about black: the allure and mystery. It is one of my signature colors. Now, I am questioning the purity of white as I gaze upon her in this mesh bra and panty set. She had straps sinfully wrapped around her stomach and thighs that formed garters to match the straps of her bra—a hint of innocence in such salacious settings. An angel surrendering to her demon.

Now, the sight of her and the countless possibilities over-whelmed me. I unbuttoned my sleeves as those alpha-type men do in those romance novels she loved so much. I saw her eyes follow my every move. I walk a perimeter around her.

"State your intentions…"

"To submit. To give power, to have you dominate me. I want you to use me, sir." She looked up and bit her lip ever so gently.

Sweet hell.

I take my eyes off her to look at my inventory—so many delicious options. I could restrain her to the bed and have my way, but that's a little advanced and can sometimes feel one-sided. I wanted her to have as much pleasure in it as I did.

I wanted mild restraint and a tease of pain. I opted for wrist cuffs and nipple clamps. I already fantasize about hearing her squeak the moment I apply the clip and the corresponding moan when I let them close completely. I hold both in my hand and continue to walk around. Now, I had to pose the same question:

"Do you trust me?"

"Yes, sir."

"Do you consent to wrist cuffs and nipple clamps? If either feels like it is too much, I want you to tell me. This amplifies pleasure for you, not harm you."

She shook her head. "But this was for you to get your power back."

I lean down and lift her chin to look her in the eye. "Don't worry… I will, but I will always make sure you verbally agree and look forward to it as much as I do. That's my job, and satisfying you brings me immense pleasure."

She nodded, but I pinched her chin. "Yes, sir." She corrected herself.

"In this room, you may call me sir or daddy. Calling me anything else without my approval will get you punished. Understand?"

"Yes, daddy."

She sounds so goddamned sinful, and I fucking loved it.

"Do you know what a safe word is?"

"No, sir."

Color me shocked. Even though she may be innocent, I would have suspected she had at least read it somewhere.

"A safe word is a word you say when play becomes too much, and you need to stop. You'll never be punished for using it."

Her eyes showed she was thinking too hard. "It doesn't have to be difficult. Any word will do. Now, what is your safe word?"

"Umm, Petey?"

Yeah, that would stop me dead. I actually may never perform again. "Let's use something else."

"Dragons."

Homage to her life at the bookstore from employee to owner. "Dragons it is. Don't be afraid to use it. I mean it, Haven." The way her body trembled. Oh, what she does to me.

I slide my belt from the loops, "Unbuckle." She reached up, promptly stuck her fingers down my pants, and unclasped the silver tongue from the loop. She also had to unbutton the inner button since all my suits were custom-tailored. I mean, what's worse than an ill-fitting suit?

With minimal effort, my pants fell to my ankles. I was primed and ready, but first, "Stand and give me your hands. I hold my hand open, and she places her tiny wrists in it. I place gentle kisses on each before wrapping them in the padded leather cuffs. The sound of the chain rattling excites me. She puts her arms down but continues this evil, but innocent look on her face. To look so innocent but ready to be tainted.

"I'm going to punish you for driving me fucking wild. On your knees, the sloppier, the better. You've read enough to know what I mean."

She comfortably rested her hands on her thighs because I didn't need any support; I was pointing toward her like an arrow with a slight curve. She reared up a bit, and her breath grazed my tip, causing it to twitch. I flinch, mildly irritated. "Do not keep me waiting." I warned.

She pursed her crimson lips like a kiss, leaning forward until they touched, then she pushed against my dick. Her warmth surrounded me, and I could barely breathe. Once she reached her limit, she held it there, looking at me.

"Relax your throat…that's right, my…mmm… mischievous book slut."

I placed my hand on her head as she bobbed back and forth at such an intense pace, trying to grant my wish to see saliva all over her and me as she worked me up. Her chains rattle as she brings her hands up to surround my cock, alternating directions while stroking. I feel my legs about to buckle; she felt so damn good. I was fighting the urge to coat her mouth with my seed. She continued to lick, slurp, and hum against me.

I ran my hands through her hair and pulled a bit which caused her to try even harder. I should have known.

"Stop."

She pulled back slowly; even that was torturous. But she complies and sits silently, her lipstick smeared and saliva covering her mouth and chest. She looked like she was fighting for her life while choking on my dick. I notice her peeking glances at the wall of toys, and I wonder... "Do you want to pick something from the wall? It's okay, take a look."

When she stands up, the thick straps of her outfit stretch and sound like tight leather or latex. She stands in front of the wall. Scanning it from top to bottom. I see her intrigued by the iridescence of quite an advanced toy. It was known as a mermaid's tail. It resembles the beautiful rainbow of green, blue, and purple scales of the mythical creature but is made of a light metal held by an O-ring for easy maneuvering. You have the choice of the smooth feel of the scales as they graze the skin or go against the grain to feel tips scrape against the skin. It was far too advanced for our first session.

"Perhaps another time when I'm testing your pain tolerance. And I WILL test it."

Her eyes widened when I brushed the scales in the opposite direction, raising them a bit, revealing the pointy tip hidden when going with the grain. I imagine the beautiful marks it'll leave.

Now, she moved over toward the whips, floggers, and paddles. I stare at her ass as she stretches her arms out and stands on her tiptoes to reach for the matte black silicone paddle with slots. The holes allow the air to pass through, so when I tag my little mate, she feels the full sting. I shake myself out of my fantasy and realize she's back on her knees, holding it up toward me.

I take it and smack it against my hand, causing her to flinch. I lean down for the last innocent kiss.

"Thank you, my love, for playtime."

I could see the adoration on her face.

"Bed, on your stomach, arms in front."

She turned around from her kneeling stance and slid her entire body across those silk sheets, purposefully keeping her ass lingering in the air. I should have marked her then, but she was expecting it. I sat on the edge of the bed next to her. I stare at the curve of her back, the movement as she breathes, rubbing the paddle against my hand before I push my shirt tails off my lap.

"Across my lap now." She scrambled to lay her heated body against me, thus warming me up further. I'm sure she could feel my dick poking her stomach. I distract her by rubbing and kneading her cheeks.

***Smack***

"OOH!" She yelps.

I didn't even give her a chance before I reared up with the paddle, spun it, and played the same tune, but got an entirely different note. "Ohhh." It was a dirty combination of a gasp/moan. She definitely prefers the paddle.

"Only five licks this session because I can't wait to devour you, my little book whore. I want to hear every sinful syllable from that dirty fucking mouth of yours."

I slip my fingers under the bra and undo it. "Take it off." I removed the cuffs so she could sit up and slip her arms out to let it fall to the floor. And now I feel their warmth. "You feel so good against me."

***Smack smack smack***

She rubbed her body against me in response. "Mmm…more, sir, please."

"Only one more. Let us not gorge ourselves on the spoils of pleasure, for you and I will have an eternity to try every dirty, filthy thing your mind can think of. But if you want to please Daddy right now," I run my fingers down her back, over then under her ass, and between her thighs, "you can cry out for me as I slide my fingers into your warmth." And I did just that; her pussy welcomed my fingers as she sighed in pleasure.

"Such a greedy pussy. Look at this; I'm soaked in you." She was at a loss for words.

"Sit up." She whimpered at my fingers slipping out. "Look at me." She watched as I wrapped my tongue and mouth around my fingers, tasting the very essence of her. I was so ready to feed her tight pussy with my cock, but first, I had one more toy to use.

"Take your panties off without removing the garters."

"Yes, sir." She hooked her thumb and slid them off. I was going to wrap my hands around those body-hugging restraints and use them to slam her against me.

I kneeled in front of her like when I worship her. Instead of devouring her, I sit her up, grabbing the clamps and staring at her already taut nipples. I hold up the clips held together by a small metal chain. Each clamp has silicone tips to hug the nipples just at the point of pleasurable pain.

I couldn't help but smirk. "These go around your nipples. It should cause mild discomfort but also feel good. Use your safe word otherwise." I looked up, and she had a wide-eyed expression, biting her lip, anticipating these new feelings.

# CHAPTER 44

## HAVEN

My entire body is buzzing; it's different from our mate bond but as electric. I watch him as he licks each clamp, pinching my nipples gently with his free hand as a distraction.

"Are you ready?"

Is he kidding me? I might orgasm from the intensity of his foreplay alone.

"Y-yes, sir." He presses down, so the clamp opens up; it's wide to make sure he places it correctly. "One at a time." He states as he slowly releases it. I felt the initial squeeze, but he still held it a bit. When he looks at me, I nod, and he lets the clamp go as it squeezes my nipples; the pressure makes me squeal loudly.

Wow, I did not expect that, but I like it.

I leaned forward toward him, and his warm breath brushed across my chest. "More." He clamped the other one more harshly, causing a slight uneasy tinge of pain. Yet, I found I liked that even more than easing into it.

Has he tainted me, or have I always been this depraved?

Either way, I have an eternity with this man, making me feel like this whenever I ask or beg.

Speaking of begging, I know he's already teetering; he's been rock hard this entire time. It's time to drive him over the edge.

I turn around and slide to the head of the bed. "Sir, please." He stared for a few moments before his resolve broke. It will never get old seeing his chiseled body stalk toward me, wanting to defile me. To leave me utterly tainted and claimed with every mark left on my sensitive, flushed skin.

I was lying on my side when he approached, sliding his hands under the tight straps of my garter. His veins bulge with every squeeze. He shook them a bit to see the movement and smirked.

Then he growled, "You know I love you, right?" I thought it was weird that he asked in that way, but I obliged.

"Yes, sir."

A devious smile rose, then a deep chuckle, "Good, because I'm going to fuck you like I don't."

I didn't even respond. What could I say to that? I knew to brace myself for an intense session. He slapped his dick on my ass before he slid himself in, a low guttural growl as he finally got relief.

The best part, next to feeling him so deep, is the groans and growls when he's thrusting hard. He's using the harnesses to slam me into him.

"Fuck! Damn it! How do you, ugh,…feel…so goddamn good?! So fucking perfect! Such a dirty, dirty girl!" He grunts every time he bottoms out, wishing he could go further.

I scream his name as he pounds into me in doggy position. I can't describe the pleasure, but I never want it to end. I knew he was being more aggressive than usual because of his rough day, and that's okay.

Ultimately, I want him to know that even if the world falls down around him, I will be there.

"So close…fuck!" He smacks me harder, and I scream into the sheets wrapped around my hands. He was getting close; I felt him getting harder, and I squeezed in response. "Don't...stop... squeezing me, my little... book... whore!"

With several more thrusts, he roared up and climaxed so hard that I thought he may have passed out until he exhaled loudly. I giggled, fully satisfied in our first playroom session.

He looked over, still breathing heavily, "Do you know about aftercare?" I tilted my hand up and down to show I knew a little about it. He nods. "Well, it's a routine that helps you feel cared for or nurtured after intense playing like this. Some people cuddle, some shower together, and some don't like to be touched at all. After all our sessions, there will always be some sort of aftercare unless you don't want it. And it doesn't have to be the same thing every time."

For a moment, I feel a certain way, like vulnerable, and all these emotions are rushing forward. My throat tightens, and I feel like I want to cry. I sniffle, and he immediately wraps me up in his arms.

"It's okay. You're okay. What happened was very intense, and I'm so grateful to you. That you wanted to make me feel better. You did so well. I love you." He ended each sentence with a kiss on my forehead, and slowly, I stopped sniffling.

I look up and give him a small smile, then comfortably bury myself under him. I really like this, especially knowing that he was satisfied.

As I drift asleep, my mind wanders back to the big dilemma: could his mom be in Tartarus? I would need to find the entrance, but they both retreat to their rooms whenever they fight. It seems like that's all they do.

Surprisingly, between their screaming matches, he and his father settled on a date to transfer power.

I worry about his mental stability. Levi makes me his priority and the reason for his existence, but he still has this big void in his heart for his mom. If there is any truth to her being alive, I have to reunite them. He might be the personification of evil, but he is still someone's son. I couldn't even fathom being kept away from my child. His father doesn't love him or show him affection. It was a lot to process emotionally.

"Haven. Wake up." I feel his lips on my shoulder.

I squeeze my eyes tight before opening them, temporarily blurring my vision. I turned over and saw Levi looking handsome in his signature red and black, when my eyes finally focused. This time, the vest was half red and black with a red handkerchief.

"Morning, beautiful. I'm going to head down. You should open your shop today to keep busy. I'll see you later." He kissed me several times, fighting the urge to stay each time.

"Have a good day, and please try to make nice with your father."

"Oh, I think that ship burned long ago. If he doesn't bother me today, I'll call it a small win."

I lean forward in a silent request, and he rewards me with several more kisses. Then he disappears. I snapped into the shower, dressed, and went into the office. I had to review resumes because I set up a help wanted sign, leaving a box where they can drop resumes off.

As much as I love owning this store, I'm in my honeymoon phase with Levi, and my focus should be on him until he's comfortable in his new position. Because of that, I need someone here as a manager.

I came in extra early to collect and review the resumes; it was way more than I expected. Who would want to work at a bookstore? A lot of college kids submitted their resumes, which made sense, but one resume caught my attention. It surprised me when I saw a name I recognized. "Claire?" I quickly dialed the number on the resume.

"Hello?"

"Hi, is this Claire Reed?"

"Yes."

"Hi, it's Haven from the bookstore. Seeing your name within the pile of resumes was shocking to me. Why do you want to work here?"

She cleared her throat. "I love your spirit, the energy you give that place. That bookstore is a safe zone for those too shy to express themselves. I want to be what you were to me with my boyfriend, I mean, my fiancé."

"Oh! Congratulations, that's so wonderful to hear. Thank you for your kind words. I would love for you to work here. I know it's short notice, but can you come in today? I want to get you comfortable with the basics; everything else should come naturally."

"Oh…oh my gosh! Really?! Oh, thank you, thank you, thank you! I'll be right there!" She shrieked before she hung up. I'm glad she's so excited.

I felt accomplished even though the day was starting. I walked out of my office to open the store and was surprised to see so many school kids. I think they saw my shock; one young man stepped forward. "Miss Haven, you helped me so much when you gave me that textbook for free, and we were wondering if we could get a special for us poor college kids. We don't want everything for free; that wouldn't be fair to you. But if we showed you our school ID, could we set a discount? You have most of the books the campus bookstore has, but you don't charge those outrageous prices. We shouldn't have to starve to learn."

I remember him; he was super sweet, and this was something that was doable. It was greedy for the college to have such expensive tuition and then add on other expenses. They should have included it.

"Tell you what? I can agree if you guys sometimes come in and help tidy up the place or stock the shelves. Maybe once a semester? If you spread the word, I think I can settle on 30% off, and from time to time, we'll do 50% off."

The applause was so loud when I let them all in. I created a suggestion jar for books we may need to order in the future. I wanted to be the go-to alternative for college textbooks.

There was a long line when Claire came in, and she observed from behind the counter. She watches me a few times, and I explain while ringing people up. I see a few of them tidying up the reading corners and re-shelving the loose books.

"Thank you, Miss Haven, seriously." I saw the absolute relief on this young girl's face.

Nobody should have to choose. I lucked out with the scholarship paying for my books and food, but it makes my stomach turn to think about being in that situation.

When the crowd died down, Claire hugged me, squealing again. "Oh my gosh, that was crazy! Why were there so many people this morning?"

"The students wanted to talk to me about adopting a new discount program."

"Ok."

After an hour of going over the fundamentals of the shop, she felt comfortable. She had to learn the genres and layout, but she had it.

During a lull, I lean over the counter, "So, tell me about the proposal!" I grab her hand to gaze at her ring. It was the perfect size for her finger.

"It was super simple. We were walking late at night on the beach near Brenton, and he was pouring his heart out. Then he turned to me and dropped to his knee. It was so romantic. Now, you owe me an update because I know something happened. Your energy changed, and you're much more confident. And you look hot…hotter." We both laugh.

"You were right about everything. Levi confessed he was in love with me and wanted me, and I gave him my everything, and I couldn't be happier."

"Oh, it's like a fairy tale!" She is swooning. I check my watch. "As a matter of fact, I need to go to his…um, office to attend a… meeting."

"Meeting, huh? One of those... clear the desk, hot and steamy closed-door sessions?" She laughed at her implication and wondered, "What kind of business is he in any way?"

"Uh, management consultation. Are you good here? Here's the key to lock up, and thanks again."

Once I got away from public view, I snapped into Hell's kitchen. I avoid his office for now, but I hear voices coming my way, angry-toned voices. I hid in the pantry.

"When are you leaving? It won't be fast enough."

"First time we agree on something. I'd like to get away from you and this incessant construction of your wretched love nest for your annoying..."

"Watch it! For all I know, you are setting me up to see if I can handle everything."

"Contrary to what you think, Levi, I don't look to create havoc for you. I have experience in every stupid thing you do, and I'm trying to warn you, but you insist on not listening, so be it. I'll be here to say I told you so. But only after I've returned from this festival where they throw their inhibitions out the window. It makes Hedonism look like vacation bible school. Good chance to find some new flesh to corrupt."

Levi looked repulsed. "I can't even count how many you have already. You'll need an even bigger whorehouse for your harem!"

"Whatever. I'll be back in five days, maybe less if I find more than I can handle. Look don't screw up. You only get one shot. I got eyes everywhere." He pointed and scolded Levi like a child. Levi just threw his hands up and walked out. I think I'll offer a massage or maybe a nice bath together. I peek to see old Petey going to his side of the... estate. Mansion? I'm still not sure what you call this spacious cavernous dwelling.

He's whistling as he walks down his hallway, but then he stops and looks behind him, so I scramble. I peek enough to see him reach for a huge portrait and lift it a bit, and it opens slightly, like a door, before he slams it back and pushes it, ensuring it doesn't look out of place.

It couldn't be that easy, could it? Plus, I assume it has millions of souls down there. How could that fit behind there? Then again, what do I know?! I'm a glorified librarian.

He shuts his double doors at the end of the hall, and that gives me time to see what might be behind that frame. His hall was darker and more macabre than Levi's; this is where evil lies. I feel a continuous sense of foreboding, like he's never really gone; even if he popped topside, he's still here. The hallway walls are a tone of black I've never seen. I'm sure a black soot would singe my fingers if I touched them and never come off. The deep black made the gold-framed paintings pop more. What I suspected to be abstract art wasn't. It looked like moments he influenced in history. One I recognized was the epic Confederate win at the First Bull Run. Then, a picture of London burning to the ground labeled Black Death. That's when the bubonic plague spread throughout it. Each image is more horrifying than the next. Chernobyl was there, Hiroshima and Nagasaki. I turned to the giant portrait he was securing, a picture of the Titanic.

What a cold, heartless bastard! I swallowed the bile rising up my throat and tried to press on. I tried to pry it open, putting my weight into it, but it wasn't as easy as he made it. Then I heard movement towards his door and scrambled back to the kitchen.

I tried to control my breathing while searching in the fridge. Maybe I will make Levi something sweet after lunch.

"Ugh, you're here. Did you not get enough torturous visions to stay away? This place isn't for the likes of you." He hissed.

He was trying to intimidate me. "Oh, Petey, what's the matter? Does it bother you to see your son happy? To know you once had that, but you were such a vile person that she walked away."

Then his eyes went completely black. If Levi could shift, then he could, too. I am not prepared to see whatever creature he turns into, and I'm sure it's unlike any tale told.

"You know nothing about me other than what those high and mighty parasites taught you. I won't waste any more time on a woman I'm not fucking. Of course, it's common knowledge that the father is always better than the son; think about it." Then he turned and walked away.

Eww! He hit on me! Although it's disgustingly vile and abhorrent, that means he's intrigued by me! This means that a woman does influence even Satan himself. She must have been powerful to deal with and love him. I was going with my gut and feeling hopeful.

I started preparing a quick bite for my handsome Devil.


*Later...*

***Knock knock***

"What?!"

I slowly opened the door and saw the absolute rage on his face before he realized or felt it was me.

"I'm sorry, my love."

He stood and looked defeated. I set the plate on his desk and wrap my arms around him, squeezing.

"It's okay."

"What are you doing here? I thought you'd be enjoying the company of those people."

"Those people? You know I was human once."

"Yeah, I fucked that right out of you." I shoved him off. "You are such a nuisance." I almost slipped up and said he sounded like his father, but that could have opened a can of worms.

"You still didn't answer my question."

"I hired a manager who is someone I know, and she's taking care of the shop while I take care of you."

I saw this twinkle in his eye, and he started to unbutton his vest. "Not like that! It's always sex with you."

"I'm..."

"The Devil. I know! I'm worried about you overstressing

before you officially take reign. I'm here to support you, honey. Whatever you need right now…that isn't sex!"

"But I'd feel so much better once I claim you all over this office. Smelling you in here and tasting you on my fingertips."

If I gave in, I would lose the opportunity to explore. I held my hands up and then placed them on his chest because he was trying to corner me against the wall. "Later, right now, you need to eat something. Do not even think about saying that, Levi! Sit down and eat…your food! Tell me what the ceremony is like. Do I have a role?"

He conceded and sat at his desk. I sat on top, legs crossed. He bites the sandwich and leans back, eyeing my legs.

"Luckily, it's mostly a verbal ceremony and the signing of a contract. I was reading through it line by line to see if he threw any ridiculous clauses or expectations in there."

"He could add it right before you sign it or after."

"No, he had to sign before I got it. Once signed, it becomes irreversible; it's practically a binding document. He knows how to word things that sound normal but are slightly off. I'm ensuring he doesn't separate or break our bond somehow. I put nothing past him. I couldn't take another loss…" He swallowed hard, and it reminded me of my assignment.

I kiss his forehead. "Nothing can keep us apart. I'm going to go. Please finish eating, okay?" I slide the plate closer to his view.

"What are you going to do?"

"Ohhh, I'm just going to wander around and explore," I said, refusing to let fear take hold every time I stepped foot here. I look back, "I'll be fine."

Was I fine? The torturous screams have become less bothersome, and I didn't react emotionally anymore. I stop by the maze to visit the pups and their pups. Who knew baby hellhounds could be so cute? I wonder if he'll let me keep one topside. Then I imagined it escaping the house and causing absolute panic and terror—maybe not a good idea. I met Khalil, their trusted handler, when Levi wasn't here. I suggested to Khalil that he take them to visit Levi to force him to take a break; he couldn't say no to them. He agreed and said he'd give them two more treats, which means souls, then take them by.

Good, reading the contract and then the impromptu visit will distract him. Daddy would never say no to his babies.

# CHAPTER 45

## LEVI

I'm thankful for my sweet Haven. As always, my dad infuriated me so much that Ares was ready to act out his aggression, and it was going to be unchartered territory. But it got me thinking about everything I'm responsible for, and I summoned Carson.

He popped in dressed in a dark crimson suit. He always experimented with color while I stuck to my classic ones. "You rang, buddy?"

"I want to see if you'd like a position once I take over. Like a senior advisor, I need a level-headed voice of reason, and since you gave me sound advice about Haven, I think you can keep me on track."

He was so shocked that he sat down in the nearest chair. "Wow, I can say I'm surprised and honored. Sure. What do you need me to do first?"

"Re-read what I reviewed from the contract. You might catch something I missed, and I'll be damned if he sneaks something past me. Here are the first 72 pages."

"72 pages?! How long is the contract?"

"It's my father. You should know he'd make it long and

painful, so I'd sign it without reading, but I'm not taking that risk, especially if he put something in there about Haven."

"Understood. By the way, how is she adjusting? I thought I saw her roaming around earlier."

"She's honestly doing way better than I expected. I thought she would die of shock before I marked her, so I waited until after she gained her immortality to bring her down. Then she changed. She became sexier, more confident, and able to hold her own. She confronted Aurora and Cherry, then stood up to my father!"

"Whoa! Never in my 4700 years would I have the balls to do that!"

"Yeah, she got under his skin. Get this; she calls him Petey."

Carson burst out laughing. It sounds so unbelievable that the King of Hell is bothered by a tiny, once-human woman. Carson is laughing so hard he's clutching his stomach. It made me wonder if my mother had the same power over him. Could she bend him to her will? Did he think showing affection showed weakness? That's what he tried to drill into my head.

Since our connection was completed, everything Haven does makes me wonder what my mom would have done with my father. I needed answers. What happened to her? Handing me this 115-page document before his trip was probably a distraction to keep me from snooping around while he was away, but with Carson taking on some of my tasks, I'll have more time to investigate.

No matter the outcome, I would find out about my mother. To, at least, allow me to grieve for her appropriately if she truly was dead.

# CHAPTER 46

## HAVEN

I HAD LITTLE TIME; IT WAS ONLY A FEW HOURS UNTIL DINNERTIME. Judging by his demeanor, it could be another long night in the playroom. I rub my arms, thinking about all the ways he marked me. There wasn't enough makeup to cover all the love marks or hickeys. I smile, knowing that under the makeup and clothes are all his markings; I am his.

I found myself back in front of the picture. I'm inspecting it because I can't believe it's that easy. It could be a trap, but I had nowhere else to start. I pull and pull; it rattles, but nothing happens. It's anchored to the wall. How did he...?

"Now, what could Levi's...pet be doing down this way? Are you lost? Sure looks like it." I almost screeched but kept calm when I saw Trevor leaning against the hallway. It was so dark that it looked like he was leaning against nothing.

"Quite bold of you to be on his side of the cavern. Maybe I had you pegged wrong. You're not the average mediocre human."

I didn't have time to dawdle; it was a long shot. "Wrong enough to where you might help me? Do you know where the entrance to Tartarus is?"

I give my most innocent smile, and he visibly cringes. Then I could see his wheels turning as he rubbed his chin.

"Now, why would you want to go there? There is nothing but anguish and utter despair down there. Far too much for someone so delicate like you. And it's not behind that photo. That's where he keeps his porno stash, like the real dirty stuff. Things you could never imagine. Power tools." He let the words hang in the air for maximum effect.

I shuddered in disgust, not noticing Trevor raising his hand to touch my cheek, but I smacked it away. "Careful, one wrong move, and you'll be the newest resident, especially by touching HIS mate. Even being this close could cause you to become a lightning rod. So, you're going to tell me everything you know. It might keep you in his good graces, especially if he finds out you knew or had something to do with his mother's disappearance. I don't know where your loyalty lies, if you have any, but remember that Levi is about to come into power. Do you want to be his permanent punishment pet?"

Trevor gives me a sarcastic clap. "Bravo, you've got balls bigger than your mate. You remind me of a young Persephone. There's a fire behind your eyes. You go for what you want. I understand, but I don't want to be connected to your scheme. In fact, I want immunity when you get caught. Your mate is one sick and twisted, demented fuck. I was under his radar once before. Deal?"

"Fine."

He smiled, and it was as fake as he was. I wonder what Levi did to poor Trevor to have him shaking in his boots.

Once we shook hands, Trevor pulled out a skeleton key. It's on a braided black cord; it looks like those black vines that grow and strangle people.

Although I'm one step closer to the answer, I must know, "Why are you helping me?"

He looks down the hall towards Levi's part, then at me, putting his hands in his pockets. His entire demeanor changed.

"Not all of us are vile, wicked creatures, but we must act a certain way. Show weakness down here, and you end up eternally fucked. Don't get me wrong; I love being an asshole. I get more ass being an absolute prick than a good guy. Who heard of a good demon, anyway? But as Levi has been coming into power, I recognize he does well with his better half, much better than his dad. Maybe he won't muck it up. Honestly, Lilith was probably the best thing that happened to Sam, uh…Satan, but he let the sinful greed of endless pussy get in the way. He's just fucking his emotions away, and that's no way to live for eternity. A leader should have someone by his side."

Wow. I would have never thought. Could Petey be more like his son than he admits, and watching Levi live his life like he was supposed to cause him greater anguish?

Hmm, now that's a head-scratcher.

"Interesting. About both of you. I will keep that a closely guarded secret." He nodded in approval. I checked my watch, and I had about 30 minutes before I needed to start dinner.

"The entrance to Tartarus is in his private quarters, guarded by Cerberus." He nodded towards the dark abyss.

*Are you kidding me?!*

As an avid lover of all things literature, mythology has always had my heart. I knew the tale of every god, goddess, and mythical creature, so that name struck a chord, not a good one.

"I thought Heracles killed Cerberus?"

"And he ended up here to guard it."

"Fucking hell! He won't let me pass, will he?"

"Well, he once belonged to Lucifer when he was in command, now Satan, and probably Levi if he wants him. But he's quite fond of his hellhounds, so who knows? Think of Cerberus as… a family pet. You've got to earn his trust, show no fear, and always look him in the eye."

"He's got three heads!"

Trevor chuckles at my uneasiness. "Always look at the middle. You know when you go to a relative's house, and they have a pet, the first thing they do is sniff you? You got to let him sniff you."

Great, I got to let the three-headed spawn of Hell that serves as a watchdog for the absolute pit of darkness sniff me.

Joy.

I got nauseous just thinking about this. The hallway was even darker before the double doors that you couldn't even make out. I would need a light even to see where I was going.

My watch beeps to alert me to my alarm set. "I know you don't hear this much, but thank you, Trevor. You're not a complete twatwaffle douchebag, but still quite a bit."

He laughed as he walked away. I needed to start my trek very early tomorrow.

# CHAPTER 47

## LEVI

I FINALLY FINISHED REVIEWING THE CONTRACT AND WAS SURPRISED to see that it was on the up and up. Carson had only reviewed about a quarter of it before he called it quits to soak in the sulfur springs. There was some pool party going on. I hadn't seen Haven since she left, but I felt her, and she wasn't in danger, so I left her alone. She was probably catering to her human customers, and I was not in the mood to socialize. I did a last-minute torture to vent my anger and frustration. I went with the classic from history's past, burning at the stake. I enjoyed hearing their screams; somehow, it calmed me.

As much as I loved my girl submitting to me last night, I realized I had brought my work and connecting stress home. Before, it wouldn't have been a big deal, but I've got to prioritize her over work.

I slip off my jacket and vest, unbutton my shirt, and roll up my sleeves to tackle this pasta dish. I could have quickly snapped up a meal, but after tasting the one she had made for me, I could feel the love in it. I would give her the same treatment.

I snap the radio on to listen to something soothing as I cook.

"Mmm, nothing sexier than a man in the kitchen."

I turn to see her sitting on the barstool.

"Hello, my handsome Devil." She smiled as I approached her, swinging her chair around to face me.

"Hello, my beautiful girl. How was your exploring?"

She ran her hands down my chest, her fingertips scraping my skin. "It was…interesting. How was the rest of your day?"

"Good, I finished scanning the contract. One step closer to taking over. Also, the 'love nest,' as you call it, is almost done."

"I consider this place our love nest, so we can think of the new place as a vacation home. Somewhere we can occasionally stay at."

"Fair enough. I told you I would dwell among the wretched to keep you happy."

"Uh huh, how much longer until dinner? I'm going to be in the library."

My hands squeeze her ass, causing her to wrap a leg around me as I steal kisses. She whimpers into the kiss, pushing me a bit. "I'll come to get you; it won't be too long. Looking for anything in particular, I could probably help."

She pondered for a minute, "Greek mythology. Preferably about ancient gods and figures."

"Oh, mythology's on the fourth shelf by the window. Start there."

She hopped up and kissed me with her nails further digging into my skin. I can feel myself rising. I tap her ass. "Go before I burn the food to take you instead."

She gave me that teasing look; her actions were getting bolder.

Oh, I'm going to make her pay for that.

# CHAPTER 48

## HAVEN

'R*OMAN* A*NCIENT* G*REEK* M*YTHOLOGY*, M*YTHOLOGY FOR* D*UMMIES*,' ah, here it is, '*Lesser-Known Mythology Figures.*'

While looking for a breadcrumb that could help me when faced with… I turn to the page and come face-to-face with their depiction of Cerberus, a gigantic, vicious-looking beast that is known as the Hound of Hades and is said to be at least ten feet tall. He is a three-headed beast with a serpent for a tail. He is the guardian of the Underworld and keeps the dead from escaping."

I fall down the rabbit hole to find every piece of information to keep myself from becoming a meal to a mythical beast, and then…eureka! I'll need to reach down deep for this to work, but I've got to try.

Knowing Levi could feel my emotions and I didn't want him asking a million questions, I read a book I knew had quite a hot and steamy shower scene. I wanted to spend the night wrapped around him in the shower. He has one of those deluxe setups with the overhead shower and body jets for overall coverage. And with it being all black tile and the lighting subdued, it has such a sexy aura. I read a few lines aloud and then daydreamed while staring out the window into the dark forest. The hot water would fill the room with steam, causing the huge wall-length mirror to fog up. I'd wipe away enough to see myself in my black silk robe. I'd run my fingers down my neck, making me shiver. I'd untie to let the fabric slide off me, but I feel hands on my shoulder instead, sliding it off as the hands caress my arms before the fabric falls. Now I am being caressed by those hands that send sparks of electricity up and down my....

"My, my, my...I could feel all that." I jumped a bit at the sound of his voice; I should have expected it.

I look to see Levi leaning against the doorway. There was that playful spark in his eye. He was curious about what his book butterfly was fantasizing about. What he knew was it got my heart racing and panties soaking wet.

Well...if I were wearing any.

I planned to wear him out tonight, tell him I was going to the store tomorrow morning, and sneak back down to find out if Lillith was being held against her will. How would his life change if he knew his mother was still living? So much time missed because of his father's heinous actions. And when he found out his dad did such an unspeakable thing, how would he react?

I knew I couldn't live another day without answers. In my heart of hearts, I don't think his dad would kill his mate. Wouldn't that kill him? That's what happens to werewolves, but I suppose demon bonds can be different. Plus, if Levi is immortal, then that means she should be, too, after mating with the King of Hell. This further leads me to believe he has her prisoner down there, but why? Why avoid unending happiness with your better half? Is the option of endless variety really worth it? No, it had to be more than that.

"Before you ravish me, I'd like to enjoy the dinner you made."

"But I'm curious... what were you fantasizing about?"

I slide the book back into its place and saunter past him on my way to the dining room. "Oh, nothing special. You, me, and the shower. I'll need help with the areas I can't reach." He growled as he followed behind me.

The following day, I got up and dressed before he even stirred. I took another shower, this one more thorough in getting me clean instead of the dirty things done the night prior. I walked out and sat on the bed. I lean down and kiss his forehead, and when I lean back, I see a literal smile on his face; it's super creepy but not off-putting. I laugh because I made the Devil smile.

"I know you're not asleep. Surprised you didn't follow me into the shower."

His eyes opened, and that smirk appeared. "I didn't have the energy. I was in my fantasies, thinking about how my dirty book slut made another appearance last night. I think she's beginning to become my favorite version. I am going to sleep in before I head down to my office. You plan on spending the day up here?"

"Yeah, taking inventory, and there's a shipment coming in. I might be a little late if we get both shipments even though I only expect one, but it's happened before. Like the day I called in sick on your regular visit day. I was so heartbroken. Seeing you is what got me through my darkest days."

"Ditto, kiddo." I snort. That's a new one.

"I love you." He pulls me down for a sweet kiss.

"I love you. See you tonight."

I snap into the bookstore about ten minutes before Claire arrives. I walk around, touching rows of books and remembering when I thought my outlook was so bleak and my life was disappointment after disappointment. But now I am confident and loved by a fantastic man whom the world sees as a black plague on society.

But to him, I'm his everything.

The bell rings, and Claire comes in with a big smile. "Morning Haven, I didn't expect to see you today. You know the big shipment is coming in." She huffed and rolled her eyes; it would be a busy day of restocking and tending to the customers.

"Yes, I thought I'd help as much as possible until around noon-ish. I have something big on the horizon."

"That sounds interesting. You think he's going to propose?" She smiled so big and wide. As much as I would love that, I think I am beyond mortal ideologies like marriage or a wedding. I wouldn't mind the ring, though.

"No, it's more like a… much-needed reunion."

"Oh. That's good, too. Nothing like seeing people reunite with loved ones. Well, I hope you are successful, but in the meantime, I'm going to walk around."

"Sure, I think only the historical fiction section needs work."

She walked to the back to put away her items before walking around the store. I changed the percentage off for students to half off; it was the start of the new semester, and they only gave them a seven-day window to get their books. I also added a special: buy three books and get the fourth free.

The shipment came in at the same time Claire opened the door. The students oohed and thanked us for the impromptu sale and deal. I could see the relief on some of their faces. I snapped some books away while they weren't looking in certain areas, such as science fiction and fantasy. I would have to refill the textbooks manually, especially since we would constantly restock them as they persuade their friends to come here instead of the campus bookstore for a better deal.

Halfway through the day, Claire joins me in restocking some biology and chemistry books. "Aren't you losing money by pricing it so low? I'd hate for the store to close because of it. I know you want to help the kids, but not at the sacrifice of something you love."

I chuckle, "I promise you, everything is fine. What I lose in book sales, I gain in customers; it more than pays for itself. Besides, Levi set aside $75,000 for expenses and anything else I might need. You should jot down some upgrades we could do. Don't fret; you'll always have a job with me for as long as needed. I can stay another 30 minutes, but then I must make a miracle happen."

In 30 minutes, I put away as many books as magically possible so Claire would only have a few boxes left toward the end of her shift, and even then, it could wait until tomorrow. And I let her know that was the case.

I popped down to Hell, but in the kitchen again, so if someone caught me, I could say I was preparing something. The whole place was quiet…too quiet. Where were the screams from the tortured and the damned? It was like I was in a museum; it was whisper quiet.

"Your mate cast a soundproofing spell on his side of the cave. He told Carson he didn't want you to hear that all the time, only when you went outside. Isn't that considerate?" I couldn't tell if he was being sarcastic, but I still didn't trust Trevor.

"What are you doing here?"

"I'm here to keep your mate distracted. Somehow, I seem to be the only suave and charismatic being that can get under his skin so much that his demon emerges." I openly laughed in his face, "Suave and charismatic being, huh? Is that code for complete pain in the ass that ruffles his feathers?"

He shrugs, "Consider this an olive branch that I put myself in harm's way so you can carry out your quest. I hope you know the repercussions of your actions if this blows up in your face or if you succeed. Either way, there will be blowback."

I stared at him, and that was enough of an answer for him. I was going to do anything to give Levi the answer he deserved.

What really happened to his mother?

# CHAPTER 49

## LEVI



If I weren't immortal, she would be the death of me.

After she went to check in on the bookstore, I laid in bed for another hour, reminiscing on our steamy escapade in the shower. The jets constantly showered us as I brought her to climax while bouncing her against me; her feet never touched the ground. If I wasn't holding her up, those legs wrapped around me as I pounded into her, water and sweat mixing with her orgasm and mine.

God, she was amazing! I roll my eyes at my faux pas and finally climb out of bed to shower and start another day of transition tasks. We'd conduct the ceremony when my father returned from his Hedonism trip with another concubine or seven.

When I snap into my office, Carson is there, ready to get the day started...and then there's Trevor. I can already feel the irritation from his presence. Ares' eyes him hungrily. I look at Carson, growling, hoping he had a good reason. "What is he doing here?"

Trevor holds his hands up. "Relax. I came to offer my services once you take over. You know, I was an advisor to your dad in his early years."

"That was a millennium ago; your thoughts and processes are as archaic and useless as you are. Plus, let's not forget that I despise you. Especially after those vile words you spat about Haven! I should gut you for disrespecting your Queen!" Ares made himself known with his claws and horns visible.

I saw Trevor shrink a little, but his arrogance reemerged. "I misspoke. I recognize I can appear a bit...condescending, but this position is powerful, Levi; it literally changes people. You may not remember, but your father was once like you. I used to think about what could have been if he had not made the choices he made.

Well, that was insightful. "What do you mean?"

"It's all moot at this point; his reign is ending. It's about you now. Let's bury the hatchet and bad blood."

I watch Carson. He seems to believe the bullshit Trevor is spouting. "Fine. You will be at Haven's beck and call for whatever she needs."

His eyes widened. "What? You want me to babysit your mate? A glorified nanny?!"

I try not to laugh at his pain. "You are the advisor to the Queen of Hell. Keep her happy and you never know, I might bring you over to my side of the operation."

*When Hell freezes over.*

"She's topside, but the moment she steps down here, it is your responsibility to keep her happy. Perhaps you should go there and relay the good news while Carson and I tend to real business. Dismissed." I could hear him grumbling on his way out, but that's none of my concern.

He wants to be in my good graces. He'll spend it groveling at her feet. If I hadn't sentenced Aurora and her buddy to Tartarus, they'd be her chambermaids. We don't even need those.

I do not forgive and forget; I torture until I'm bored with you, and then I pass it off to someone else. The punishment never ends.

# CHAPTER 50

## HAVEN

 Lillith away, but why?

From what I read, she was an ethereal beauty, strong-willed and curvaceous, but then when she sought refuge down here, she turned into a different kind of beauty, a haunting beauty… she visually portrayed the torment and pain of her circumstances. It says she wrapped her naked frame in thin layers of sheer black or royal purple fabric. I wear a purple and black Grecian-style gown with a high-waisted split on both sides. If Levi saw me, he would claim me where I stood. I also don a replica of a crown, weaving and interlocking vines and placing them on my head. A future Queen should always pay respect to her predecessor. I pray she is alive so I can learn how best to take this role.

I wear the key necklace; it dangles between my breasts of the low-cut gown. I gather the fabric and walk down the hallway's darkness toward his bedroom. I don't think Heaven's light could penetrate this level of darkness. I tried to stay in the middle of the corridor, careful not to run into anything that would show I was there.

I took a deep breath and pushed open only one of the enormous chamber doors, which I only opened enough to slide through. It was freezing in there! Ironic to be in Hell. I was expecting to be confronted immediately by the beast, but he was nowhere in sight. I looked around and saw only one other set of doors that resembled the other, most likely the bathroom. I had no choice; the door creaks loudly, and that sends shivers down my spine. It is an opulent bathroom bathed in black and red. There was even a very ornate black crystal chandelier. The jacuzzi bathtub was a deep red and resembled the after-effect of a ritualistic blood sacrifice. It was both sexy and terrifying.

I look around to see no other door. Where could it be? I double back out of the bathroom and back into his bedroom. I noticed two things I hadn't in my rush to get to the other door.

Now I see where Levi gets some of his kinks, although we don't have a Sybian machine or a bench for advanced bondage play. As my eyes adjust, I realize he has a collection we don't have...of self-help aids. Could it all be a front? All the tales of orgies and sex at any and all times? Would he rather have the touch of his mate, and this is his punishment? Self-pleasure. Self-torture.

I don't want to feel pity for him because this could have easily been avoided had he not locked her down...

Then I felt it before I heard it: heavy breathing. The warm, humid air rushed forward, moving my gown, and warming me with it. The growling was another giveaway. I take a deep breath and say a quick prayer. I wonder if he still listens to me. At this moment, I really hoped so.

I turn slowly, not to move suddenly when I'm face-to-face with the beast. He had lowered his three heads, and they were now growling and baring their teeth. He sniffed me again and again while I kept focusing on the center head.

"I am Cerberus, guardian of Tartarus! State who you are and your purpose!" He roared as his serpent tail whipped around behind it.

I push my shoulders back, standing tall, but literally terrified.

"I am Haven, mate to Levi, the Prince of Darkness and future King of Hell."

His eyes grew wide. "Has he already grown tired of his mate and sent her down to the depths so that he can partake in the pleasures of endless sin?"

"Absolutely not! If he did, would I willingly show up at the door?"

"Then why have you interrupted my slumber by breaking into the bedchambers of my Master? I should devour you for trespassing."

"I don't think the future King would like that. He would surely rip you apart for doing so."

He inhales my scent and ponders. "So the man child believes strongly in the mate bond, interesting…"

"I seek Lillith to return her to her son."

"And what makes you think she wants to see her son? How do you know she didn't choose to be where she is? She is the mother of Hell, and all of us are her children."

I believed old Petey had spun his own story to Cerberus to keep her down there, but one thing he revealed was that she was down there! He could have easily said she was not there and banished me.

"I'll never believe a mother left her child unless someone forced or blackmailed her in some extreme way." Tell me I'm wrong?" I arch my brow to see if he would lie to my face.

He bows. "You are as wise as you are beautiful. As the future Queen of Hell, I cannot deny you entrance. I hope you allow me to continue my duties when you reign."

I was concerned. "Will you get in trouble if Satan finds out that you let me in? I don't intend for you to be punished for my undertaking. I have no ill will towards you; your position is essential."

He was a product of his environment, and deep down, I know there is some good in him. "I will not shy away from my punishment if so be it. I will only end up in the land that I secured for centuries. True torture is being regarded as a pet, not the powerful mythical entity I once was." The light shifted off his serpent scales, showing a different type of beauty; it was magnificent!

"Levi will know that you aided me in rescuing his mother. Levi will know you assisted me in rescuing his mother. You will receive a reward, not punishment.

"The entrance will open when you rotate the key in the light fixture next to the bed."

I bow, "Thank you." I feel like I had been here for hours, but it had only been minutes. Levi told me that time was twice as slow down here, but I still wanted to get in and out. I walk to the right side of the enormous platform bed and admire the gothic-style sconce with intricate lace detailing hanging off with black pearls.

Nope, that wasn't lace detail; that was someone's thong! I bit my tongue to stop from screaming or dry heaving.

I look back to see Cerberus chuckle at my misfortune. I aggressively wipe my hands. I find the keyhole, insert the key, and wiggle it to find the relief, which is a quarter turn to the left, and then the wall slides back. It's glowing ominously down there. The screams are different, and they sound more tortured, if that's possible. I hesitate, but then remember why I'm doing this. I pick up my dress, square my shoulders, and proceed down the stairs; maybe I should have worn shoes instead of going barefoot. The stairs are icy cold; I can see my breath. It's the opposite of everything I knew about the depths of Hell. Is this what they mean by Hell freezing over?

The stairs descend deep into an open cavern, with everything covered in ice. The demons who are torturing the double damned stop when they see me. They, too, are a bluish hue, adapting to their frigid environment. I keep my head up as I walk around, trying to locate her, but it isn't too hard when she's caged in the center of the chaos.

A body lying in a fetal position facing away from me was on

the cold ground. It's astonishing how someone with such great strength can be reduced to a state of weariness and defeat, but when someone forcibly takes you away from your child, eventually, you concede. I ran up to her cage, rattling it to get her attention.

She's barely moving. I clear my throat, hoping it would cause a stir, but it only makes her shift a bit, not face me.

"Lilith?"

She pulls herself up and turns around. She looks at me and hisses, "Who are you? Another one of Sam's whores coming down to torment me! You may have free rein of his body, but I will always have his heart, even if he has me locked away like he doesn't care!" Her voice cracked at the end; she was emotionally exhausted. She snapped her fingers and became as beautiful as portrayed in the books. I was in such awe that I didn't notice she had rushed up to the bars, gripping them tightly, and her breathing was forceful.

"You're one of the bold ones, standing there mocking me by dressing like me! You think you'll even come close, you pathetic…"

I let her project her anger and hatred, calling me every hateful name in the book. She yelled until she had nothing left. I couldn't even imagine how I could continue in her situation.

I bow, gracefully lowering myself to one knee with my hand over my heart, "I am not mocking you, my Queen. I seek your guidance. I am Haven. I am mated to your son, Levi. He will soon become the King of Hell, and I will be his Queen."

Her face softened, and her eyes filled with tears quickly. "Levi? My sweet, sweet boy. He's still alive? You're…his mate? I went against my better judgment and prayed to HIM so that Levi would be nothing like his father and that he would lean into his bond and not lock his mate away."

"I'm here to get you out. He needs his mother; he missed out on so much, and the pressure of becoming the next King, it's… it's something I can't do alone. He needs you."

She chuckled and patted my hand, which was holding the bar. "You can't break me out. You need to bring Levi down here; this cage is warded. Sam used his blood to activate it. Only the blood of a male heir can short-circuit the hold."

"I will go get him now."

I turn to snap myself to his office, but she grabs my hand. "Thank you, Haven." I only nod, feeling the tightness in my throat because he needed his mother, and I did, too. I snap into his office, and he rambles off while Carson is taking dictation.

"Per Order of the sanctions of Hell..." He stopped dead in his tracks, and his eyes flashed golden. They are curious.

"I was wondering what you were up to. I couldn't pinpoint your emotion. Is this for the ceremony...or after?" His devilish smirk let me know where his mind was wandering.

I think my adrenaline was wearing off. I faced a huge, ferocious beast, walked into the deepest, coldest pit of Hell, and found his mother, who looked so worn down and beaten. I could feel my stomach churning, and now I was going to...

I slapped my hand against my mouth, praying to get there quickly. I crumbled to the floor and expelled everything as if all the dark secrets kept from Levi emptied into the toilet along with my breakfast. I heard him behind me, feeling his hands hold my hair back; it was just too much.

I was so close.

"My love," He picked me up, carrying me to our bed. "Get some rest."

"No..." I felt so weak, but I had to push beyond it. "I need you to follow me." I tried to stand, but he stood in front of me, preventing me from getting off the bed. I noticed Carson at the door; he, too, seemed concerned. He was also Levi's other voice of reason, and I needed them to listen!

I was panicking; his dad could come back early with his conquests and lock her away even further or punish her! I can't let that happen!

I got so frustrated, and time was of the essence! I blurted out,

"I found your mother, Levi! I...found...Lilith." I felt like I couldn't catch my breath. When her name left my lips, he looked enraged, as if I was playing some cruel joke on him.

He stepped away from me. "You lie! She left me here to rot with my father!" Then he turned his back on me. Nothing hurt more than that.

I tried to keep calm, to be supportive. "You never said she was dead! He held her captive...in Tartarus, but I'M A LIAR?"

I couldn't believe it when he called me a liar with no hesitation. I felt an anger I hadn't felt in a long time and snapped, "You think I would joke about something like this? A person who has NO parents! I'm an orphan; I'd sell my soul for another day with them! At one point, I wished I had died with them!" Admitting a dark part of my past made me choke up, but I pushed through, "I only wanted what's best for you, and for you to think so little of me is goddamn telling! You need your mom for things I can't fix! You try to smother me with your love when you've been without for so long! Like I'm going to disappear like she did. WHY WOULD I LIE TO YOU?! TELL ME!" I screeched so loud and angrily wiped the tears from my face. He tried to walk to me, to console me from his baseless claim. "Don't even fucking bother. Follow me. I know where the entrance is."

I picked up my dress and stomped toward the other side, with him and Carson following me into the bedroom.

"Cerberus," I called, and he came from around the bed where the gate lay.

"My future Queen." He bowed, but his demeanor changed when he noticed my expression. "Is everything okay? You seem upset."

"Nothing you can fix but thank you for your genuine concern." Cerberus looked past me to see both of them, and they looked shocked. He sat next to the door as I turned the key in the sconce, and the door slid back again. I hurried down the icy steps as they took their time to take in the surroundings. The gasps and whispers from the demons who were torturing others now witnessing the Prince of Hell and their future King enter this place.

"Lillith," I say as I run to her cage. She turns around to face me. I have him blocked from her view, but she nods, and I step aside so she can finally see her son. He paused to lay his eyes on his mother. Carson slapped his hand over his mouth. Levi's mouth fell open as he took baby steps. His head tilted in different directions, as if she were a mirage that would disappear at the right angle. I could see the emotion building up as he approached.

It was so much for both of them to take in.

"Levi. Levi Gideon, I gave you that name, and look at you; you grew up to be so handsome." She smiles through the tears, reaching out for him.

"Mo...mom? What did he do to you?" His hands are over hers, holding the bars, and then they slide off hers as he rattles the cage, the anger resurfacing. "He locked you away?! In here, away from me?! ALL THIS TIME?" His eyes flashed red this time, showing Ares' overwhelming disapproval.

"We'll talk about that, but first, you have to break the cage. Only the blood of a male heir can release me. Let your demon out!"

Ares emerged, and his wings burst forth. He let out a monstrous roar, which made all the nearby demons scatter, leaving their subjects stranded in their current punishment.

"Free me, son. Free your mother from the shackles built by your father. Release me!"

He sliced his hand with his claw to smear blood on his hands. Once he grabs the cage, this once invisible barrier breaks and shatters into a black mist, then fades away. He uses his claws to rip the cage open, and she steps over the remnants. Overwhelmed by everything, she faints in her son's arms, and a wayward thought passes:

*He doesn't need you; he has his mother now. SHE is the most important woman in his life, not you.*

I had blocked my feelings from Levi to let that thought utterly rip me to shreds as he carried her back to his side of the cavern. He laid her down and pulled the blankets over her. She whispered his name, and he kissed her hand, hoping to coax her awake.

Trying not to burst into tears, I slipped out of the bedroom and snapped to my apartment.

Maybe this wasn't my happy ending after all.

# CHAPTER 51

### LEVI

I can't believe my eyes! My mother, my beautiful mother in the flesh! She didn't abandon me; my father kept her locked away where I couldn't find her!

The swirling storm of rage being conjured for my father knows no bounds.

I sit and watch my mother sleep; she is more beautiful than I imagined her to be. Her story is unique; she started out as human but became the Queen of Demons and the mother of Hell, but I was her only legitimate child, a *campion*, born out of love. My father always chastised my human side, and I turned that into hatred of myself and humans.

There was so much time to make up for, so many stories to tell and listen to. I'm so thankful to my sweet book angel for getting me the answers I so desperately needed; I'm in utter debt to her. I look back but only see Carson there.

"Haven?" No answer. I checked my office, kitchen, and even outside in the torture maze, but she wasn't down there. Maybe she had gone topside.

After putting Carson in charge of my mother's care and notifying me immediately if my father returned, I snapped to our place, but it was eerily quiet. I called her, but there was no answer. She must be at the bookstore. I snap myself there behind the building and walk in.

"Welcome to Book Lair of Dragons. How may I help you?"

Ugh, I don't have time for unnecessary human interaction. "Where's my Haven?" This must be the girl she hired to manage the store; she seems…adequate.

"Oh! You must be Levi. Haven said you were devilishly handsome and well-dressed. Nice to meet you; I'm Claire." She gave me a little wave, which was better than shaking her hand. Then her expression changed. "Um, I haven't seen her since earlier. You can check her office, but I'm pretty sure she's not here."

I head right to her office, and it's empty. Now I was worried. Where could she be? I walk out without acknowledging her and look around. I remember that maggot who tried to take her from me. Could she have gone to him?

Then I felt something different; it was like despair, hopelessness, and anger, and I remember why. I had called her a liar when she said she found my mother. I had directed my anger toward her, and all I wanted now was to hold her, but she had already shut me down.

My head was swimming. When she admitted she wished she had died with her family, it gutted me. Not just because I never would have had her, but because she felt so alone in the world that she thought death was her best option. And now, I made her feel alone. Where could she be?

Her apartment! I snapped myself there, and she was in her beautiful gown, staring out the window. She didn't even bother to look my way.

"It's over. I'm, uh…I'm delighted you got your mother back in your life." She says mechanically, with the tears rolling down her cheek. I knew she was serious when I felt the sharp pain stabbing my heart. It was the first time we both clutched our chests in agony. It was pre-cursor pain before the anguish of rejection. She hadn't said it verbatim, but it was close enough to cause us pain.

No. There was no fucking way she was going to end it like that. I pull her to her feet by her arm, cradling her close. She tries to fight me, but I hold on and let the sparks course between us to remind her.

"Don't you think for a goddamn second I'm going to just let you go! I shouldn't have called you a liar, my love. I am so used to being betrayed, and I directed my anger at you."

She shoves me super hard. "You got what you wanted! She's back. What do you need me for? Just leave me alone!" She squeaked out, still never looking me in the eye. My harsh reaction and words had ripped her confidence to shreds, and I had to build it back. I tip her chin, "Look at me, Haven Marie."

I never called her by her middle name; she didn't know I knew it, but I needed her to know I was serious. As she looks, her eyes fill with tears, and I catch a glimpse of the once insecure, shy girl hiding behind her sweater, fantasizing about her knight in shining armor.

"I'm not letting you go, and you are not leaving. I will beg on a floor of barbed wire, bleeding from my knees, until you forgive me. You gave me the missing part of my life, but you are my bigger piece. I will put no one above you, and that includes her. And my mother knows you are critical to my future as King. I cannot rule without you by my side. Look at me, I can't."

# CHAPTER 52

## HAVEN

"...I cannot rule without you by my side. Look at me, I can't."

He held my face with his hand, rubbing my cheek until I completely broke down. There was so much emotion: happiness, anger, doubt, uncertainty, love, and fear. He's in front of me, pouring his heart out, which is a sign of his undying love. Maybe I panicked, thinking he would toss me aside. My circumstances never allowed me to be comfortable. There was always some sort of change outside of my control. I was trying to lessen the pain by striking the first blow.

"Hey."

I look at him and try to smile. His lips pressed against my forehead while squeezing me. "Thank you, my sweet book angel. You have no idea how much you have changed my life for the better. None of this would be possible without you."

My handsome devil loves me, and I love him; it would have killed me to end it. What was I thinking?

"I was scared."

"I know."

"Scared that you'd replace me because what's stronger than a mother's love?"

"Yours. I love my mother, but her bond differs from ours. Like knowing that you're practically naked behind those paper-thin pieces of cloth right now, tempting me to defile you here or in your office at the store. Why are you dressed like that?" He growled.

"I was paying homage to your mom as the original Queen of Hell. She thought I was one of your dad's concubines, but as soon as I said your name, she was so awestruck. I'm sorry I blew up at you."

His hands slide over my barely covered curves. "The apology is mine for doubting you. How about I make it up to you with a sea of orgasms?"

"Your mother is in our bed. I don't think that's going to happen."

"Lucky for us, we have a home up here. I don't mind spending the night...begging on my knees in front of you...for your forgiveness."

"I will let you another time. The big question I have is, what are you going to do when your dad finds out? You know Sam is not going..."

He froze. "What did you call him?"

"Your mom called me one of 'Sam's whores'. I figured that was his actual name."

He shakes his head. "Wow, I haven't heard it in so long. He forbids anyone from using it. But that is only part of his name, but let's refrain from calling him by his God-given name. I watched him rip the leather wings off of one of his close associates. He thinks it, too, is a curse from above."

"O...kay."

"Speaking of okay, are we okay? Can you ensure the future King of Hell that his love won't abandon him at the first sign of trouble, that their relationship is strong enough to withstand anything?"

I only chuckle, "Taking relationship advice from the Devil?

Sure, whatever you say. Let's go back. I'm sure your mother wants to spend as much time with you as possible."

"I can split my time between you. Don't step off your pedestal because I'll always place you back where you belong. Yes, I'm going to spend time with my mom. I need answers, but you…you are my world."

"I know. I meant I was going to cook while you catch up. I should change." I snap into a simple dress, but he snaps the scandalous dress back on. "Don't think I overlooked the lingerie mid-switch. Keep this on; I like it."

"Oh, you mean this?" I snapped, the soft fabric of the tiniest thong brushing against my skin, the cool air caressing my exposed breasts. I hurriedly covered up, smirking as I teased him.

He ran his fingers through his hair, tugging at the end. "Fucking tease." He grabbed me and snapped us back into his room, where his mom was alert and resting comfortably.

"Mom, how do you feel?"

She patted the bed, and he sat down immediately. "You too, Haven. I still feel pretty weak, but my powers are returning, and soon I'll be at full strength. I thought I'd never see you again. I can't believe how much you look like Sam, a spitting image."

# CHAPTER 53

## LEVI



"Why, Mom?"

She sat up and sighed. "Your father thought my hold over him was too powerful and that I would be his downfall. He didn't understand that my only responsibility was to love and help him sustain Hell. He deemed it witchcraft, but he couldn't...or wouldn't, formally sever the bond. I know it sounds crazy, but your father still loves me, and his solution was to contain our bond within only me and keep me alive. He removed the bond from himself without breaking it! Only I feel love and admiration toward the man I should loathe and despise." She tuts and then looks away. When she looks back, there's a smile. "Seeing you with Haven warms my heart. I gave my soul to make sure that you embrace such a beautiful gift. I apologize, Haven, for calling you those horrible things. You have only the kindest heart and eyes for my son, and for that, I am grateful."

She holds her hand out, and Haven leans to take it. "Thank you. I only want to be his encouragement when he's down and the guardian of his heart."

"See, such a perfect reply. I only wish you the best, my future daughter-in-law. I'm so excited to have a new daughter!

Speaking of, when are you going to…" This mischievous smile formed on her face.

"Mom!"

She holds up her hands, "Alright. Too soon, too soon." Haven clears her throat. "On that note, I'm going to whip up something to eat while you bond." She kissed me on the cheek. A torrent of indecent, lewd thoughts consumed my mind. It was as if an uncontrollable surge of desire had taken hold of me, clouding my judgment, and overriding any sense of propriety.

Haven's eyes filled with compassion and understanding, her body language displaying both empathy and restraint. She was sharing the struggle I was facing, torn between our desires and the need to show respect to the woman who had given me life. In that moment, I realized how lucky I was to have someone who cared so deeply about my renewed relationship I held dear. She turns to leave.

When the door closes, I partially shift, allowing Ares to vent a minute portion of his rage. He balances several fireballs on his blackened fingertips like a sinister juggler. I feel his horns shoot out from my head. "I'm going to eviscerate him, Mom! I haven't let Ares burst out completely because last time I destroyed part of the palace, and I don't want Haven to see that side of me."

"Well, has she met Ares?"

"She's the one who named him, but I want to keep my innocent book bee away from some of the heinous things I do. I don't want to tarnish her."

"Is that what you think? I was like her in the beginning; I was very meek, terrified, and impressionable, but once I claimed my power, I was a force. Whether or not she gains powers, she will grow into her role. Even though I've been locked away this whole time, I can mentor her." She looked away, placing her hand on her chest. "You know…all I ever wanted was for your father to love me, but he chose lust. Every act of adultery I felt! It felt like I was a pin cushion until I was numb to it. It's happening right now; he's screwing some bimbo, and my heart mends right over the infinite layers of scar tissue, hoping he'll come to his senses. The real Hell is the heart that continues to beat inside a dead horse."

She looks away, and the tears fall. I didn't know what to say. To know that she felt the sharp stab of betrayal every time infuriates me more. Feeling that for a moment was excruciating, I couldn't imagine it consistently. I squeezed her hand and kneeled beside her bed. "I love you, Mom. I never stopped."

"I know, my sweet boy. I knew it was your love that kept me alive. Sam went to great lengths to keep you from searching for me or knowing anything about me, essentially wiping me from history, but it's okay. I have a plan."

# CHAPTER 54

## HAVEN

Dinner was great with the three of us. We laughed and talked about the last six months of our lives because it would bring her down if we talked about anything further. She couldn't wait to tell us about her dream, him ruling, and me being barefoot and pregnant with her first biological grandchild. As the mother of Hell, they were all her children, but Levi was the only child she gave birth to. She used spells and pure evil to create the rest.

"So, Mom, do you feel any stronger?"

"I am just about at full strength. By tomorrow, we should proceed with our plan for your father." They both nod and look forward to dessert.

I decided on a chocolate cream pie, and he insisted on feeding me in front of his mom. Of course, it felt super awkward, but she just swooned at his attentiveness to me. Besides, I love chocolate.

"Son, we hadn't talked about it, but I don't want to be down here if your father returns early. I need time to calm my emotions and not immediately act out and torture him. Does he have a place topside? I can stay and ward for my safety."

"No, but I do. You can stay at my house; it's dark and

secluded, with everything you need. There is a guest bedroom on the left side of the hallway."

Then it suddenly hit me, "Levi! The playroom…did you lock it?" I whispered. He turned his hand in a locking motion. "Thank you."

Could you imagine?! I'd be completely mortified.

"What about you two? I don't want to take away your love nest, especially if it's your safe space."

"I've been meaning to take Haven to the new place down here, and we also need to have…that talk about tomorrow." She nods at him, and they share another identical look. I feel uneasy about what this could be about.

She stands and places a kiss on his forehead. "Tomorrow is a new dawn, a new day, my son." Then she looks at me, "My precious daughter, from fear, you will find your strength, I promise you." When she touches my forehead, I feel the warmth of motherly love. It was a feeling I hadn't felt in so long, so I basked in it.

"Yes, ma'am."

She disappears, and Levi takes my hand to take me to our new accommodations. It's actually beside his dad's place, but not connected to it. He opened the massive double doors; they reminded me of Sam's bedroom doors. When I walk in, my steps echo along the walls.

"It's a bit…big, don't you think?"

"More room to grow." He snapped his fingers, and the three massive chandeliers above illuminated the open space. It looked like his home above, but with much higher vaulted ceilings. If our place above was a space for a couple, then this was for that couple who now had three kids and two dogs and room for even more.

"Did you make a backyard space for the pups? I'd like to see them when they're not working, just acting like normal pets."

"Of course I did. They are my first set of children. II tried to include everything that would keep all my most important beings happy and contemplate future possibilities.

I touched my lips as my mouth fell open. I slowly walked into the space, looking around. "It's a nursery. A nursery." I whispered the last part, and he nodded as I continued to touch everything there: the crib and mobile, the chair and ottoman, the changing table. Everything was a neutral grey that could be accented in any color. I opened the closet door to see a closet full of baby clothes in neutral shades. He thought of everything.

"Haven."

He calls me out of my fantasy and holds out his hand. He stands us in the middle of our future and caresses my cheek before signaling me to sit on the ottoman.

"We need to talk." The irony of him saying it and not me was funny, but he didn't smile. He stood firm in his serious state. Then he paced in front of me. "First things first, it wasn't until you asked me about children that the idea bore into my thoughts, my every waking moment, so I decided why not express my readiness for whenever it happens? It is not to rush you, only to say I'm in this whenever you are."

He smiled, but was expressionless again. "I also brought you here to discuss something pivotal. When my dad returns tomorrow, we will hold the transfer of power ceremony. The ritual won't take long, but that's not the issue. The issue is that after I come into power, I will unleash Ares upon my mom's command. She will seek revenge on my father, and I'll be ever so happy to help her. I may go into a blackout rage, Haven. The anger and utter hatred I have for this man has been eating away at my sanity since I laid eyes on my mother. I have a desire to tear him apart, to inflict suffering until he pleads for mercy, and to persist until I find solace where my soul should live. Ares has had one uncontrolled outburst in my existence, and I do not want you there. I know you met Ares, but I don't want you to see the monster psychopath that we become."

I knew what he meant; he was worried that if I saw him, a

fully unleashed demon, I'd run for the hills. "It's a fair assumption, and I understand." He sighed in relief to know that we shared the same concern, "But, how am I supposed to support you if I don't see every side of you, including the rage-driven demon who is just an angry boy for what his father did to his mother? No matter what you have planned, I will be there."

"No, Haven, he's going to hurt me by hurting you, and I guarantee you, if he hurts you or worse, I'll kill everything moving. I won't spare anyone, not even myself. It'll be an atomic bomb full of rage."

Well…that's dark.

I stood tall in front of him with my arms crossed. "I want to be there."

He's teetering with my decision. "Fine, only if you do exactly what I say. No exceptions, Haven, I mean it. I'll lose it." I see the weight of the situation in his eyes, and I nod in acknowledgment. "Yes, Sir."

My attempt to lighten the mood worked as he adjusted himself before putting his hand in his pocket. I try to take my mind off the importance of tomorrow's events and the endless outcomes. None of them had an entirely positive outcome. There would be some sort of damage, whether physical or mental.

I can't focus on the negative, so I walk toward the door as he stays in the center of the room, observing my movements. I look back, "So…is there a playroom down here, too?" He's on me in the blink of an eye, carrying me somewhere.

After that, I was tossing and turning all night. I wandered around the new place early that morning. I have to admit that this kitchen is the one of my dreams with double ovens and a huge island where it could serve as a place to set out all the food buffet style.

But as lovely as the Hell house is, I'll always favor the one above ground because of all the critical milestones. It's where he poured his heart out, told me he loved me, and claimed my body and heart as his. As weird as it sounds, it's the refuge from the insanity down here. It'll be where we ward ourselves for even just a moment's peace.

"Haven." I jumped and turned around to see Lillith, but she looked more powerful, more alluring, and seductive than before. I knew she was at her full power.

"My Queen." I bow gracefully.

"Oh, that part of my life is over and will soon be yours. I have something special to pass down to you before the ceremony."

She holds her hand out and snaps her other fingers, and a beautiful crown appears. The fires of Hell forged the tips of the antique gold, causing them to be blackened. It was stunning.

No. I shook my head. I was not worthy.

"Yes, I want you to have this. This was the crown placed on my head when Sam took over. The only time I was without it was the opportunity Sam took to lock me away. It was my shield and sword."

I saw her other hand squeeze tightly; I don't know if she was repressing her disappointment or trying to forget what awful things he had done to her.

"I don't know what to say. It's beautiful." I bend down a bit, and she places it on me. Once it was secure, she stepped back, and I stood straight, hands clasped in front.

"Ahhh, perfect for the new Queen. That crown is special; it holds special powers that only reveal itself when needed. As long as you wear it, the crown will always protect you.

"Have you decided what to wear for the ceremony? A Queen should wear two colors to signify the powerful principles of the new reign. I wore black and purple for his ceremony, black for the divine evil, and purple for regality."

I turn and face the mirror, wearing this headdress, a beautiful gesture between two women. She stands behind me in silence.

I cleared my throat. "All I ever wanted, besides true love, was to have parents again. No one could ever take the place of my own, but I imagined that my true love's parents would love me as their own. I know I am asking for so much, but…"

Her arm wraps around me and squeezes me tight while looking at me through the mirror. "You never have to worry. You are my child, special than my other children, as you have the love of my son. I am honored to fill that role for all eternity."

She turned and embraced me. It was a feeling I missed so much that I let the tears fall. It was cathartic just to let someone hug me, to feel the warmth of a mother's love. I step back and wipe my tears away. "I'm sorry. Thank you for that; it's been so long. I think I want to wear his signature colors in solidarity, black for divine evil and red for the sacrifices made." Lilith waves her hand, and my sleep gown turns into another Grecian-style gown with a low back and fabric gathered at the small of my back and flowing from my shoulder straps; a belt accentuated my waist and crown. The front wasn't as plunging as the back, which was good so as not to distract my King. I wore a thin gold chain underneath my dress that wrapped around my neck and my waist connected in the middle. It peeked out from the side and neckline as a tease. And to finish the look, I wore a smokey eye and bold blood-red lip, my hair in loose waves with the highlights peeking out.

Lillith clapped her hands. "Utter perfection! Are you ready to witness Levi come into his power?"

"I think so; he's just so worried about my safety after the ceremony is over; he thinks Petey is going to hurt me." She raised her brow, and I explained, "I gave him that name to make him seem less scary. He hates it."

"Duly noted, and Levi is correct; he will do anything to get his son to partake and indulge like him, even break his heart… but I am the ace in the hole."

"Are you going to hurt him?"

"I'm going to make him feel everything he tried to avoid."

"Do you…do you still love him?"

"With every fiber of my being. A mate bond is stronger than

any bullshit he might try to pull. I'm simply going to remind him, but enough about that. Levi is requesting you in his office. I'm going to get ready. I'll see you soon."

I smile, feeling that familiar blush on my cheeks, "Okay, Mom." I snap myself in to see him in a blood-red smoker jacket and black slacks, his hair slicked to the opposite side, quite a distinct look than I'm used to. He turned to look at me, and I did a curtsy with my bow, "Good morning, my King." He was so quick I couldn't do anything but gasp when his hand wrapped around my throat and then slid shamelessly down between my breasts. I look around but don't see Carson. I could also see he struggled, trying not to rip my new gown. He took time looking over my outfit. "So, this is what you chose to wear for my ceremony?" I couldn't tell if he approved or not. "Ye-yes, sir. I can change if it doesn't meet your expectations."

"Oh... tsk tsk tsk...this is far beyond my expectations, my book bee. You are in for a long night later. In the meantime, my father should be back any moment. I need you to stay on this circle rug. There is an invisible ward and protection spell. Do you understand that no matter what he does or throws at you, do not leave this area?"

I second guess my confidence and his ability to protect me from his dad's wrath. The rug was big enough for me to take a step in either direction, and that's it. I felt fidgety but tried not to do anything to express my hesitation.

"It's okay if you feel nervous, Haven. You've never been in a situation like this, but I have done everything I can to keep you safe. Trust in me, trust in us."

I saw a brief glimpse of uncertainty, which was okay because he was comfortable letting his guard down. I grab his hands, and he looks down. "You can do this. It's your time, and I'll be waiting no matter how this plays out." I knew he needed to be reassured.

Then there was a door slam. I jumped and yelped. I look

down to ensure I'm within my protective area, moving the excess fabric away from my feet.

LEVI GIDEON!

Levi rolled his eyes. "Here we go. Carson, it's time." Carson appeared immediately and stood beside me. "My Queen." I nod, but then Carson points at me, "Uh, shouldn't Trevor be in attendance? He is her advisor."

"He's my what?!" I whip my head around. Obviously, it was a conversation I missed. Levi looked a bit panicked. I could hear his dad's footsteps and feel his presence. "Never mind."

He and Carson adjust their suits and stand in front of his desk. Both doors burst forward, and Petey drops his arms after his excessive display.

He was not happy.

"I was going to enjoy the hottest threesome of the millennium until I couldn't reach my bedroom! Why have you warded my side of the house?"

Levi walks around to his side of the desk, leaning forward. "I wanted to do the ceremony the moment you returned. If given the opportunity, you'd drag it out, and I don't have the time to wait for you to finish banging whatever poor soul you tricked."

He looked at me, "Tuh, you are missing out, son. I met a set of twins who were sin incarnate! The things done to me and what they did to each other...I may have to make them my number one go-to."

I try not to look disgusted, but I am. He's a walking STD.

"No one here cares. Let's get this over with." Petey huffs, annoyed with Levi's disinterest. I look down to make sure I am in my safety circle. My senses tell me it is about to go left, and fast.

# CHAPTER 55

## LEVI

I'm glad I knew how to block Haven from feeling my emotions, especially this ungodly amount of anger, rage, and resentment. I could barely contain it or Ares. Any wayward comment or insult could break the levee to centuries of emotion.

I had already signed the decree and strategically placed it, so when he confirms my signature and signs the third and final spot, I'll have him right where I want him. He turns the pages to the end, where the signatures are. He signs the last part. "Looks good. All you have to do is recite the incantation after me. Last time to back out." I glare at him.

"You take everything too seriously. You'd be less stressed if you had more than one option to suck and fuck you dry." He cuts his eyes to Haven, who stiffens up. She's jumpy because she doesn't know what to expect.

"What's her problem?" He asked, but he didn't want an answer. "Okay, let's get this over with. Repeat when I point at you. *Impevindus requiem vios refnirium.* My reign as the King of Hell, ruler of the great Underworld, is complete. I hereby pass the power over to my son, Levi Gideon Asant. Repeat after me, as my father's sun sets, I rise as the new King of Hell."

"As my father's sun sets, I rise as the new King of Hell."

"I accept my fate; the Kingdom of Hell shall forever thrive under my rule!" He sounds so fucking dramatic; he hasn't seen anything yet.

"I accept my fate; the Kingdom of Hell shall forever thrive under my rule." Then, a black mist rose from my dad and floated toward me until I watched it disappear into my skin. I wheezed, it's as if it sucked out my breath. I panicked a bit but regained my control. Ares's power overwhelmed me, and he unleashed a vicious roar that echoed throughout the lands. I felt like a Mack truck hit me and it gave me an adrenaline rush! I felt the power radiating from my core, but that wasn't even the best part.

Then my ears trained on my dad…laughing. A deep, dark, sinister laugh I've never heard before. "I knew you'd take the bait. Do you really think I'd hand over my rule to a pathetic excuse for a demon? You're incompetent and weak! I cringe every time I call you my son! Smoke and mirrors for you to let your guard down, and I could poison you! Force you to reject the bond!"

Suddenly, I felt this hatred, not my usual hatred toward my dad, but a strong distaste... for Haven. Just looking at her made me sneer.

*What good was she to me? She's just a woman. They're no good, nothing but a dumpster for my seed. Why stick to one when I can fuck anyone I want?*

These were my father's words, not mine! I shake my head and feel a moment of clarity before the swirling hatred comes back. And then I realized I had said those words out loud. He forced me to speak his truth. I turned to see Haven absolutely heartbroken, and then I felt it, the excruciating pain leading to rejection. I wanted to run to her, but I couldn't move!

No! These aren't my words! These aren't my thoughts!

*I love Haven!* **Worthless human whore**

*She's my world!* **Filthy fucking flea**

*I can't live without her!* **Then you'll die with her!**

"Nothing like a good old-fashioned possession to make a

man feel great! Why didn't I think of this before? I should have possessed you and fucked her out of spite, stealing her precious innocence. I could have, but I didn't. You're welcome." He stated like he did me a favor.

Haven clutched her stomach, dry heaving at the thought; it almost brought her to her knees. I wanted to scream how much I loved her, but now I couldn't speak! Ares is fighting the forced hatred for control while listening to these vile words from my father. "Shut up! I'll kill you if you fucking touch her!" Despite being frozen in place; I found my voice again!"

"Still fighting, huh? Well, I'm stronger than you. You'll fall to my will and indulge in carnal pleasure whether or not you want to. Maybe I'll even make her watch? Ooh, with Aurora and Cherry, now that would be devastating. A triple dose of reality that sounds like the perfect cure for this mate bond."

I could feel the ability to move increase, but only faintly. As he spews his hate-filled speech, he takes his concentration off of me.

Just need a few seconds more…

Carson stood in front of Haven, who had now fallen to her knees; the pain was pulsing between us. I wish I could take it all away from her, for her to never hear what he said, those vile and vicious lies! I wanted her to look me in the eyes to see that I was fighting! That, in my eyes, is the truth; she's my everything.

"What's this? You got your lackey protecting the frail, helpless creature now? Last chance to save yourself." He spoke to Carson, further giving me time to regain my power.

Carson stood taller and whispered something behind him to Haven.

"So be it! *Sotictum veloria petris!*" A wave of electricity sped toward Carson, and he put up a force field, but I knew…

It wasn't strong enough.

*Haven!*

# CHAPTER 56

## HAVEN

I know the words leaving his mouth weren't his. I knew his father was forcing him, but his face broke me; it looked so convincing, like he wasn't even trying to fight back.

Was I crazy? Or was I delusional to think that a demon could ever love me, especially the Prince of Darkness? My stomach was churning, and I felt so sick because of the sharp pain in my heart.

Then Petey said something so vile about taking my virginity while he possessed his own son. I lurched forward, almost puking on the floor. Who would say something so disgusting? Then, I remembered who he was, but it was despicable even for him.

Carson stood in front of me to protect me. He saw how badly the words broke me down. He shielded me from both of them. Had I already lost my Levi? I prayed. I prayed long and hard.

"What's this? You got your lackey protecting the frail, help-less creature now? Last chance to save yourself." He directed his threat at Carson, but he just stood taller.

He's such a great advisor and friend to Levi.

"Whatever happens, my Queen, know Levi loves you unconditionally, and this isn't the end." He raises his hands, and a bubble forms around us. I believe it's a force field, but for what?

"So be it! *Sotictum veloria petris!*" And this electric blue wave raced toward us so fast I couldn't even inhale before I was in mid-air. I could see I was hurtling away from my refuge. I was no longer safe or protected.

# CHAPTER 57

## LEVI

At that moment he attacked them, I was able to get complete control back, and I watched in horror as her body bounced off the ground and became still; by some miracle, the crown stayed in place.

Ares let out a monstrous inner roar as he sprinted forward. I knew he would express the rage of seeing Haven lying unconscious. I gladly sidestepped out of his way. My demon shot up to full height, letting my horns grow but withholding my wings. My veins did not glow red this time. They were as black as my skin. As if fueled by the darkness of Tartarus. All the hatred, malice, and vengeance replaced my blood. For the first time, I wanted to kill my father. To rip him into pieces, chew him up, and spit him out. He wasn't worthy of being torn apart by my hellhounds.

When he saw I had regained control, he quickly shifted, but failed to remember how I was taller, stronger, and now much more volatile.

"Now you die!" I tell him as I grab him by his throat. I hold my other hand up so he can watch my massive claws grow. I wanted to slice him open and tear out his entrails, bathe in his blood!

Then the doors burst open with a powerful gust of wind, and a feminine form approaches.

What can I say? We are a family of dramatic entrances.

My father's eyes widened when he saw my mother. Beauty incarnate, a type of allure you couldn't shy away from, like a siren calling all within her grasp. Of course, being her son protected me, and I cast a spell on Carson earlier to keep him immune. Any man my mother wanted could genuinely be hers, but fate had chosen someone like him for her.

I watched my father shrink back to his human form and fall to the ground, battling those feelings he once had. He looked like he was swallowing shards of glass and rusty razor blades, and they were ripping him open mercilessly.

Good. I have no problem dismembering his human form either, as long as the bastard was dead.

I plucked my weak, pathetic excuse for a father up, ready to rip him to literal shreds when Ares rose off the ground! I looked to see my mother with her arm up. She was slowly closing her hand, restricting my airflow. How powerful was she to lift my 20-foot-tall frame? My sudden need to breathe causes me to panic and Ares to retreat. My human form is still struggling in her grip. "Mo-mom!" Was she going to kill me? For him! By now, I had released him, but she was still holding me and keeping me from breathing and, even worse, checking on Haven.

That angered me more than her defending dad against me. I slam my arm past the invisible barrier in front of me and fall to my feet, grabbing my neck. I was livid at her actions against her own son! I lashed out with a fireball in their direction, which knocked them off their feet. I wanted to obliterate everything in sight.

Now, I had two enemies instead of one. They were both responsible for harming my precious book bee. I didn't give a fuck who they were!

Did I love my mother? Yes. But did I need her? No, especially after she protected him.

I turned to face her as she stood in front of my father. How could she after he tried to hurt us all? Is this what love is?!

"Step aside, Mother, that bastard is going to die for harming her! And you, too, if you get in my way!" Of course, I didn't want to hurt her, but if it came down to it, then she was sailing on the same boat as my father.

I meant it when I said I only need Haven.

My dad stumbled to his feet, and my mother stepped away to make sure her back wasn't toward him. She didn't trust him not to trap her again. Now it was a three-way standoff.

"You're a fucking psychopath like your worthless mother! You almost killed me!"

My mom caught my attention before I incinerated him where he stood. "Stick to the plan! Levi, please." I knew she felt bad about attacking me, so I relented and put my hands down. She needed her vindication for all he had put her through. That distraction let my mom cast an energy absorption spell. It left him weak and on his knees.

She paced in front of him, "Even after a millennium of repetitive wounds every time you fucked some whore, I can still look you in the eye and say that I love you, Sam! It's a gift and a curse you left me to bear alone. What was I supposed to do with our love?"

"Choke on it, I hoped!" He spat.

The shriek that left my mom's lips would send banshees running. Then she started laughing, not a normal or even a hysterical laugh. No, this was dark and ominous.

"Oh no, Sam, you see, it'll be you who chokes on it!"

He roared up, "Die, you wretched wench!" Then he exploded, and the force knocked us both down. I coughed, finally looking around to see my mother on the ground.

Motionless.

No.

My dad lifted his hands, and her body rose. "You're a sorceress, a siren, the bane of my existence!" He spoke with so much venom, making me wonder if he ever loved her. "I am going to sever this wretched bond and rid myself of you permanently, and then I'll rip him apart." He pointed at me. I wanted to get up, but the powerful blast weakened me.

# CHAPTER 58

## HAVEN

I sat up slowly and realized I was in a dark room. Cavern? I could hear an echo; it sounded like people talking.

"Greetings, my Queen." I hear a voice.

"Who said that?! Where am I?" I look around but see nothing.

"I am your protector now that Lillith's crown belongs to you."

"Like Ares? A demon?"

"No. I am not a demon; think of me as a powerful entity that is available to you in times of distress. This is one of those times. Your mate needs you." I was now looking out from the inside! I saw all three with their hands up like in an old Western showdown. Then she cast a force that brought Petey to his feet, but as she was pouring out her anguish, he hit them with a force, knocking them both to the ground. He seemed to cause more damage.

"Levi!" It echoed off my consciousness. "What do I do? I have to help them! But I'm just a former human."

"You are much stronger than you know. You will be the new Queen of Hell, or you're about to be…"

Then, a form resembling me emerged, except she had fiery

red hair, and black vines covered her skin. Her eyes were gold, and they were mesmerizing. She bowed. "I am your guardian. You may name me as you please."

I didn't need a moment; it made perfect sense, "Athena, sister to Ares. Goddess of Wisdom."

"Thank you. Call my name whenever you need me, but since you were knocked unconscious, and this is our first meeting, I wanted to make my presence known. Your mate needs us."

"Then you do what you need to save him. He's all I have!"

"So be it!"

# CHAPTER 59

## LEVI

I spent my last conscious moments searching for Haven. If this was it, I wanted her face to be the last thing I saw.

"Haven," I whispered. Then, a sudden gust of wind made me close my eyes to shield them from the dust. I turned my head in the direction the wind came from. I felt like I was on a slow charge, my energy slowly returning. What I saw shocked me!

I barely recognized my sweet, innocent girl. She had fiery red hair, and her once warm skin was paler and covered in black vines. She exhaled, tilting her head to the sky, then left and right. Then, she set her sights on my father. By this time, I had enough energy to follow along without being in excruciating pain.

She laughed, "Oh, Petey, you've gone and done it now. So much for Haven being a weak, human flesh bag, huh? Now that I've assumed my rightful place on the head of the future Queen of Hell, you can't hurt her anymore. I'd sooner slit your fucking throat before she's tortured again. Like I should have with Lillith! I won't make that mistake again."

I look down and notice she's hovering a few inches above the ground. I force my head to turn and look at my father. He was as shocked as I was!

"Of course you're a witch! You cannot defeat me. I am the

King of Hell! Bow before your master or face the same fate as his worthless mother."

I wanted to expose him to the same pain and torture he put my mother through, but Haven looked at me, and I knew to stand down. She held out her hand, and with quick movements, my father was being held down by an invisible force. He grunted and roared as he tried to move even one inch but couldn't budge.

"I am the protector of the future Queen of Hell as I was protector to my goddess Lillith until you tricked her and withheld her powers, and for that, you are my enemy." She lifted her hand, squeezed it, and twisted it. He shrieked, clutching his chest. "Am I weak now, Petey? All you had to do was simply sign over the position and be on your whorish way, but instead, you wanted to hurt all of us. Well, you can't hurt me. The surge of power from this crown kept you on a leash, but you didn't like it, so you tricked Lillith into taking it off. But now it belongs to me, and I can help her with whatever she had planned for you."

She may not look like herself, but those words were from my brave girl. I loved the power and confidence she received from the crown.

She gently floated over to my mother, who was still not moving. She knelt beside her and whispered in her ear, then waved her hand over her body. Her body jerked, and she coughed violently as she shot up, "Whoa!" She took a few breaths before she looked up. "Haven?"

She shook her head and bowed. "I am Athena, her protector." My mom stood up and bowed back. "Good, the crown did what I expected. Thank you, Athena, for reviving me. Now I can complete my mission."

My mom placed her hand over her heart and pulled out this black and red orb. Then she crosses her arms in front of her face. When her arms slam down to her side, she's engulfed in flames, and her beauty is now deadly. Her skin was marked black by her veins, much like Haven's. I looked to see Haven was back to her former beauty, but knowing she had this intense amount of power made her stand taller. She kept my dad bound for my mom, whose grin could fuel nightmares for the darkest of demons. It was as if her display was a representation of her emotional anguish.

My dad just scoffed, finally being allowed to get to his feet. "Huh, was your little transformation supposed to scare me, Lily? What are you going to do…kill me?" Haven tightened her grip, and he was once again on his knees.

"You know I can't kill you. We're immortal, you stubborn jackass! But I can do something much worse, Sam, MUCH worse…and I intend to. Watch the floating orb; look familiar?" She waves her other hand over the orb and pulls away, separating the orb into a red and a black orb.

"This should look very familiar, Sam…it's our mate bond." She approached him slowly. He wanted to get as far away as possible but couldn't. "Get that away from me, Lillith!"

"SHUT UP! I'm tired of your fucking whining, the lies, and I'm sick of your cheating! But I'm tired of harboring your poison and pain about love. And now that I'm free, I will enjoy watching you suffer!" The two orbs circled each other as my mother paced before the love of her life.

In this moment, she realized that this emotional warfare she had embarked upon was not just about breaking him, but about breaking free from the chains that had bound her. It was a desperate attempt to reclaim her own power, to regain control over her heart and mind. And though the tears flow, they were no longer solely tears of pain but tears of defiance, a declaration that she would no longer be held hostage by her own emotions.

"Do you know what I felt every time you screwed someone else, Sam? A hot, searing pain in my heart. Every. Single. Fucking. Time! Hundreds, thousands, hell millions because you became such a WHORE! Is that your legacy? Being a promiscuous slut?! Trying to fuck your feelings away, it left me with so much anger, so much rage! You put me in Tartarus where

Levi couldn't find me...but where I could feel every indiscretion, and now I want payback. I want revenge. I may love you, but I'm going to hurt you in every way possible and not the way you think. Let's call it emotional warfare, and I damn sure am going to break you!" Her trembling hands clenched into tight fists, knuckles turning white with the intensity of her emotions. She visibly clenched her jaw and ground her teeth together, physically manifesting the pent-up frustration and anger that had consumed her for far too long. Beads of sweat formed on her forehead, a testament to the sheer exertion required to contain the storm raging within her.

As the tears streamed down her face, they carried with them the weight of years of suppressed emotions, each droplet releasing a small fraction of the pain and anguish that had been festering deep within her soul. The salty liquid traced intricate paths down her cheeks, leaving trails of glistening despair in its wake. Her eyes, once vibrant and full of life, were now blood-shot and swollen, a reflection of the internal battle she had been waging.

Her body language spoke something a blind man could see, undying love. The pain, like a relentless fire, consumed her from within, searing her heart and leaving an indelible mark on her spirit. But amidst the agony, there was a glimmer of relief, a sense of freedom in finally allowing herself to release these emotions that had held her captive for so long. What an ordeal to love and hate your mate at the same time.

She closed her eyes, inhaled, and exhaled deeply, then returned to her unequivocal beauty.

He growled, "What are you going to do? Shove the dead part back into me, hoping it grows to love you again. Ha! I'll fight it every step of the way."

"Oh noooo. That would be too easy, Sam. I'm going to subject you to the same sentence you gave me! *Emvidium loranter vibratim!* I sentence you to an eternity of love filled with hope-lessness!"

Then the red orb started infiltrating the black one before she combined them again. She violently shoves it into my dad's chest. He heaved, falling to the ground. He inhaled deeply, but there was no exhalation. It was as if it was choking him to death! He gasped and gurgled, scratching at his chest, writhing as if he was in the most absolute of pain.

My mom only laughed at his agony.

# CHAPTER 60

## HAVEN

This is the most twisted thing I've ever witnessed. Making the one you love suffer after being freed from your emotional prison.

It all makes me feel sad for everyone involved. Unfortunately, Lillith had to resort to inflicting pain to get his attention, and she lost so much time with Levi. And it makes me wonder if their relationship is in the least bit healthy. My Levi witnessed his parents battle not only with each other, but their emotions. I hope we never come to this point. But I don't have to worry since he leaned into our bond. And poor Carson is just collateral damage.

"Ares!" She called, and he appeared as if Levi wasn't just on the ground writhing. His roar echoed across the cavern. "Do it now!"

What was he going to do?

At full demon, he points to his father, "I sentence YOU to Tartarus!" And just like with Aurora and Cherry, his claws sliced through his father, and he was gone!

"Holy shit!" I screeched, then clapped my hand over my mouth. I hear groaning and see Carson attempting to sit up. He had missed everything, but I was glad he was okay. I helped him up. "What'd I miss?"

# CHAPTER 61

### LEVI

I laughed when Carson asked what he missed. "I'll fill you in later, but first.," I pulled Haven to me to feel her against me, but her body shook. "Are you alright, my love? Are you cold?" She shook her head. "I think it's adrenaline. I'm okay, are you okay? What about the ceremony? Was it real?"

"I'm not sure."

His mother approaches us, "Since you sentenced your father to Tartarus, you, as his heir, are King of Hell effective immediately. It's in the by-laws. In the event of a coup. She closes her eyes, and then a contract appears in her hand. She turns to the last page where both of his signatures lay. "But how?"

"When you're forced to be in love, you do anything to make your mate happy. Sign here, and it's official, binding, and irreversible." I signed it but wondered, "What will you do next?"

She touched my face. "My sweet boy, now the prestigious King of Hell. I'm so proud of you, proud to be your mother. I am proud to be the mother of both of you. I'm returning to Tartarus to spend time with just the two of us. It'll take a long time and effort; he may have both parts of the bond, but I'm not stupid; he's still fighting it. Trying to poison it, just like when his part tried to get me to despise the man I love. I need uninterrupted time to build our bond and research a more permanent solution."

"How long will that take?!" My heart was breaking at the thought of losing her again.

"I don't know. It isn't forever, I promise you. I will seal off his bedroom to deny anyone access, but don't fret, I will be reachable through Haven and her crown, Athena knows how. You take care of my special girl. You leaned into your bond, and she fell in love with you. Don't take it for granted how blessed you are."

I arch my brow.

"What your father thinks about HIM is his opinion. Do what you will with that information. And Haven…"

She held her hand out. Haven stepped forward, placing her hands in my mother's. "You're going to grow into your newfound powers with Athena. You and I have the power to communicate. Just speak my name and recite the spell."

She bowed so gracefully before standing so elegantly. My mom kissed her forehead, then mine, as I felt the sting of abandonment even though I knew she wasn't gone. It was bittersweet, watching her smile with tears.

She blew a last kiss, and then she was gone.

# CHAPTER 62

## HAVEN

I braced for an outburst from Ares, expressing Levi's contempt at losing both parents. I expected him to lash out and possibly destroy his part of the cavern, his roar echoing throughout the land of tortured souls. Carson was also cautiously observing.

Levi exhaled long and hard, his shoulders dropping before he turned to face me.

His hand caressed my face, and the sparks jolted me into feeling bliss at the touch of my mate, my love.

Before I could ask, his body bolted forward. "Whoa!" He shook his head, and when he opened his eyes, they were glowing gold before returning to normal.

"What just happened?"

"The completion of the transfer, you're looking at the new King of Hell, baby." He smiled, wrapping me even tighter, leaning down for a much-needed kiss, each one hotter than the last. I felt his hand slide down from my waist, searching for the split so his hands could squeeze my…

"Excuse me! Hello?! Still here." Carson waved. I break away from Levi to run over and hug him. "Thank you for everything." He bowed. "Whatever my Queen needs." We laugh until I feel

Levi grab me and pull me back. "Remember, you are MY advisor, not hers."

That reminds me, "Speaking of advisors... Trevor? Really? He's a class A douchebag."

"I agree, but it tortures him to be at your beck and call, so consider that."

Then I remembered, "To be fair, he told me where the entrance to Tartarus was. I owe him a thank you."

"A BIG thank you, actually. Without my knowledge, you wouldn't be where you are." Trevor appeared arrogantly in a nice cobalt blue suit in the chair by the fireplace.

I grit my teeth, "Hello, Trevor. Yes, thank you for your help. I couldn't have done this without you." I responded like I was reading a script, cold and emotionless, because he would hold this above me. He rolled his eyes and waved his hand. "Guess that's as good as it'll get. And you're welcome...my Queen." He bowed so dramatically. I wave him off with a smile.

Levi stepped forward. "Why did you help Haven? I thought she was the downfall of my reign. What was it you called her...a pity fuck?"

"WHAT!" I screamed, feeling Athena's anger, but I calmed her and waited patiently for his response. It better be good, or she will boil him from the inside out.

Trevor stood up slowly. "I apologize for my premature assumption. I was operating on events in the past and what your father always said. But the fact is... your father was wrong. Early on, I told him how his thought process was a vicious cycle from his dad. Levi, when you fought to find your mate, I knew the cycle was broken, but I feared the consequences for both you and me if I stood by your side. Especially because not only was I his advisor, but I was also his best friend. I saw Haven in the kitchen and planted that seed about your mother. I knew she'd find out information and, inevitably, find her for you. That's why I gave her my key."

Levi laughed, but when he looked at Trevor, he was not

laughing. He actually looked hurt. "It may not seem like it now, but your father was like a brother to me. He should have listened to only me; I had his best interest, and his father only wanted him to suffer. Sound familiar?" He sighed. "I'll never forgive myself for not trying harder! Lillith was his saving grace, and I'll do anything now to make sure their bond is indestructible. He's nothing without her...and you're perfect WITH her." He stopped, looking away. We were witnessing a break in his cocky demeanor.

What is happening right now?

I clear my throat. "Well, thanks for your vote of confidence. I'm sorry about your friend. Listen, you are not obligated to be my advisor. I'll understand."

"You know, I rather enjoy our banter and perhaps I can take some credit in the Queen you become. I am honored to be your advisor." I stepped forward to hug him, but he recoiled violently. "One step at a time. I don't think my stomach can handle… affection." He dry heaved, causing me to laugh.

"Fair." I hold out my hand, and he shakes it.

Levi claps his hands and I jump, "Awesome, one big happy family, blah blah blah. Now, if you'll excuse me, I'd like to fuck my wife."

They both instantly disappear, and I turn to face my demon love. "How barbaric! I like it...say it again..." I stroll toward him, stopping and swaying. He's watching my chest. "Excuse me, sir. I noticed something...you said wife, and as far as I know..." I look at my bare hand and then at him, implying.

He stepped back. "I planned to do this right after the ceremony, but the turn of events was not what I expected." He kneeled in front of me and then stood back up. "Wait!" He snapped, and we were in my store! Surrounded by the books of the past and present, witnessing our future. Now we were standing in the romance section circled by candles and roses!

"Haven Marie Evers, this is the exact spot you stood when I first saw you through the window. It's where our love story grew between the pages of these books, and now you are the light to my darkness, the reason I live, and the future mother to my children. Marry me, my beautiful book bee, and say yes to an eternity, living in nothing but love and adoration." He opens the green velvet box to a black diamond surrounded by rubies on a blackened silver band representing his signature colors, a perfect fit for his Queen.

I gasp, tears streaming down my face in absolute joy. I take a few seconds to soak in the moment. "Oh, Levi, it's my dream to be your wife! Yes! Absolutely, yes!" I lunged at him for a hug and knocked him to the floor. He growled, "If you wanted sex, all you had to do was ask."

"Oh, brother. I'm pretty sure I never have to ask..." I help him back up, hold my hand in front of his face, and let him slide on the ring. It's gorgeous!

"Honestly, I don't need a wedding. I just wanted the ring!"

"Whatever you want, however, I want something from you."

"What is that?" I'm suspicious.

"Well, there's one very special place we haven't marked. The one spot I fantasized about every night I lay in bed without you. How I imagined the way you felt, how you'd sound, mmm, how you'd taste." He unbuttoned his cuffs and then the top button of his shirt. I was shocked, because I was super shy back then; but now the thought of a half-naked man made me blush, and I watched hungrily.

I point, trying to sound innocent. "Here?"

He only nodded as I stepped back, and he stepped forward.

"In my office?"

As I stood there, I could feel the cool wood of the ladder pressing against my back, a stark contrast to the electric warmth of the surrounding air. The sound of my steady breaths filled the silence as I contemplated my next move. I take another step back, and then, with his determination, he takes another step forward.

"Uh uh."

I pondered, "One of the reading chairs?"

He stopped. "No but added to the list. You see, I fantasized about setting you right here." He sits me on the ladder and spreads my legs so he can step in between. He inhales hard, and his eyes flash gold when both my legs peek out from the high splits, the fabric covering my essence. His thumb grazes my lips, then down my chin and throat. His movements slow from my collarbone to in-between my breasts. My body shuddered to his touch. A smirk appeared. "Mmm, there's your arousal. Now, unbuckle me." I do, but slowly to torture him. Slipping my fingers between the fabric and his skin, unclasping and unbuttoning, he sighed in relief. "Haven..." He muttered. We both exhale, moaning loudly when he slides in. He slips the straps off my shoulders to expose my breasts as he holds my waist, sliding in slowly. The pace was slow and methodical as he finally claimed me in the bookstore.

He took me where he created a plan to infiltrate my sad, bleak life and give me something to look forward to, meaning. I look forward to eternity with the man who broke me from my shell, who never gave up, and when he screwed up, practically groveled on his knees for my forgiveness. He didn't listen to the naysayers and stood his ground about me. He loves me, and I love him. He's the new King of Hell, and I am his Queen. I'm going to show them I'm not as innocent as they think I am. I have some torture methods I'd like to try out.

Maybe he can conjure Aurora and Cherry back...for scientific purposes.

# CHAPTER 63

## HAVEN

*One year later...*

"Ugh, so many left! Claire, is the coast clear?" Claire walked around the part of the store that wasn't filled with boxes, looked out the windows, and closed the blinds on the door. She gave me the thumbs up. I sigh in relief as I snap my fingers and put away the 36 boxes of books. "Ahhh, another hard day's work." We both laugh.

"I still can't believe your turn of events! I mean, who you are now. My upbringing wasn't very religious. Maybe that's why it doesn't bother me. I should be terrified, but I'm not. Pretty sure Levi still doesn't like me." She shrugs her shoulders.

"Well, what we learn and what is are two different versions. Some of it is true! Down there is exactly what you'd expect, and even though we have the house below, I still prefer being up here. And he hates all humans, but I told him you were the exception to the rule and that he had to be nice to you or else..."

Claire's so invested after I felt comfortable telling her the truth. I admit she reacted better than I did when Levi told me.

Her brow raised. "Or else what? What could possibly scare the King of Hell?"

I step back and allow Athena to step forward before pulling her back after the revelation, and Claire's expression said it all. "Yeah! That would work."

"Don't worry. She knows you're my closest friend. Athena's my protector, that's all.

"Neat."

I stretch. "If we're done here, I'm headed home."

"Here home or down there home?"

"Down there, but plan to sleep topside. Levi's been sad. It's been a year since the incident, and he hasn't heard from his parents, so I plan to cheer him up."

"Must be tough, but I know you'll have just the thing to bring him out of it."

She's right. I snap myself down to his office that he had moved to our home instead of a part of his dad's place. He felt a sharp pain of abandonment when he worked there. I suggested he move and start fresh. It improved his attitude, but not by much.

He would take out his frustration on the damned. I knew he was hurting when he allowed me to witness instead of suggesting I do something else. And I appreciated it because I needed to understand all his moods. My love was just a boy with a broken heart.

# CHAPTER 64

### LEVI

It isn't easy being the King of Hell! My dad neglected to tell me about all my duties, but I think I'm doing a decent job. No one had the balls to say otherwise. I've been trying to allow Haven to witness all my duties, including the brutal torturing. I remember her words; how can she help me if she doesn't see all of me? Let me tell you, when I started tossing victims onto the *Mons Cultri,* she let out a scream to rival a banshee, and then she fought to keep her breakfast down. It's been several months, and I think her stomach is getting stronger. We even have date nights where I would do live demonstrations, or we would do a hands-on activity so she would experience it.

My sweet girl is quite vicious. I think she's still venting from her life with Cherry. I gently remind her not to feel sorry for them and reveal their sins, and she continues. Speaking of Cherry and Aurora, she spent several months focusing her torture on them after I rescinded their sentence to Tartarus. We found out that you can come back through an intense ceremony. Anything for my wife. She implemented every torture method she could think of, but it wasn't enough, and I "suggested" some darker methods to try.

Carson snaps his fingers, and I realize I zoned out while

reviewing decrees and amendments. He and Trevor waited for me to respond.

Yes, Trevor is still alive. After finding out that he was the voice of reason and his douchebag attitude was to keep himself safe, he became quite the asset. He now holds the title of Advisor to the Queen of Hell and liaison to the King of Hell. He was very appreciative that his opinions and thoughts mattered.

"I'm sorry. It's a…tough day."

"I know. It's been a year, and you haven't heard from either of them?"

"Not a peep. So he's either making her work twice as hard, or maybe they're blissfully in love."

"I pray for the latter, but Sam is… well, Sam's an asshole. He'll fight tooth and nail, but Lily, she's a pit bull. It's probably very loud down there." Trevor chuckles, which makes us all laugh.

I sigh, "I just want to know she's okay." Everyone went silent until my door opened, and there was my book angel. She bowed gracefully and then giggled; she loved acknowledging my title. "My King."

Trevor and Carson disappear immediately. There's been a few close calls where it was almost an exhibition for all to see.

I could use a pick-me-up. Or to pick her up and claim her on my desk…again. I stood, and she held her hand up. "Stop! Don't even think about it. I've got a surprise for you. Come on." She held out her hand, and I noticed she was wearing a floral dress and sweater coat, referencing her old bookish charm instead of the skin tight or corseted dresses of the present. I took her hand but pulled her to me instead to wrap my arms around her, but she broke free and pulled me out of the office.

"What are you up to, Haven?"

She paused and looked back. "Haven? That's not what you call me. Say it…"

She folds her arms, tapping her feet until I relent; how could I tell her no? "My beautiful wife, the heartbeat of my life. My bookbee, bookworm…and naughty little bookslut. Does that cover it?" She nods as she pulls me to an unknown location until we are in our nursery. She snaps her fingers, her crown appears on her head, and she takes my hand. "I know it's been a long, arduous year for you. You try to keep yourself busy to block out the feelings. Feelings of the unknown, of regret that it couldn't be any other way than what it is. I want you to know how proud I am of all your hard work. You are becoming the man I knew you would be: strong, powerful, and sadistic. Who knew it would be so sexy? Now, before you try to ravage me, I want you to wait.

She knows me well as she sidesteps and does some weird hand motions while reciting what looks to be a spell.

"*Valarium pendenses allo!*" A portal appears, with smoke surrounding it. "I humbly request Lillith, the Queen mother of all who dwell here. Her daughter awaits."

My heart raced a mile a minute, my mind was completely blank, and I'm sure I was holding my breath.

Then, a figure showed within the cloud and stepped forward, and it was the beauty and grace of my mother just as I last saw her.

She clapped her hands. "Whew, sorry for the wait. Sam is still yelling about how the thumping in his chest and the sharp pain are all my fault…blah blah blah. Anyway," She hugs Haven and kisses her cheek. "How's my beautiful daughter?"

"I'm good, but I knew it would be good for him if he saw you and got a status report."

My mom turns and hugs me real tight. It's what I needed. She pulls back and puts her hand on my cheek, "My handsome son and King! I'm so proud of you."

"I miss you, Mom. Can't you come around more? A year is too long."

She was about to answer, but she looked around and gasped. "What a beautiful nursery!"

"I had it put into the plans when we started construction. I'm sorry you didn't see the house sooner. I was planning for our future, you know?"

She does the same thing Haven did, touching various items. "It's beautifully decorated. The colors have muted tones but can complement any other color. The chair and ottoman look so comfortable! I'd probably fall asleep with the baby against me in something so comfy. I remember the little time we had together. You were such a quiet baby, Levi. I would sing and rock you until you fell asleep in my arms." She mirrored her motions as if carrying a baby version of me. "Then I would lay you down…" She stopped at the crib and gasped. She spun around with a look of shock, and the tears formed.

"No way!" I had no clue what she meant. She covered her mouth and then hugged me.

"Somebody want to tell me what's going on?"

They share a knowing look, and my mom takes my arm. We step toward the crib, and she points.

I look to see a onesie that says Daddy's Little Angel.

I scoffed at the words then shook my head violently. "What?" My voice wavered. Is she saying…

My mom squeezes my arm. "I guess I'll be visiting more often! Congratulations, son, you're going to be a father. That means I'll be a grandma! Can you believe it?"

I can only hear the sound of my increased breathing as the world seemed to waver in and out and so did their voices.

I'm brought back by the sparks of her reaching for my hand. She squeezes in between us, peering up to gauge my reaction.

I was going to be a dad. A father.

Nothing like my father, that I could guarantee. The pain, suffering, and torment ends with me. My child could do whatever they wanted when it comes to their life.

I kiss her forehead, and she smiles at me in relief. I place our hands on her stomach.

I look at the smiles and tears of the women who made me who I am today.

The King of Hell
Ruler of Demons.
And I owe it to them.
"Thank you, my beautiful bookbee."
"Thank you for loving me."

THE END

# ABOUT THE AUTHOR

Thank you for taking the time to read Devil in the Bookstore. I hope you enjoyed the book and would love if you could leave a review on any retailer or Goodreads.

If you would like to hear more from me about new releases and sales, you can visit my website.

Website: https://www.scourtneybooks.com/

www.ingramcontent.com/pod-product-compliance
Lightning Source LLC
Chambersburg PA
CBHW032349310726
48973CB00007B/1928